Until Ashlyn

Aurora Rose Reynolds

Cover and Cover design by Sara Eirew
Designs: Formatted by BB eBooks

Dedication

To every single person that believes in the *BOOM*

Table of Contents

Until Ashlyn

Prologue

"LARGE ICED COFFEE, cream and two sugars." I smile at Melissa behind the counter of my favorite coffee shop and pull cash out of my purse as she types my order into the computer.

"Anything else, Ash?" She looks up, and I try to fight it, but I can't.

"Two cake pops, both chocolate. Oh, and a cranberry scone."

"Got it." She grins, knowing me, since I come in and order the same thing almost everyday, unless it's fall—then I always go for something pumpkin. "You can pick it up at the end of the counter."

"Thanks." I give her one last smile and tuck the change into the tip jar in front of me then make my way down the line to wait. Pulling out my cell phone, I type a message back to my dad letting him know I'll be over after work.

"Coffee black, one sugar." A deep male voice slides over every inch of me and my head lifts. The moment I spot the commander of that voice, my body freezes. I've seen thousands of good-looking men in my life, but with long, dark-blond hair, sun-kissed skin, broad shoulders covered in a tailored suit jacket, a slim waist, and long, thick legs encased in slacks, I know he's the most spectacular.

"Ash… Ashlyn?" Turning my head and coming out of my daze, I find my order in front of me and Dane, Melissa's husband, staring at me with concern. "Are you okay?"

Oh, God. I probably look like an idiot. "Yeah, sorry. I spaced out." I smile, taking my drink and the bag holding my goodies, then reach over and grab a straw.

"No problem." He grins then I feel heat hit my side, and my eyes travel up and up, until I find the object of my sudden fascination looking down at me through crystal-blue eyes.

"Hi," I breathe, feeling myself involuntarily lean toward him. His eyes scan my face and he lifts his chin ever so slightly before turning back to the counter.

Feeling like a total moron, I book it out of the coffee shop and down two doors to the dental office I work at, unlocking the door and turning on the lights as I enter. Heading to the reception desk, I set my coffee down on my desk along with my bag of goodies and stow my purse as I start up the computer.

"Hey," I greet Gregory as the chime sounds and he steps into the office.

"Hey, darlin'." He smiles, taking off his hat and suit jacket. "We need to have a quick chat."

"Sure," I agree as he walks past me, back toward his office, and I follow with my coffee while shoving a whole entire cake pop into my mouth, chewing quickly.

"I've got some news."

"Okay." I take a seat, watching him tuck his coat away and put on a scrub jacket that is in major need of ironing.

"I found someone to buy my practice."

"That's great." I smile, feeling relieved. Gregory isn't as young as he used to be, and we are constantly losing patients. People are fearful of him, with his thick glasses, shaky hands, and his old school attitude that no one really needs to be numbed before a procedure.

"He's going to be here soon. I just wanted to give you a heads up."

"Thanks, Greg."

"You know I adore you, darlin'."

"I know," I concur. "The feeling is mutual." I smile, and he smiles back then looks toward the door when the chime signals someone came in.

"That's probably him," he mumbles, buttoning the jacket up.

"Do you want me to send him back?"

"Yep, business as usual. He can talk while I get stuff set up," he says, and I nod then head out toward the front of the office. As soon as I reach the reception desk, the smile on my face slides away and my steps falter. The guy from the coffee shop is standing with his hands on his hips, looking around the reception area with a look on his face that says it doesn't meet his standards. Taking in his expression I can't say I blame him for his distaste. The paint is peeling in spots and the furniture is worn and out dated. The whole office needs an update.

"Hi, can I help you?" I ask, and he turns at the sound of my voice. As soon as his eyes meet mine I see something flash behind his gaze, but it's gone before I can read it.

"I'm here to see Gregory. He should be expecting me."

Oh, God. This cannot be happening.

"He's in the back. Let me take you to him."

"You are?" he asks, raising a brow.

"Oh," I let out a short laugh filled with nervousness, "Ashlyn." I stick out my hand and his eyes drop to it before his fingers wrap around mine. A zing surges through my body, leaving me paralyzed.

"Dillon."

"Huh?" I breathe, staring at him once more.

"I'm Dillon."

"Right." I tug my hand free, shaking it out, then turn on my heels, hoping he's following me, but I'm too afraid to check. Once I reach Gregory's office, I point. "He's right in there." I wait for him to enter then reach in and close the door, wondering what the hell is wrong with me.

"DARLIN', DILLON WOULD like to have a word with you," Gregory says, and I look up from Jane, who is having her teeth cleaned, to find him standing in the doorway and pull my mask down.

"Now?"

"It won't take long. I'll take over for you until you get back."

"Sure." I give Jane's shoulder a reassuring squeeze when her eyes get big and fill with fear. "I'll be right back." I slip off my gloves, tossing them in the trash, then take off my mask and head past Gregory and down the hall to his office, finding Dillon leaning against the desk.

"Gregory said you wanted to speak with me?"

"I do. Have a seat." He nods toward one of the chairs. I really want to say something about him being bossy, but instead, I move to the chair and sit with my hands folded in my lap.

"I understand you've been working here for a while."

"I have," I confirm with a nod as he crosses his arms over his massive chest.

"With me taking over, things around here are going to change."

"Good," I state, really meaning it. This office needs change if it's going to last much longer. There are dental offices popping up all the time, taking business away from us.

"If you want to keep your current position, I'm going to need to re-interview you."

"That's fine."

His eyes scan the length of me slowly, making my skin feel suddenly too hot and too tight. "I don't need pretty objects around to look at. I need someone who knows what they're doing working with me, and I need to make sure you understand that." Blinking, I stare at him wondering if I heard him correctly. "I'll be in town this week. Hopefully that will be enough time for you to get a resume together."

"Absolutely," I grit out, faking a smile that says I really want to take his head off and use my four-inch heels as soccer cleats.

"Great, I'll call the office and schedule a time for us to meet."

"Great," I agree, standing. "Is there anything else?"

"Not at this time," he mumbles, watching me closely.

"It was nice meeting you," I lie, while plotting his untimely death in my head.

"You too." He lifts his chin, and I turn and walk out the door, wondering why the hell I thought he was attractive when he's obviously a *major dick*.

Chapter 1

Ashlyn

"HEY, MOM," I greet, tucking my phone between my ear and shoulder as I shove another dress and matching heels into my suitcase. I smile while I do, because Dillon will likely flip his lid when he sees my choices in attire for the weekend, but there is not one damn thing he can do about it since we won't be in the office. So technically, his stupid rules don't apply.

"Are you all packed?"

"Almost," I sigh, looking at the clock and realizing I only have ten minutes to finish before my cab is set to arrive. I wasn't planning on going to Vegas for the dental convention, but Dillon insisted he needed me with him, and like an idiot, I agreed.

"Is Dillon picking you up?"

"No, I'm meeting him there. His flight left a couple hours ago."

"Oh." She lets out a defeated breath. "Is it just you and him going?"

"I hope so. I swear if the Wicked Witch shows up, I'll sell her on the strip to the highest bidder, or pay someone to take her out to the desert and drop her off," I grumble, digging under my bed for my tickler—just in case of an emergency.

"Call me if you need an alibi." She laughs, and I smile, shaking my head, because I know she's not lying; she would find a way to be my alibi if something happened.

"I'll call," I mutter, heading to the bathroom so I can gather my shower supplies.

"Dillon's so nice," she says quietly, and I grit my teeth.

Dillon is annoying, bossy, and… fine, he can be nice sometimes. Plus, he's uber-hot, but I hate him. Okay, I don't hate him… but I really, really *want* to.

"How long are you going to be gone for?" she questions, breaking into my internal rant.

"Just four days. My flight gets back Monday night around seven."

"Promise you'll call everyday and check in."

"I'll call or text," I agree, grabbing my cosmetics case from under the bathroom cupboard, filling it with all of my makeup.

"Please try and have some fun while you're there. Make Dillon take you out to a nice dinner or dancing."

Snorting, I mutter, "Sure, Mom. I love you. I'll message when I land."

"Okay, honey, and don't forget your dad and I leave Monday for Florida and we'll be gone for three weeks."

"I haven't forgotten. Have fun, kiss Grandma and Grandpa, and tell Dad I love him."

"Will do," she promises softly before I hang up and shove my cell into my back pocket. Looking at the clock I let out a quiet curse, getting my ass in gear to finish packing so I don't miss my flight.

DRAGGING MY BAG behind me toward the reception desk, I'm stunned by how many people are here wearing nametags stating they're attending the dental convention. Dillon mentioned this weekend is one of the largest gatherings of dentists in the United States, but sheesh, this is crazy. Finally making it to the front of the line, I smile at the cutie behind the desk.

"How can I help you, gorgeous?" he inquires once I'm close, and I set my purse on the counter and pull out my ID, handing it over to him.

"Hi, I have a reservation." I yawn, covering my mouth while I listen to the sound of slot machines going off in the distance. I love the slots—or penny slots to be exact, since I'm too chicken to play the real ones.

"I'm sorry, but there is no reservation under your name. Are you sure you're staying with us?" he asks, handing me back my ID, and I frown.

"I'm positive. It may be under my boss' name, Dillon Keck. He made the reservations," I say, and he starts to type again then smiles.

"Got it. I see here that Mr. Keck has already checked in and requested we give you your own key to the suite upon arrival."

"Uh… what?" I blurt, feeling something close to dread fill my stomach. "Are you saying he's staying in that room too?"

"Yes, it's a suite with two kings."

"I don't care how many kings are in the room. It's one room. Right?" I panic, leaning half over the counter, trying to see his computer screen. "Please tell me you have another room available?"

"I'm sorry, but we're completely booked. This is one of our busiest weekends of the year."

"Of course it is." I shake my head. "Can you recommend another hotel nearby?"

"Sorry, but I really doubt anywhere else has an opening."

"Oh man… oh man," I breathe, squeezing my eyes closed. "It's not a big deal. You can share a room with him. You're an adult, and it's not like you even like him, right?" I whisper, balling my hands into fists.

"Um, so do you want me to get you your key?" Opening my eyes, I nod once and his face softens. "Call down and check. Sometimes we have people call off their reservations last minute. You never know. Something might open up between tonight and tomorrow."

"Sure, I'll call," I agree, wondering what the hell I did to deserve this kind of karma as I wait there for the room key.

Standing in the hall outside the door to *our* room ten minutes later, I pause with my key card in my hand, not sure if I should knock or just go in. I seriously cannot believe Dillon booked us in a room together. Actually, I can believe it, because I think he gets off on annoying me.

"Screw it. It's my room too," I mutter to myself, shoving the key into the card reader, watching the light turn green. Pushing down on the handle, I turn, using my shoulder to hold the door open while I drag my suitcase into the room, fighting with its weight as the door closes, trapping it half way through.

"Shit!"

Turning my head, I look over my shoulder and almost fall on my ass when my eyes find Dillon standing in the middle of the room, completely naked, with a pair of boxers in his hand. His once long hair now short and wet, and a tattoo I didn't know he had along his muscled ribs on his side.

"Oh, my God," I breathe, turning quickly while attempting to shove my suitcase back out of the room. I totally did not need to know Dillon looks hotter without clothes than what my mind had made up, and believe me—my mind had unfortunately tormented me with thoughts of him naked many times.

"Christ, you're a mess," is muttered from behind me while a very strong arm wraps around my waist, lifting me off my feet, and my suitcase is tugged from my grasp. Before I know it, my suitcase and I are both in the room and the door closes with a soft hiss, trapping me inside.

"Please tell me you're not still naked," I whimper, squeezing my eyes closed, feeling his arm release me and his heat leave my back.

"I'm not naked."

Opening my eyes, I close them again when I see he's only got on a pair of form-fitting black boxers and nothing else. "Put some clothes on."

"Don't tell me you've never seen a naked man before." He chuckles, and the sound of his laughter makes my teeth grind and my hands drop to my sides.

"I don't want to see you naked." I glare at him while he buttons up a pair of dark slacks that fit him perfectly.

"You could have avoided all of this if you had knocked."

"Really?" I raise a brow. "You could have 'avoided all this,'" I make air quotes, "and gotten me a separate room."

"They messed up the reservation." He shrugs like it's no big deal, and I feel my eyes narrow further.

"You should have called to tell me that, so I could have—"

"You would have avoided coming," he cuts me off. "If you knew we were sharing a room, you would have found an excuse, and I need you with me this weekend."

"Whatever," I grumble, knowing he's right. I would have canceled the trip if I knew we were sharing a room, even knowing that being here is a great way to build connections with other dentists. Especially, if I want to open my own practice in the future. "We need to set a few ground rules." I cross my arms over my chest while I watch him walk across the room toward the bed near the window.

"Later." He picks up a dark-blue, almost black, dress shirt and starts to put it on, which is unfortunate, because now that I've seen him shirtless, I'm thinking he should never cover up again.

"No, now," I growl, annoyed with myself for being attracted to the dick.

"Later." He holds my glare. "Right now, you need to get dressed. We have reservations in forty minutes." He takes a seat on the side of the bed and starts to put on his shoes.

"What?" I look at the clock on the wall. It's after seven at night and

I'm exhausted. All I want to do is climb into bed, order room service, and watch some bad TV.

"We have a reservation in forty minutes," he repeats, then stands. "The restaurant is twenty minutes away, so you have twenty minutes to get ready, unless you want to wear that." He motions to my sweats, flip-flops, and hoodie. "I suggest you change."

"I hate you."

"So you say," he says, just barely loud enough for me to hear, as he goes to the dresser, picking up his watch and putting it on.

"What did I do to deserve this?" I shake my head, pulling out my hair tie and running my fingers through my knotted hair.

"You may want to hurry."

Holding his eyes for a minute, I give up my glare then drag my suitcase to the middle of the room and unzip it. After pulling out one of my favorite "going out" outfits along with my makeup bag, I go to the bathroom and try to slam the door closed, but it's on one of those thingies that prevents me from doing that, which pisses me off even more.

"Stupid door. Stupid dick," I mutter once the door is closed, then get to work on making myself look halfway decent.

Twenty minutes later, I look at my refection and lean forward, putting my face an inch from the mirror, and use my dark-red lipstick for the final touch on my dramatic makeup look. Since I didn't have time to do anything with my hair, I brushed it out and put it up in a bun on top of my head then pulled out a few pieces to frame my face. Looking at my now blonde hair, I smile. I wasn't sure I would like having blonde hair but Kim insisted it would look great on me, and she wasn't wrong. Standing back, I place my hands on my hips and take myself in. My black sleeveless-top, with triangles cut out of the center of the chest and sides, is sexy but classy, and my red skin-tight pencil skirt, with its slit up the thigh, shows off just enough skin to draw attention while leaving everything to the imagination.

Slipping on my black, pointed-toe, four-inch pumps, I open the door to the bathroom, and mutter toward where I know Dillon is sitting, "Let me just change my purse and we can go."

"You're not wearing that."

"Pardon?" I ask, pausing in my squatted position in front of my open suitcase to look at him.

"You're not wearing that outfit. Go change."

"I'm not changing." I stand, moving to the desk so I can transfer what I need from my bag to my clutch. Hearing no reply, my eyes move to where he's sitting on the edge of the bed, and I feel my skin warm up and butterflies take off in my stomach as our eyes lock and his darken.

Licking my lips that have suddenly gone dry, his eyes drop to my mouth and his jaw clenches. "I'll meet you downstairs." He stands abruptly and moves past me out the room quickly, letting the door close behind him with a swoosh without another word.

"What the fuck was that?" I ask the door, gaining no reply—not that I need one. I know exactly what that was; I just have no idea what to do with it. Dillon has always acted professional with me. There has never been a time that I've seen him look at me like he's interested, but the look in his eyes a moment ago was primal and not one an engaged man should give another woman, or a boss should give his employee, ever.

Shaking off the strange feeling in the pit of my stomach, I finish changing out my bag then leave the room and make my way through the casino and into the lobby. Not finding Dillon inside, I head outside to the area the cabs and limos pick up and drop off, and spot him standing with a group of people. I'm not surprised he's surrounded by a gaggle of women and a couple of men. He tends to draw attention wherever he goes, and it's something else that annoys me. I hate being the center of attention, and I don't really like people who need it to feel important. Needing a minute to get my head together, I stop a few feet away and tuck my clutch under my arm.

"Where you going, gorgeous? 'Cause wherever it is, I'm there," a drunk guy, who can't be much older than twenty-one, slurs, stumbling up to me. His clothes are rumpled, his hair in disarray, and if he wasn't such a mess, he'd be cute. But sadly, sloppy drunk works for no one.

Ignoring him, I untuck my purse, open it, and pull out my cell phone, knowing better than to engage with men like him in his current state.

"So you're to good for me?" he slurs, snatching my cell out of my hand, and my eyes fly up.

"Give me my phone," I say evenly, holding out my hand, and his eyes travel the length of me and his face scrunches up.

"Ho here thinks she's too good for me."

"Mike, come on. Give her the phone and let's go," someone says off to the side, but I keep my eyes on Mike, with my palm out toward him. My dad insisted I take martial arts with Jax when I was little. I hated it; I wanted to be a ballerina, not a ninja, but he was adamant about me being able to protect myself. Over the years, the skills I learned back then have come in handy, like now, when all I really want to do is kick the crap out of Mike but know better. One of the first things I was forced to learn was control, to never lose my temper. The second thing I learned was to keep my eyes on my enemy at all times. I was never really good at either, but I still got a black belt in the end.

"Mike," I say softly, taking a step toward him. "I'm going to ask you nicely, once, to give me my phone. If you don't, I swear to God I will unleash the Kraken, kick your ass in front of your friends, and send you home crying to your mother."

Laughing, he looks around then his eyes widen as they move behind me. I really, really want to know what he's looking at, but I refuse to turn my head and give in.

"Give her the phone." The deep rumble of Dillon's voice sends a chill down my spine. I've only heard him pissed a few times, and I know he's pissed right now without even looking at him.

"I… I… w-was just playin' man," Mike stutters out, tossing my phone toward me. Missing my hands and causing my phone to crash to the ground, and my nostrils to flare as it shatters at my feet.

"Oh, shit. Oh, Christ. I'm sorry." He drops to his knees and begins gathering the pieces of what used to be my phone then tries to get up, but falls face forward into my crotch, causing me to stumble back.

"I can't believe this shit," Dillon grumbles, catching me before I fall, then tugs me out of the way as Mike's friends decide to finally step in and pick him up from the ground. "You had to wear that outfit."

"You can not be serious right now?" I hiss, swinging my head back and finding him glaring down at me.

"Deadly."

"Let me go." I try to get free, but his hand on my waist tightens as his eyes leave mine. Swinging my head in the other direction, I find one of Mike's friends standing a few feet away with my phone, looking anywhere but at us, and Mike off to the side, puking in a trashcan.

"Let me go," I repeat, and his arm tightens for a moment before he finally lets me loose. I really want to scream or throw a fit, but instead, I calmly take my clutch and open it, holding it out toward the guy and letting him dump the now useless pieces inside. "You need to get him some Gatorade and toast," I tell him, nodding toward Mike.

"Um, yeah sure. Than…" his words taper off, and the smile that was forming on his lips slides away as he looks over my shoulder. Rolling my eyes, I watch him turn quickly and go to Mike to help carry him away, feeling Dillon get close once more.

"Limo's waiting," he mutters, placing his hand against my lower back, making me tense.

"I'm not going." I try to step away, but his hand slides around my waist, bringing my side into his middle.

"You are."

"I'm not."

"You are," he growls, leaning forward, close… way too close.

"Fine, you want me there? I'll go, but just so you know, I plan on getting completely wasted, so you have just become my chaperone for the evening."

"You're not getting drunk."

"Wasted, not drunk. And you better make sure I don't do anything stupid." I pat his chest, ignoring his flashing eyes. With that, I step out of his grasp and start toward the line of limos then turn to look over my shoulder at him, realizing I have no clue which one to go to.

Smirking, he crosses his arms over his chest and raises a brow. "What's wrong, blondie? Confused?" His mocking tone and the look of triumph in his eyes does it. I turn on my heels and head to one of the limos with the driver standing outside leaning against it. The moment the driver spots me coming in his direction, his back leaves the car and his eyes rake over me, making my teeth snap together.

"Can I help you, Miss?"

"Ashlyn Mayson, get your ass back here," Dillon snarls behind me, making my palm itch to smack him.

"I'm sorry, pumpkin. I thought you said this was our limo." I fake pout, turning to look at him and tossing my head to the side for good measure.

"Christ, you drive me fucking insane." He walks to where I'm standing, tagging my hand, and then starts to drag me with him, grumbling under his breath.

"You know all I want in this whole wide world is to make you happy, pumpernickel," I whine, batting my lashes while watching his jaw tic.

Leading me toward another limo with a driver holding the back door open, he growls, "Behave."

"I swear I'll be your good girl from now on if you don't spank me," I stage-whisper, and his hand spasms in mine as a smirk forms on his lips.

"You don't behave, I'll bend you over and tan your ass right here." His words ring through my ears, making my insides liquid, and then I hear the sound of a male chuckle as I'm gently forced into the back seat of the dark limo before I can reply.

"You're such a jerk," I hiss, adjusting my skirt as I move across the leather seats.

"You started the show we put on. I just ended it," he mutters, sitting down across from me and unbuttoning his suit jacket.

"You started it with the whole 'blondie' thing." I cross my arms over my chest and glare at him.

"Can we not do this tonight? Can we get along for one damn evening?"

"You tell me. I'm not the one who's bossy and annoying all the damn time."

"No, you're just crazy."

"Crazy?" I snort, and his lips twitch ever so slightly. "*I'm* not crazy."

"Babe, you told that kid you were going to unleash the Kraken on him then went on to tell his friends to get him Gatorade and toast. You're the definition of crazy."

He may have a point, but instead of agreeing with him, I turn my head to look out the window and watch the city of Las Vegas slide by.

"TURN IT OFF. Turn it off," I croon sleepily as my hand sweeps out in the direction of the noise blaring from the alarm, missing it over and over as the beeping continues to torture me.

"Jesus, shut that shit off." An arm comes from around me, and silence fills the room as my body freezes and my eyes spring open, only to close again when the room spins.

"Oh, God, why are you in my bed?" I hiss, trying to calm my stomach that feels like it's getting ready to empty.

"You're in my bed," Dillon grumbles, sliding his arm around my waist, pulling my ass back into the crook of his thighs.

"Why am I in your bed?" I breathe as bits and pieces from last night flash through my mind, and none of them are good. *None of them at all.*

"You wanted to cuddle." He buries his face in my neck then moves his hand up to cup my breast. I know I don't have any clothes on when I feel the hair from his thighs tickle mine and his finger runs over my nipple. Oh, God. A memory of me telling him we have so much in common while we both got naked for bed fills my mind, and then another one pops in and my hand flies up to my face.

I force my eyes open, trying to focus, and see it there—the small, plain, white-gold band from the memory of him sliding it on my finger.

"We got married?" I shout, pulling his hand from my breast.

"We got married," he agrees, not sounding upset, but instead, almost proud.

"Oh *shit!*" I fly out of the bed and trip over our clothes scattered across the floor, feeling him catch me right before I land on my face.

"Ash, calm down."

"Calm down? *Calm down?* Are you insane? We got married last night. Married, Dillon. I got married to a man who is engaged to another woman!" I yell, then cover my mouth. "Oh, God, I'm going to hell. I'm so going to hell for this."

"I'm not engaged," he says calmly, giving me a shake.

"I know your fiancée!" I screech, attempting to get away from him, only to have him hold me tighter.

"I'm not fucking with Isla. Now stop with the crazy."

"You're not with her?" I stop, and he runs a hand through his hair.

"No," he states, holding my stare, and my body uncoils just slightly.

"Fine, I'm not going to hell." I move away from him and resume pacing. "We need to find an attorney. I saw loads of advertisements on the strip. We'll get one and get this taken care of. It's no big deal. People get married in Vegas everyday then get divorced. We will just be one of the ninety percent," I ramble while pacing.

"We are not getting an annulment."

"Annulment, right." I snap my fingers. "That's even better. No one has to know about this."

"Listen to me." He grabs onto my shoulders, giving me a shake, and my eyes focus on his. "We are not getting an annulment, or divorced. We got married and are staying that way."

"Oh, God, you were drugged." I rest my hands against his chest and drop my voice, "Don't worry. We'll go to the hospital and they'll give you something. Once you're better, this will all be taken care of."

"Jesus Christ." He rubs his hands down his face, tilting his head back to look toward the ceiling. "I'm married to a nut."

"Hey, that's not nice." I plant my hands on my hips. His head drops, his eyes scan the length of me, and I realize I'm naked… that we're both completely naked. "Dillon." I take a step back when his eyes meet mine, and his arms swing toward me. "What are you doing?" I shriek, sidestepping him, only to stumble onto the bed, where I attempt to roll. But he flips me to my back, his giant body moving between my legs, and his hands pin my wrists to the mattress over my head. Panting, I look up into his beautiful blue eyes.

"We are not getting a divorce," he snarls, leaning down so his face is mere centimeters from mine.

"Be rational." I lift my hips and my arms, trying to throw him off. "You're obviously on—"

Before I can say more, his head descends and his mouth is covering mine, stealing my breath along with my soul. The feel of his lips, the taste of him on my tongue, ignites something deep inside of me, and I kiss him back with everything I am. Ripping my mouth from his, I pant, "Please let me go."

"No." The word sounds almost primal, and I lean up, placing my mouth back against his.

"Please, I want to touch you."

Groaning, his hands release my wrists, and my palms fly to his chest and slide up and over his shoulders, pulling him closer to me as my legs wrap around the back of his thighs. He kisses me again, this time using his tongue and teeth to torture me in the most beautiful way possible.

"How is it possible you taste as good as you look?" he questions, pulling back, but I have no answer for him. He tastes amazing and having him covering me, his hardness pressing against my softness, is making my brain short-circuit. Palming my breast, he slides his thumb over my nipple, causing my hips to jerk forward. Rolling us again, he settles me on top of him, palms both my breasts, and then leans up, pulling my right nipple into his mouth, releasing it with a pop. "When did you get these?" he questions, flicking the tip with his tongue.

"When I was thirteen." I smile, and he smiles back then moves to my other breast, doing the same, only sucking harder, almost punishing.

"When?" he asks again, and I know he's asking about my nipple piercings. I got them with my cousin April a few years back. I wanted a piercing, but needed to be able to look professional to the outside world, so I got both my nipples done with simple, almost elegant-looking gold barbells.

"Three years ago," I breathe as he tweaks the tiny piece of metal.

"Before me."

"What?" I try to focus, but every time he touches me, my body gets hotter and my focus depletes. Grabbing my hips, he tugs me forward, dragging my wet center along his length.

"Soaked." He nips my nipple then wraps his hand into the hair at the back of my head, taking control of my movements as he pulls my mouth to his and thrusts his tongue between my lips. Lost in his kiss and the feel of him between my legs, so close to where I need and want him, I squeak when he flips us over and slides down my body, not giving me a chance to think as his mouth covers me.

"Dillon." My hands move through his hair and my hips lift off the bed, offering myself up to him without thinking about anything but the way his tongue, lips, and teeth feel as he fucks me with his mouth. "Oh, God. Oh, God, I'm going to come," I pant, feeling my toes curl into the bedding and my hands grip his hair. The touch of his finger rimming just the inside of my entrance sends me over, shouting his name as I go.

Feeling him kiss my inner thigh then my belly, over my breasts then shoulder, I come back to myself lazily.

"Tell me you want me." Looking into my eyes while his hand moves between my legs and his fingers slide though my folds, I know I'll give him anything. "Tell me you want me as badly as I want you."

"I want you," I hiss, feeling the very large head of his cock at my entrance, and then watch his eyes drop between us before my eyes do the same, and I know I need to tell him. "I—"

Oh, God, too late… way too late. I bite my lip as he fills me, stretching me.

"Tight, so goddamn tight." He pushes in farther and his jaw clenches.

"Hold on. Please, hold on," I breathe, and his body stills above me as his eyes search mine.

"What's wrong?"

"I just need a minute." I squeeze my eyes closed, feeling like an idiot.

"Baby." His fingers slide along my jaw and cheekbone, into my hair. "Do you want to stop?" he asks gently, making tears sting my nose.

"God, no." He feels good, so good. But he's huge, way bigger than any of my toys. "You're just big. So big." I wiggle my hips and he hisses out a breath, grabbing my waist.

"Don't say that shit when I'm inside of you," he groans, dropping his forehead to mine.

"I have to tell you something, but please don't be mad."

"Christ, what now?" He pulls back, gritting his teeth.

"Stop being a jerk and let me talk." I smack his shoulder and he looks down at me, thrusting in another inch.

"Never mind. I don't want to know."

"What?" I moan, wrapping my legs around his hips as he slides in a little more.

"If it's going to piss me off, I don't want to know." He slides out then back in, and my back arches off the bed as his thick cock fills every inch of me.

"You're such a dick!" I cry out as he tosses my leg over his shoulder, changing the angle of his thrust.

"I don't give a fuck about that either." He drops his mouth, covering mine and stealing my reply—not that I have time to think about that as his mouth leisurely travels down my neck to my breast, which he pulls and sucks until I'm once again shouting his name and hearing mine groaned from his lips as we both come.

"ASH, WE NEED to get up. We've already missed the conference this morning, and I have to speak in two hours at the next one."

"You have to speak, not me." I pull the pillow over my head in an attempt to drown him out, along with the fact I married and slept with him then spent the last two hours cuddled into his chest like a damn puppy.

"You're coming with."

"I'm not." I roll to my stomach.

"You are." He tugs the pillow away then rolls me to my back, looming over me. "What do you want for breakfast? I'll order up, and we'll eat before we go down."

Okay, this is getting really weird, and I wonder if he didn't get a concussion at some point last night. "I think we need to talk about what happened, about what we're going to do."

"Not this again." He sighs, looking over my head.

"It's kinda a big deal!" I cry, and his hand slides between my legs, cupping me.

"We got married, consummated that marriage, and now we need to get to work. If we didn't have to deal with work shit, we would spend the rest of the weekend in this bed."

Feeling my eyes grow wide, I breathe, "You've lost it, totally lost it."

"Tell me that you haven't been feeling this pull between us. Tell me that I'm the only one who feels this, and I'll get up and walk away. I'll even call a lawyer myself and have our marriage dissolved by tomorrow."

Oh, God, I want to tell him that I haven't felt it, that I don't know what he's talking about, but I do. I've felt it since the moment we met. A pull toward him, like the universe had tied a string between us, linking us together. But I never knew he felt it. "You can't. I know you can't, because it's been there since the beginning."

"We got married. *Married.* That's more than us just dating and seeing how things go, Dillon."

"Yep, and now it will take a lot more than you just walking away to get rid of me."

"What is that supposed to mean?" I frown.

"You date all the damn time, baby. I've seen you run men off for not wearing the proper socks or for parting their hair the wrong way."

"Excuse me?" I have never done that, not once. Okay, yes, I'm a little picky, but what woman isn't?

"Just saying, it will be a lot harder for you to drop me, now that you have my last name."

"You're crazy," I breathe, and his face moves close enough that his lips brush mine.

"No, I've finally got you where I want you." He grins, and my heart rate speeds up.

"Fine, if you want to see how this goes, I'm going to pretend like we didn't get married and that we are just dating."

"We are married."

"Not in my head we're not," I grouch, and his nostrils flare. "I'd like to remind you that you think I'm crazy and don't even really like me." I know I drive him nuts, and that he thinks I'm off my rocker most days, so I don't understand why he wants to stay married, or why he even married me to begin with. That memory is still fuzzy, but I swear he is the one who insisted we tie the knot after I made a joke about us getting married.

"Oh, I definitely like you." His finger flicks my clit as his mouth touches mine. "Now, what do you want for breakfast?"

Rubbing my hands down my face in frustration, I mutter, "Pancakes, bacon, and eggs. And coffee, the largest pot they have."

"Got it." His fingers slide away and his mouth touches my shoulder before I feel him exit the bed. Pulling my hands from my face, I watch him move across the room to the phone and place the order for our food before he walks to the dresser and opens it, pulling out a pair of boxers.

"No one is supposed to use those dressers," I inform him, sitting up and noticing his suitcase is nowhere in sight, while mine is still open on the floor in the middle of the room with items scattered out around it.

"Pardon?" His eyes come to me then drop to my breast. Rolling my eyes, I tuck the sheet under my arms and nod toward the dresser.

"No one folds their clothes and puts them away in those dressers when they are on a vacation or a trip. Everyone lives out of their suitcase."

"Says who?"

"I don't know, everyone."

Grinning, like he thinks I'm cute, he opens another drawer and pulls out a shirt then steps toward the bed. "You wanna shower with me?"

"No." I shake my head, even though I really do want to. "I told you, from this moment on, we are just dating. So no more naked anything, and definitely no showering together."

"If you say so." He walks to the bathroom, the mirror on the wall across the hall from him allowing me to continue watching him until I get annoyed with myself and pull the pillow from the bed next to me, put it to my face, and scream. Swearing I hear him laugh as I do.

Chapter 2

Ashlyn

"BABY, PLANE'S LANDING," Dillon says into my ear, and my eyes slowly open as my head lifts off his shoulder, where it dropped as soon as the plane left the ground. Putting my feet to the floor, I look around the first class section, watching the flight attendant pick up empty glasses and trash.

"I missed the champagne," I complain, looking at Dillon. "I told you to wake me up for that part."

"You were tired. You needed sleep. You can have champagne at home."

My nose scrunches and I make a gross face, gagging, and mutter, "Ewww no, I hate champagne."

Chuckling, he leans toward me. "Then why'd you want to drink it now?"

"'Cause we're in first class. I wanted the full experience." I shrug. I've never flown first class, and I've always wondered what it would be like. It's honestly no different, just bigger seats. Well, plus free champagne, which I didn't have.

"You're a nut."

"Stop calling me that," I say for the billionth time, glaring at him.

"A cute nut." He leans in, kissing the side of my mouth, then runs his fingers down my cheek and I see his wedding band sitting at the base of his finger, which makes my stomach turn. The weekend went by in a flash. Between conferences and dinners, there wasn't a lot of time to think about the fact we are now married. Well… there was time to think about it, because he insisted on introducing me as his wife to anyone and everyone, which completely freaked me out.

"Where are we sleeping tonight?" he asks, dragging me out of my head. I pull my eyes from his ring and lean down, picking up my bag from the floor, pretending I didn't hear his question. "Ashlyn." His hand moves to my denim-covered thigh, squeezing.

"Hm?" I pull out my compact and flip it open.

"I know you heard my question. Where are we sleeping? Your place or mine?"

"You're sleeping at your place and I'm sleeping at mine," I mutter, pulling out my chapstick, only to have it snatched out of my hand. My eyes fly to his and I swallow when I see the look he's giving me. I tried over the last three days to insist we sleep in different beds. That didn't happen. He would join me in mine or drag me to his, each and every time. And each and every time, I put up a fight, knowing I would lose.

Okay, so I may not have fought that hard.

There was something about sleeping next to him that made me feel oddly whole—something I liked a little too much, if I was honest with myself.

"Fine, we're staying at my house." He sits back, buckling his seatbelt.

"No." I shake my head. "No way am I staying at a house that you bought for another woman. No freaking way." I snap my compact closed and toss it in my bag.

"I did not fucking buy that house for her," he growls, setting my teeth on edge.

"I can't do this." I shake my head; even the thought of her makes me mental, makes me want to kill someone, mainly him, because he is the one who was engaged to the woman—a woman I'm almost positive has the devil inside of her.

"You're very wrong, *wife.* We're already doing this."

"Dillon." I soften my voice, leaning closer. "We each need some time to think about this, to really think about what it is we're doing. Maybe having a night apart—"

"Not happening." He cuts me off with a shake of his head then leans across me, pulling my seatbelt over my lap and locking it.

"Yes it is." I smack his hands away.

"It most definitely is not." He tags the back of my neck, pulls me close, and kisses me until my body melts into his. "We'll stay at your place," he whispers against my lips, and my eyes flutter open.

"You're so annoying," I breathe, seeing him smile before he lets me go and grabs my hand, holding it tight until we've landed, and then keeps ahold of it until he's forced to release me so he can carry our bags.

"A limo, seriously?" I roll my eyes when I realize what car he's leading me to.

"It's just a car, baby."

"No, a *car* is just a car. This is a limo, there are only two of us. We should have used my Uber. It would have cost a whole lot less," I mutter to his back as he drags our suitcases behind him toward the driver.

"Maybe they have champagne inside." He grins at me over his shoulder, and I don't want to think he's funny, but I find myself smiling back at him anyway.

"You went to Vegas single and came back married." Our driver, who apparently knows Dillon, laughs, giving him a handshake and a pat on the back. My breath freezes in my lungs and the sound of their voices fades away.

Yes, we have been married for three days and sixteen hours, but it felt different when we were in Vegas. It felt, almost unreal. But now we're back in Tennessee. Tennessee… where my family lives. Tennessee… where my dad, who owns a plethora of guns, lives. Tennessee… where no one knows about our marriage, but where my very nosey family all resides and is liable to find out. I know my mom is already wondering what's going on. Dillon had a phone delivered to me at the hotel the afternoon we woke up married so I have been able to talk to her everyday as promised, and she knows Dillon and I were sharing a room, since Dillon wouldn't keep his hands off me or mouth closed when I was on the phone her.

"Baby." Coming out of my daze, I blink as his hand comes to rest against my cheek. "Hey," his face dips closer and his eyes search mine, "are you okay?"

"How am I going to tell my family about this?" I hold up my hand and point at my ring, which I took off once, only to have it shoved right back on my finger with a growl telling me not to take it off ever again.

His face softens and his hand slides around the back of my neck. "We'll tell them together."

"My dad owns guns, lots and lots of guns. This isn't going to end well for you."

"It will be okay."

"I think something happened to you. I'm pretty sure you've lost your mind." I start to panic as visions of him being chased by my dad, wielding a shotgun, flash through my mind.

"Stop worrying. It will work out."

"It won't."

"It will, trust me."

Snorting, I mutter, "Last time I trusted you, we ended up married."

"Well, that can't happen again, now can it?" He smiles smugly, and I let out a huff.

"At least there's that." Chuckling, he takes my hand and helps me into the back seat then gets in behind me as I move to sit across from him.

"Come over here." He pats the seat next to him as the driver shuts the door.

"Why?"

"I want to tell you something."

"You can tell me from here."

"Come here," he repeats, and I raise a brow then squeak when he leans forward, wraps his hands around my waist, and drags me to straddle him.

"Dillon!" I snap, and his hands slide up under my shirt, causing goose bumps to break out across my skin and butterflies to dance in my stomach.

"You're so damn beautiful," he mumbles, and I still while one of his hands slides farther up the back of my shirt and the other moves to rest on the underside of my jaw. "Far too perfect to be real. I thought that since the moment I first saw you."

"You did?" I question, leaning forward, lost in the look in his eyes and his softly spoken words.

"I did," he confirms, sliding his fingers through the hair at the back of my head, pulling me closer. "I didn't know all of you then. I had no idea how damn smart you are, how funny you are, how caring and compassionate—"

"You forgot crazy," I whisper, cutting him off, and he smiles.

"Crazy, so damn crazy." He closes the minute distance between us, kissing me gently then pulling back.

"I didn't know you even liked me," I tell him, running my fingers through his hair, and his body stiffens. "Dillon."

"I couldn't tell you. I needed to take care of a few things before I even attempted to get into your head."

"What?" I lean back, and his hands move to my waist, holding tight.

"Isla and me, there's—"

"Nope." I attempt to struggle free, but his grip tightens. "Let me go."

"Never," he growls, pulling me closer.

"Dillon."

"I won't talk about her now, but we will be talking about her. You need to understand."

"I really don't," I hiss, grabbing his hands and trying to pry them off of me. "I don't want to talk about her—not now, not ever. She's... she's evil."

"Calm."

"You calm! You were engaged to her, were going to marry her," I taunt, tugging at his hands.

"I wasn't."

"Oh, my God," I growl, leaning as far back as I can go. "Do you know how often she flashed that obnoxious ring in front of my face? How often she reiterated that you were hers to me? Like... like I wanted you!"

"You did want me," he whispers, and my hands move to his shirt, where I grab on with both fists and lean close until my face is an inch from his.

"Do not do that. Do not even say that. Never in a billion fricking years would I ever approach a man who I knew was married, engaged, or had a girlfriend." I pull him forward, hissing, "Never. Even if I was attracted to you, I would never *ever* go there. Not ever." I let him go then move quickly off his lap. "I'm not a slut, a whore, or a home-wrecker." I hold his stare. "And until you," I point at his chest, "I had never even been with a man, so put that in your pipe and fucking smoke it!" I yell, dropping to the seat behind me, feeling my chest heave, completely missing the look of shock and satisfaction on his face.

"Baby."

"No, do not 'baby' me, and do not come near me." I hold out my hand when he starts to sit forward. "I swear I will take out your eyes if you touch me." Pressing his lips together, I can tell he's trying not to laugh and that he thinks I'm funny, but I'm dead serious. "I can't believe I'm fricking married to you."

"Believe it," he barks, pushing up the sleeves of his navy blue Henley up to his elbows. "We're married, baby, and you better get use to the idea, 'cause that shit is not changing. *Ever.*"

"You're not letting me go, *blah blah blah*… You've said it before." I roll my eyes, crossing my arms over my chest.

"Glad you're starting to understand." He leans forward, and I brace myself. "And just so we're clear and you understand completely, you sealed your fate. You're mine. That brain of yours is mine. Your body is mine. *And*," he growls, leaning closer, "that pussy only I've had is fucking mine. You've been mine for a long fucking time, baby. You just didn't know it."

"And you think I'm the crazy one," I mutter, turning my head to look out the window.

Feeling his hand on my thigh, my eyes fly to him. "Our pasts do not have one goddamn thing to do with what is going on between us now, and one day, when you're ready to listen, I'll explain things."

"Sure." I shake my head, pushing his hand away and turning my eyes back to the window.

"Jesus, you're a pain in the ass."

"And you're a dick," I mumble to the glass, resting my forehead against it, lifting it only to turn and glare at him twenty minutes later when I see where we're headed.

"I told you I'm not staying at your house," I hiss as soon as I see the limo turn down the long driveway that leads to his place. I wouldn't even call his house a house; it's a mansion, one of the only ones in town. The size of it is ridiculous for just one, or even two people to live in. It has to be over eight thousand square feet with upper and lower balconies, giant pillars in the front, along with a fountain in the circular driveway. Who the hell has a fountain outside their house unless they are the fricking Kardashians or the Fresh Prince of Bellaire?

"We're getting my car, and I need to get some clothes," he says while pulling out his cell phone, typing something on the screen that makes the whole house light up, inside and out, as we park out front.

"The driver can just take me home."

"No," is all he says as he shoves his phone back into his pocket and opens the door. Ignoring his hand that he holds out for me, I get out on my own and head to the trunk where my bag is stowed.

"Thank you," I tell the driver as he sets my bag on the ground, doing the same with Dillon's.

"Would you like me to help you inside?"

"No, thank you. We've got—"

"That's fine, Tim," Dillon says, and my teeth snap together.

"It's really not a problem." He smiles at me, picking up both pieces of luggage and carrying them toward the house.

"We could have carried our own bags," I say, turning to glare at Dillon.

"Are you itching for a fight?" he asks when the driver is out of ear-shot, grabbing my hand and preventing me from walking away.

"No." I attempt to shake him free but his hold tightens as he tugs, forcing me a step closer to him.

"Then relax with the attitude."

"Don't tell me to relax."

"Baby," his voice softens and his face dips closer toward mine, "I can tell you're ready to go to war with me, but I don't want to fight with you. We've had a really good weekend and we're home now. All I want to do is get some clothes, go to your place, get something to eat, fuck you, and go to sleep with you pressed against me."

"We are not having sex," I grumble, looking over his shoulder. That is one thing I've stood firm on. Yes, somehow I'm still married to him, but I refuse to continue having sex with him until I feel more secure in what's going on between us.

"Can't blame me for trying." He grins, and I let out a deep, frustrated breath, blowing a piece of hair out of my face.

"You're not funny."

"Stop being pissed." He tugs my hand, causing me to fall completely into him, and his hand slides around my back so he can hold me close. I try to fight the feeling in my stomach as his mouth lowers toward mine, but as soon as our lips touch, I'm once again lost in everything that is him.

"Now," he says softly against my lips, leaning back just an inch, "Tim has been my driver since my first flight to Tennessee. He has a daughter with autism and works days at the airport doing security. The money he makes at that gig doesn't give him enough to get her the extra help she needs, but driving and tips do. He's a proud man. He won't take handouts, so I let him help with my bags if I've got them, or give him extra, even if I don't."

"What?"

"I'm not highborn, baby. I could have carried our bags or driven to the airport and parked myself, but I like helping him out the only way I can."

"Oh," I whisper, something altogether different settling over me, and I feel myself melt into him.

"Jesus, should I tell you about the charities I donate to?" he asks, searching my face with a smile.

"Maybe." I smile back, and he shakes his head.

"Nut," he mutters, before kissing me once more and leading me toward the house, where Tim is coming down the stairs without our bags but a smile on his face. "It was good to see you, man. I'll call and give you my travel schedule in a few days," Dillon says to him, palming him some money.

"Sounds good, and have a good evening." He gives us each a smile then heads toward the limo, where he gets in and takes off down the driveway as Dillon opens the door to his house. Stopping with the door open, I squeak as he scoops me up with an arm behind my back and one under my knees.

"What are you doing?" I latch on to his neck and he laughs.

"Carrying you over the threshold." He pecks my nose then sets me down before stepping back out to bring our bags inside. I try to tell myself his actions are not sweet, but my stomach still flutters.

"Holy crap." I spin in a circle, taking everything in. I knew from the outside that the house would be absurd to most, but with shiny marble floors, two curved staircases leading to the second level, a giant crystal chandelier hanging from what must be twenty-foot ceilings, it really is ridiculous. I mean, there is even a dark, antique round table in the middle of the space with an obnoxiously large vase of fake flowers in the center of it.

"Do you like it?" Dillon asks and I stop my spin to look at him, resting my hands on my hips.

"Honestly?" I don't want to hurt his feelings, but I would never live in a place like this. It's cold and reminds me of a museum in some ways.

"Honestly."

"No." I shrug then look around again. "I mean, I know some people like these types of houses, don't get me wrong, but it doesn't feel like a home. To me, it feels like a hotel lobby. I can't imagine kicking off my shoes and walking around, and no way can I see kids here. I would be afraid they'd break something or hurt themselves on these shiny floors," I say, shuffling my foot against the shinny marble.

"Kids?"

"Mini people. Kids." I nod, and his eyes change ever-so-slightly before leaving mine.

Scanning the room, he slides his hands into the pockets of his jeans and leans back. “It reminded me of my grandparents’ home in Westchester, New York.” He smiles then looks at me once more. “I loved their house growing up. My brother and I used to spend our summers with them. We spent most of our days skating across floors just like these, playing indoor hockey.”

“Oh.” I look around, trying to picture a younger him doing just that, laughing and having fun, goofing around and being a kid. It seems almost impossible; he’s always kind of uptight and acts like he’s much older than he is.

“Those were some of my favorite memories, and when I found this house, I could see my kids doing the same thing right here.” He pulls one hand free and sweeps it out to encompass the room.

“How many kids do you want?” I ask without thinking.

“Four, if not more.”

“More than four?” I squeak and he grins, causing my legs to quake.

“Or however many you want to give me.”

“Slow down. I haven’t even come to terms with the fact we’re married.”

“You will.” He shrugs, pulling his hand from his pocket and walking toward me. “Now let me show you around.” He takes my hand, not giving me a choice, then leads me through one room after another, including a library with big, oversized couches, fluffy chairs, and a fireplace making the room feel cozy. A kitchen, with a huge island in the center, tons of counter space, and appliances the likes I’ve never seen in person, including a glass front fridge and a pizza oven. Before we even make it to his room I’m half in love with the house, but when I see his bedroom I’m done. The room is three times the size of mine, with a masculine four-post bed in the center of it covered in crisp white sheets and a simple pattern white and gray duvet, but by far my favorite thing is his closet that is so big it has an island in the middle. By the time the tour is over and he's packed some clothes, I'm wondering if it wouldn't be so bad to stay at his place.

"WE ARE NOT watching this garbage."

Pausing the television, I turn and glare at Dillon, who's sprawled out next to me with his back to my headboard. His bare chest on display, tight boxers leaving nothing to the imagination, and his feet crossed at the ankle.

"This is not garbage. This is the truth, and you just need to expand your mind." I point the remote at him, letting out a huff. My cousin July got me hooked on this show, and ever since I watched the first episode, I've become an addict.

"Aliens, babe, seriously? *Ancient Aliens*? What the ever-loving fuck is that?"

"The government has been covering up the secrets of the universe for years. These people," I point back at the TV, "are letting us in on what's really been going on for centuries."

"That guy there?" He points at the TV, and I look at the screen. Okay, so he looks a little strange with shaggy brown hair and beady eyes, but that doesn't negate the fact he's a genius and I may have a little crush on him.

"Just watch."

"Can we find something else?"

"No, this is the newest season and I have to catch up. And then I want to watch *Naked and Afraid*."

"*Naked and Afraid*?" His brows snap together, and I roll my eyes.

"Have you been living under a rock? It's only one of the best shows in the world."

"I'm seeing we have different tastes in TV," he mumbles, looking at me like I'm crazy.

"Whatever. You'll see," I mutter back, pressing play on the DVR and turning back to watch my show, all while resting my elbows on my knees which are crossed in front of me.

"If I'm forced to watch this garbage, you're going to cuddle with me." He tags me around the waist then settles me against him. I don't put up a fight; there is no point. Besides, I like cuddling with him, even though his constant grunting and disbelieving huffs during my shows are annoying.

"Can I have the remote now?" he asks, three hours later, when *Naked and Afraid* comes to an end.

"Yeah." I sleepily hand it to him then watch, with my cheek to his chest and my arm thrown across his abs, as he flips through channels until he finds Conan O'Brian and drops the remote to his stomach. "And you thought my shows were lame." I cuddle closer, feeling his chest shake under my cheek as my eyes slide closed and I fall asleep.

WAKING SUDDENLY WHEN the doorbell rings, I roll across the bed and off, landing with my feet to the floor. "What the fuck?" He sits up, looking at the clock next to the bed, and my eyes follow his, seeing it's just two minutes after seven. I totally forgot about telling my brother, Jax, to bring my cat, Leo, back to me this morning before he went to work, and I know that's him at the door. And under no circumstances do I want him to see Dillon in my house.

"Stay here." I point at him while skirting the bed and slipping on one of my zip up hoodies over my sleep shorts and tank.

"Stay here. Has she lost her damn mind?" I hear him ask as I open the door, closing it behind me as I slip out. Jogging down the hall to the front door, I open it just an inch and poke my head out.

"Hey." I squint one eye closed as the early morning sun almost blinds me.

"Sorry about the time," Jax says, holding a hissing Leo out toward me. "I had to sneak him out of the house before Hope got up."

"Hey, baby," I greet my cat, settling him against my chest, kissing the top of his hairless head and hearing him hiss before looking up at Jax once more. "Tell Hope she can come see him anytime she wants." I smile, using my free hand to grab the edge of the door when it looks like he's going to try and come in, and his eyes move to my hand.

"I'm going back to sleep before I need to get up for work. I'll call you later."

"What?" His hand shoots out, preventing me from shutting the door, and his eyes narrow. "What the hell is going on?"

"Nothing," I huff. "I'm just jet-lagged. I'll call you later this afternoon."

"Are you okay?"

Feeling my face soften, I nod. Most of the time, having a brother is annoying, but I would be lost without him. He's my best friend, and has been since we were little.

"I'm fine, I swear." I cross my fingers over my heart.

"Call me when you got time today."

"Will do," I agree, shutting the door before he walks off, and then flip the lock back into place.

Holding Leo up in front of my face, I walk down the hall toward my room, murmuring, "I missed my baby so much," as he hisses. His paw swipes at a piece of my hair hanging near my face. "Are you mad at Mama?" I ask, and he hisses again, making me smile. He's always mad when I leave him for any length of time. Okay, he's really always mad, but I love him.

"So I take it you're not going to tell your bother about us." Dillon's voice startles me and I turn, finding him with his bare shoulder resting against the doorjamb of my room, his arms crossed over his chest.

"I'm going to tell him." I shrug, leaving out *'at some point,'* since he doesn't need to know that part.

"Yeah?" he questions softly, and I hate the disappointment I see in his gaze.

"I'm going to tell everyone we're dating, and then once they're used to that idea, I'll explain we're actually married."

"Married?" Jax's voice rings through the room behind me and I spin, finding him at the end of the hall, having obviously used his key to get in.

"Jax—" I caution, and his eyes swing to Dillon.

"Married? You fucking married my sister, when you're engaged to someone else?" He lunges forward, and I watch in slow motion as his shoulder hits Dillon in the stomach and he uses his forward momentum to take him across the room, where they crash into my nightstand and lamp, causing the nightstand to bang back into the wall and my lamp to topple over and shatter at their feet.

"Jax, stop it now!" I scream, dropping Leo to the ground then running toward the two men wrestling in my bedroom.

"Get out of here, Ash," Jax snaps as I try to pull him off Dillon, who's not even attempting to fight back.

"Screw you, Jax." I shove him, wishing I were bigger since it does absolutely nothing to move him.

"If she gets hurt, I'm going to kick your ass," Dillon barks at Jax, and like his words have spoken to the devil himself, I take a step forward to shove Jax again and my foot slides across a shard of glass.

"Fuck." Tears fill my eyes. "You stupid fricking jerk," I whimper, squeezing my eyes closed, too afraid to move as I freeze in place.

"Get the fuck off me!" Dillon snarls, and I hear someone stumble back before I'm up in arms that I've grown accustomed to and carried across the room.

"Are you okay, Ash?" Jax asks, and I hold Dillon tighter as pain throbs through my foot.

"No, she's not fucking okay," Dillon snaps, then light filters through my closed eyelids as I'm set on the counter. "Fuck, baby, take some deep breaths for me." His voice is gentle, and I hear someone else inhale sharply.

"She's gonna need stitches," Jax says, and I open my eyes and feel them widen as I see blood, so much blood, running down my foot and dripping onto the white tiles in my bathroom.

Swallowing down the nausea I feel come over me, I look up at Dillon as the room starts to spin. "Breathe, baby, you need to breathe for me," he says calmly, grabbing a towel, wrapping it around my foot, and lifting it onto the counter near my inner thigh. "Keep pressure on it." He tenderly wraps my hands around it, and I nod once more.

"Fuck, Ash." Jax moves toward me, but Dillon puts a hand against his chest, preventing him from getting to me.

"Stay the fuck back," he growls, then turns to me and his eyes flash as my head grows dizzy.

"God dammit." Dropping his hand from Jax chest, he grabs ahold of my face as his gets close. "Take a breath. A deep breath in, then let it out." I hadn't even realized I was holding my breath until that second. Until I pull in a deep breath and feel the oxygen burn through my lungs. "Good girl," he whispers, touching is forehead to mine briefly, then he grabs another towel and ties it around my foot tightly. "Keep breathing for me. I'll be right back." He leans away, waiting for me to agree. Jerking my head up once, I watch him move, using his size to force Jax out of the bathroom.

"I'm taking her to the hospital," Jax says, trying to shove his way back toward me. I don't hear Dillon's reply. My eyes drop to my foot, wrapped in two of my plush white towels, and I watch red soak through the two layers of fabric.

"Dillon," I whisper, "there's way too much blood." I start to panic as he comes back, wearing a plain blue T-shirt, shorts, and sneakers that aren't even tied. Scooping me off the counter, his mouth moves to my ear. "You'll be okay."

"Yeah." My head drops to his shoulder, too heavy for me to hold up, as we head down the hall toward the door behind Jax.

"I'll drive," my brother states when we're outside, and I feel Dillon's chest expand and a growl of annoyance rumble his chest. I want to tell him to stop being a dick, but I'm too tired to even try to speak. Opening the door to Jax's truck, I expect him to set me down. Instead, he gets in and settles me on his lap as Jax jogs around and gets behind the wheel.

"I'm sorry, Ash."

Tossing my hand out, I wave him off. I know he feels bad enough already, and I honestly don't have it in me to tell him he's an asshole right now.

"Just drive," Dillon snaps, and I rub his chest when it rumbles again. His body relaxes, ever so slightly, as his hand moves to the back of my head, holding me there.

"Fuck you. This is your fault," Jax retaliates.

"Me? You came at me like a deranged lunatic."

"You're engaged to another woman!" Jax roars.

I bury my face against Dillon's chest and his arms tighten around me. "I'm not fucking engaged. If you gave me a half a fucking second, I would have told you that."

"Damn fucking straight, you're not engaged anymore, since you married my goddamn sister."

"Fuck! Just fucking drive and shut the fuck up," Dillon hisses, and I squeeze my eyes closed, feeling a headache coming on. Feeling the tension in the car growing with each mile, I'm more than thankful when we reach the hospital and Jax drops us at the ambulance bay where Dillon get's out, still holding me.

Carrying me through the automatic emergency room doors, I hear them swish closed behind us, then seconds later, a woman gasp.

"Oh my, come on. Follow me." I try to lift my head to see where we're going, but Dillon's large hand holds down my head, keeping me in place.

"She needs a doctor," he barks as a curtain slides open, and I'm gently placed on a hard mattress. Wrapping his hands around my foot, my eyes squeeze closed.

"The doctor will be right in," the woman murmurs before leaving.

"Baby, look at me." Opening one eye then the other, I focus on Dillon's worried face above mine.

"Stop snarling at everyone," I whisper, and his eyes slide closed while his forehead drops to my chest. Running my fingers through his hair, I pull back, forcing him to look at me. "I'm okay. It's just a cut. I'll be fine."

"I know," he agrees softly.

"Ashlyn."

"Could this morning get any better," I groan, knowing the person attached to that voice.

"What's going on?" David, my ex, asks.

I look at him and then Dillon as he mutters, "Fuck me," while resting his hand against my chest, keeping me down when I attempt to sit up.

"Are you the doctor on duty?" Dillon asks, and David looks between Dillon and me.

His brows snap together as his chest puffs out, making me roll my eyes. "I'm a doctor at this hospital," he informs us, like we don't know, when of course we do. Everyone in town knows he's a doctor, because he brings it up any time he's got a chance. But that's not why I broke up with him. Nope, we broke up because he thought any woman lucky enough to snag him would praise Jesus for her good fortune. *Not so much.* He was rude, condescending, and a big, fat cheat.

"Get someone else."

"Pardon?" He narrows his eyes.

"You heard me."

"Dillon." I try to sit up again, and his eyes snap to me.

"He's not touching you."

"Dillon," I warn as Jax comes in, narrowing his eyes on David.

"Why the hell are you in here?"

"I'm a doctor," he grumbles, tugging on the collar of his dress shirt.

"Find someone else to take over for you," Jax says, and Dillon grunts in agreement.

"Christ." I cover my face, letting out a breath of annoyance. "I'm going to fricking bleed to death in a damn hospital."

"Just move and let me have a look at her," David snaps as Dillon's hand on my foot tightens.

"David, what are you doing in here?" A woman wearing a doctor's coat frowns at him as she comes through the open curtain, followed by the nurse who left earlier. "You're supposed to be off duty."

"Yeah, David. You're supposed to be off duty." Dillon glares as I rub my hands down my face in frustration.

"We've got this covered. You can go," the new doctor dismisses him, taking a step toward me. "I hear you're going to need some stitches." She smiles softly, putting on a pair of gloves as the nurse rolls over a cart with supplies and begins to set up things on the top.

"I don't know, but there's a lot of blood," I tell her, and she nods then moves her eyes from the hands wrapped around my foot, up the arms attached to those hands, and blinks when her eyes meet Dillon's.

"Lord, save me," I mutter as her eyes widen, and she blushes.

"My wife needs a doctor. Are you a doctor?" Dillon grumbles, and she clears her throat.

"Ye… yes, of course," she stutters out as her blush grows deeper, and her eyes drop to my foot. I can't even blame her for her reaction, since I had the same one when I saw Dillon for the first time. "Foot injuries tend to bleed a lot. It may not be as bad as you think," she continues after a moment, unwrapping the towels that are swaddling my foot, but she's wrong, it is that bad. And it's not until an hour and four stitches later that I'm finally sent home with an extremely annoying overbearing man, who also happens to be my husband.

Chapter 3

Ashlyn

"MOM, I'M FINE. It's just a few stitches. Dr. Woods assured me I'll be up and about in just a few days." I put my cell on speaker and set it next to me on the bed as Dillon grabs the pillow on the other side of me. Leo, who isn't happy about having his sleep interrupted, stands and hisses, batting his paw in his direction. Placing the pillow carefully under my foot, he reaches over my legs and runs his hand down Leo's hairless back.

We got home from the hospital a little less than an hour ago, and when we got back to my house, Dillon deposited me on the couch while he and Jax cleaned up. While they were cleaning, I could hear them talking but couldn't make out much of anything, which was annoying, since I knew they were talking about me. Jax was still mad when he left, but there was nothing I could do about that.

"Maybe we should come home," Mom says, cutting into my thoughts.

"No!" I shout then lower my tone. "That's not necessary." I lean back against the headboard, taking the remote from Dillon when he hands it to me. I don't know if my karma is taking a turn for the better, but my parents' trip to Florida couldn't have come at a better time.

"Fine, I'll send a message to Jax and let him know I expect him to look out for you while we're away," she says, and I pray that if she talks to him he keeps his mouth closed. I told him before he left, after helping Dillon clean up the mess in my room, that if he said one word to Mom or Dad about Dillon and I, I would never talk to him again and I meant that.

"I'm here with Ashlyn," Dillon says, and I feel my eyes widen before narrowing on him as he shrugs, picking up his bag from the floor and setting it on the end of the bed.

"Dillon's there with you?" Mom whispers, and I let my head fall back as my eyes squeeze tight.

"He's here," I confirm with a sigh, since I obviously can't say he's not.

"Is there anything you want to tell me?" she questions softly. "I mean, you two were just in Vegas together, and now he's at your house?"

"Um." I feel my stomach twist. I don't want to lie about this to her, but I know the truth will have her and my dad on a plane back to Tennessee within hours.

"Ash and I are seeing each other," Dillon cuts in rudely, and I swear if I had the ability to get out of bed, I would kick his ass. Instead, I open my eyes back up and glare at him.

"Did... did he just say you two are seeing each other?" Mom whispers, apparently losing the ability to speak above that decibel.

"Sorry, Mom, hold on a second." I hit mute and glare at Dillon, holding up my hand. "Do not say anything else."

"I'm not hiding us from them, or from anyone," he replies, not even looking up from his bag as he digs through it.

"I'm not hiding us," I lie, and his head lifts. His eyes meet mine, narrowing, making me fight the urge to squirm. "I don't want to tell them about us over the phone."

"Fine." He shrugs, but he doesn't look fine. In fact, he looks pissed.

"Fine," I mutter back.

Shaking his head, he lifts his hands over his shoulders, pulls off his shirt, and then kicks off his sneakers and shorts before he heads for the bathroom naked, without another glance to where I'm seated.

"You're really flipping annoying!" I yell, hearing the shower turn on. Gaining no reply in return, I take my phone off mute. "Sorry about that, Mom."

"So..."

My bottom lip goes between my teeth, and I grumble, "Yes, we're dating."

"Honey—" I look at the phone to make sure I didn't lose the call when she doesn't say more.

"Mom?"

"You know I adore Dillon, but this is not okay. He's engaged to another woman," she murmurs, and I roll my eyes toward the ceiling, letting out a long, frustrated breath.

"He's not with her. He hasn't been for a while."

"Are you sure?"

God, I hope so. Otherwise, Dillon is going to die a very tragic death, I think, running my fingers over Leo's head when he presses against my side.

"I'll explain everything when you're home," I mutter, leaving out the fact I plan on getting her drunk before I tell her, in hopes she doesn't remember anything the next day.

"Okay, honey, I trust you."

Shit.

"Mom." I fake yawn. "My pain pill is starting to kick in. I'm going to take a nap. I love you, and tell Dad I love him."

"I will," she agrees softly. "Love you."

Hitting end on the call, I stare at the bathroom and listen to the shower while I wait for Dillon to reappear. I feel like he's made it perfectly clear that he wants everyone to know about us, but what about his family? I've never even heard him mention them. Hearing the water turn off, I watch him step out of the bathroom with a towel wrapped around his waist a minute later. I lose my train of thought for a moment as I watch him put on a pair of gray boxers and walk across the room to my closet, sliding open the mirrored doors, where he stored some of his clothes last night.

"Why did you cut your hair?"

His eyes come to me over his shoulder, and the look on his face makes my stomach twist with unease. "Is that really what you want to ask me right now?"

Actually, it isn't. But I'm not sure I want to know the answer to my real question, since that would make this thing between us even more real.

"I've been wondering." I shrug, and he mutters something I don't catch then pulls a pair of his dark slacks off a hanger and steps into them, grabbing a dark gray button-down shirt and shrugging it on.

"Are you mad?"

"Nope."

"You seem mad," I mutter as he buttons up his shirt, then grabs his belt that is hanging over the back of the chair in the corner of my room before he loops it through his waistband, tucks in his shirt, and buckles his belt. Taking a seat, I watch him put on his shoes without sparing me a glance then watch him stand and grab his wallet off the dresser near the door, I'm at a loss. This would be the moment in any of my previous relationships where I would say, 'Fuck you,' and never talk to the guy again. But Dillon was right. I can't do that with him now, not without a crap-ton of paperwork and maybe even a broken heart.

"I'll be at the office. Your pills are there; take one and try to get some rest." He nods to the bedside table, where he left me a bottle of water and pills, then heads for the door. My stomach twists uncomfortably as I watch him turn to leave.

"When are we going to tell your parents about us?" I blurt without thinking, and he turns to face me, the pain in his eyes catching me off guard.

"Both my parents are dead," he states evenly, and before my brain catches up and his words register, he's gone.

FEELING THE BED shift, I blink my eyes open and find Dillon sitting in the crook of my lap, softly gazing at me. I called him multiple times after he left, but he didn't answer his cell. And when I called the office, Matt, our new receptionist, told me he was with patients, but always made sure to ask if I was okay or if it was an emergency. I knew that was Dillon, not Matt. I knew if I played the 'it's an emergency' card, Dillon would have rushed back to the house.

"Hey." He lifts his hand and slides his fingers softly across my forehead as his eyes follow the path of his touch.

"Hey," I reply softly, studying him. He doesn't look angry anymore; he looks apprehensive, making me wonder what he's thinking. Scooting back, his hand drops to rest on the bed near my hip, and his eyes scan my face before meeting my gaze once more.

"I didn't know about your parents. I'm really sorry for being insensitive," I whisper, and his face softens.

"You weren't being insensitive. You didn't know, and I don't talk about them often… to anyone," he confesses gently and I nod, chewing the inside of my cheek.

"Will you tell me about them?" I question delicately when he doesn't say more. His face softens further, and he kicks off his shoes and climbs up next to me on the bed, tucking me into his side.

"My moms name was Lacey and my dad was Paul, they met at summer camp when my mom was fourteen and my dad was sixteen. They disliked each other from the moment they met. My mom was outgoing, happy, and the center of attention, while my dad was uptight, high-strung, and slightly antisocial." I hear the smile in his tone, and I smile a little myself, thinking they sound a lot like us. "Both their parents sent them back to the same camp every summer, and every summer, the animosity between my mom and dad grew a little more."

"And then they fell in love?" I tilt my head back and look at him, and he shakes his head.

"No, they eventually got too old for summer camp and forgot about each other."

"Oh," I mutter, thinking that's a total letdown. His arms give me a squeeze and I hear him chuckle before his lips touch the top of my head.

"When my mom was twenty-two and my dad was twenty-four, they met again at a party. My mom was going to Wellesley, and my dad was going to Harvard, when they ran into each other. Mom was drunk and spilt her drink on him," he says, and I giggle, pressing my forehead to his chest, picturing his dad's face and imagining it looked a lot like Dillon's. "My dad hadn't changed at all. He was pissed and demanded my mom pay for his shirt to be dry-cleaned."

"Did she tell him where to shove it?" I smile.

"Yeah." He laughs, running his hand over the top of my head. "That did not go over well with my dad. He left the party and went back to his dorm. The next day, he took his shirt to the dry-cleaners then tracked down my mom's address and sent her the bill."

"Oh, Lord, I see where you get your personality from," I murmur, feeling his chest shake under my cheek.

"The day she got the bill in the mail, she went to his dorm."

"Go Mom." I whisper, tucking my hand under my cheek. "They had a blowout fight in the middle of campus. My dad, hating the attention, gave in and told her just to leave, that he didn't want her money. She did leave. She took off, only she didn't go back to her school right away. Instead, she went to the dry-cleaners and picked up his shirt."

"Your mom was awesome."

"She was," he agrees softly, running his fingers through my hair. "When my dad went to get his shirt, he found out it had already been picked up, and he knew it was her. He thought she was insane."

"But he liked her, didn't he?"

"He didn't know how he felt about her until the fall, when my mom graduated from Wellesley and started at Harvard Law School, and they ran into each other again. My dad swore my mom did everything within her power to annoy him. She would always stop to talk to him, always do crazy things to get his attention or bug him."

"And he fell in love with her."

"He did, but my mom was having none of it. She gave him a run for his money. It took a year for him to catch her. She wasn't exactly easy to hold onto, but my dad persevered and one thing led to another. They started dating then moved in together, got married, graduated college, and had Parker and me."

"Parker's your brother?"

"Yeah, you'll meet him." He squeezes me again and my stomach fills with butterflies. "He's five years older than me and lives in Chicago with his wife and sons. He was a doctor, but after he and his wife had twins, he decided to stay home, and his wife, who is a plastic surgeon, works."

"What about your dad? Your mom was in law. What was he?"

"My dad was a dentist."

"Is that why you wanted to be a dentist?" I ask, tilting my head back catching his smile.

"No." He chuckles. "I wanted to be a lawyer."

"I could see you as a lawyer." He smiles, and I question, "So why did you become a dentist then?"

"After he and my mom passed, I got into Harvard. I decided law wasn't for me, so I followed in Dad's footsteps instead."

"I'm sure both of them would be proud of you."

"I'm sure they would too," he mutters, dropping a kiss to the top of my head.

"Can I ask what happened to them?" I question after a moment, and his hold on me tightens.

"They were coming home from a New Years Eve party. My father had been drinking and insisted he was sober enough to drive. He wasn't, or maybe he was. Their car hit a patch of black ice, went off the side of the road, and rolled down a ravine. They both died instantly." Hearing that, I wonder how much that changed who he was. I can't imagine how a tragedy like that would affect someone.

"I'm so sorry."

"Me too." He rests his mouth at the top of my head, then whispers, "Your family reminds me a lot of how my family was before."

That makes heart hurt for him. I don't say anything else or ask any more questions. Instead, I lay there holding him for a long time, with my ear to his chest, listening to the sound of his heart so long that my pain pill wears off completely and my stomach growls, reminding me I haven't eaten anything since the few crackers I had this afternoon.

"Do you want to order in?" He laughs, hearing another loud growl come from my stomach, and I nod against his chest.

"Chinese, if that's okay with you."

"That works. When did you take your last pill?" he asks when I wince as he gets off the bed.

"A little after you left this morning," I admit, watching him strip off his dress shirt and slacks and put on a pair of loose workout pants.

"You shouldn't wait so long between to take them."

"It's not that bad. Just a little pain, nothing I can't handle."

"It's not something you need to handle," he grumbles, putting on a form-fitting white tee.

"They make me tired. I don't want my sleeping schedule to go all wonky, since tomorrow I plan on going back to work."

"You're not working tomorrow."

"I am."

"You're not," he disagrees, shaking his head, and I let out an annoyed breath.

"I don't want to fight with you right now."

"We're not fighting. I'm telling you that you're not working tomorrow. You need to keep off your foot so it has time to heal."

"I sit most of the day. It will be fine, Dillon."

"Yes, it will be, since you're staying home."

"Does everything with you have to be an argument?" I question, tossing my legs over the side of the bed so I can stand.

"You're the one who loves to argue, babe. This wouldn't even be an issue right now if you'd just listen to me."

"You're right. You don't like to argue. You just like to boss me around, tell me what to do, and then get pissed when I don't listen. Even better," I huff, standing carefully, making sure to keep the pressure off my foot, and then I grab one of the crutches leaning against my bedside table.

"You got four stitches in your foot this morning, four stitches that need time to heal properly. I'm not bossing you around. I'm concerned about your wellbeing."

"Fine, I won't work tomorrow, but only because I don't want to," I grumble, making sure he knows it's not his choice but mine.

"Good," he mutters, then looks at the crutch under my arm and frowns. "Where are you going?"

"The bathroom then the living room, so we can eat there."

"We could eat in here." He nods to the bed, but I shake my head.

"No eating in my bed."

"No eating in your bed?" He raises a brow, and I really wish I didn't find him so attractive, especially when I'm annoyed with him.

"I don't like to sleep on crumbs."

Smiling, he takes a step closer to me and places a kiss to my forehead, muttering there, "I'll meet you in the living room with the menu."

"I know what I want. Should I text it to you?" I ask, grabbing my cell.

"I think I can remember."

"Okay. Peanut noodles, fried dumplings, egg rolls, hot and sour soup, ginger—"

"I'll wait for you to come out to call," he cuts me off, smiling. "Do you want me to help you into the bathroom?"

"Nope, I got it." I limp, using my crutch, and head for the bathroom, ignoring the fact that he follows behind me until I'm inside and have shut the door. Once I'm done taking care of business, I wash my hands and open the door, not at all surprised that he's standing outside the door waiting on me. "I told you I'm okay."

"I know I just wanted to make sure." He shrugs taking my crutch from me, leaning it against the wall next to the bathroom, before scooping me up into his arms.

"I can walk," I halfheartedly inform him while wrapping my arms around his neck.

"You can walk tomorrow when I'm not home to carry you," he says, carrying me to the couch in the living room where he settles me against his side as he places the order for Chinese food.

Unloading the bag of Chinese food the delivery guy dropped off twenty minutes later, I watch Dillon come back with plates and forks, taking a seat next to me on the couch.

"Are you going to really eat all of that?" he asks, and I turn to look at him and nod.

"Not all of it right now, but yes. Between tonight and tomorrow for breakfast, none of it will go to waste."

"I've never seen a woman eat as much as you do," he states, and my hand lingers over my styrofoam dish containing peanut noodles.

"Is that bad?"

"No, I like that you eat. I like that you're not afraid to eat in front of me."

"Oh." I move my hand to his container of beef and broccoli and brown rice, and hand it to him, holding his stare as he takes it from me. "I work out," I inform him, not sure why I feel the need to tell him that, but I'm suddenly uncomfortable with his comment.

Setting his container of food on the table, he leans forward and takes hold of my chin. "You're beautiful, Ashlyn. You could weigh a hundred pounds more and you'd still be gorgeous. I'd still be attracted to you."

Studying him, I can see he's being sincere, and those stupid butterflies take flight once more as my body leans into his touch.

I've never needed a man to tell me I'm beautiful, to pay for my meals, open doors, or take care of me, but having him do those things is playing havoc with my emotions and making me pray this thing between us works out.

"What are you thinking right now?" he questions softly.

That I'm stupidly falling in love with you.

"I don't know," I lie, looking into his beautiful eyes and wondering what he's thinking.

"Hmm," he hums, leaning in and touching his mouth to mine briefly. "Let's eat before all your food is cold."

"Okay," I agree, but instead of doing the smart thing, I lean forward and press my mouth to his, sweeping my tongue across his lips. The instant I do, his hold on my chin tightens, his free hand slides into my hair, and he takes over the kiss, sweeping his tongue into my mouth. I don't know how long we make out, but by the time we get around to eating, our food is cold.

"GO BACK TO bed," Dillon bosses as I lean against the front door.

Rolling my eyes at that, I grumble, "I already told you I would." I just catch his lips tip up, which annoys the hell out of me. He knows he's won. Then again, he's won for the last week. I haven't worked all week long, and today is my last day at home. My foot is much better. I can put weight on it without wincing, and I don't need to take the pills I was prescribed anymore to deal with the pain.

"I have to stop at my place when I get off work to pick some stuff up. Do you want me to bring dinner home?"

Home. Okay, that word makes those pesky butterflies take flight again, but I shouldn't be surprised. He's calling this home since he's been here with me every night.

"Um, I may try to cook," I murmur, watching a familiar car pull into my second driveway.

"I'll check in on you today, before then."

"Okay."

"Okay," he repeats softly, dipping his face and brushing his lips over mine once, twice, then a third time, sliding his tongue across my lips, making me moan. I latch on to his dress shirt, and his hand on my ass squeezes. I have no idea how much longer I will be able to hold down the no sex rule. Every time he touches me, my whole body begs for more, and it's not helping that we are sharing a bed and he walks around half naked most of the time.

"I'll see you tonight," he speaks against my mouth, giving my ass another squeeze before sauntering off down the steps to his car. Watching his ass in dark slacks, his broad shoulders covered in a burgundy dress shirt, and his confident gait, I hold my breath. I definitely won't be able to hold out much longer.

"Um… what the hell was that?" Michelle, my very best friend in the whole wide world, asks from the sidewalk with her hands on her hips and her brows arched. I totally forgot about seeing her car pull in a moment ago. She's been away with her boyfriend, Luka, visiting his family in Colorado, and we haven't really talked since she's been gone.

"Um…"

"Do not 'um' me, woman. Are you insane? That was Dillon the Dick, with his tongue down your throat and hands on your ass." She swivels her head, watching Dillon back his shiny black Mercedes out of the drive and onto the road. "You have some explaining to do," she hisses, tossing her long red hair over her shoulder while stomping toward me on her wedge-covered feet, and I cringe.

I can't lie to her. I don't even want to lie to my parents about this. As she forces me back into the house, I let her in and close the door before turning to face her.

"Spill it now. Obviously, your relationship with him has changed."

"I may have married him in Vegas," I say quietly, and she blinks.

"What?" She presses her hand against the wall dramatically, like she needs it to hold her up. "Did you just say you married him in Vegas?"

"Maybe." I shrug, and she slides down the wall to the floor and rolls to her back.

"I knew this would happen. I knew it, I knew it, I knew it." She laughs, kicking her legs up and down like a toddler throwing a fit.

"When you're done, I'll be in the kitchen," I mutter, moving around her and down the hall toward the kitchen so I can put some food out for Leo, who has been in hiding all morning.

Coming around the corner a second later, she climbs up on one of the barstools and grabs a banana from my fruit dish—which had always been empty until Dillon started staying here. "Please tell me he has a big penis."

"How are you my best friend?" I scoop out Leo's food into a dish and set it on the ground in his spot.

Taking a bite of her banana, she chews and swallows then points the uneaten portion at me. "As your best friend, I need to know you are married to a man who has a big penis."

"You don't seem to think it's a big deal that I married him."

"You guys have been pussy-footing around each other forever. I knew it would happen." She shrugs. "Now answer my question."

"Yes."

"Yes what?" She smirks, and I roll my eyes.

"Yes, he has a big penis. Are you happy?"

"Not really, since his super-sized penis and hotness isn't mine, but I'm happy for you."

"Are you really?" I whisper, and her brown eyes soften.

"Very. He's the only man I know who's ever made you feel any kind of emotion besides your family. Any other guy, you couldn't care less what they think. To me, that says a lot."

"It's way too fast."

"Yeah." She nods. "I mean, I thought you two would end up together, but I had no idea you'd marry him before actually dating him."

"I didn't plan it."

"I bet not, Miss ADD, but then again, some of the best things in life are unplanned."

"I guess we'll find out. So how was your trip with Luka?"

"Amazing," she breathes, resting her chin in the palm of her hands and I blink.

"Is that… Is that what I think it is?" I whisper, pointing at the giant rock on her finger.

"This little thing?" She holds up her hand, then screams, "I'm getting married!"

"Oh, my God, you finally said yes!" I shout, launching myself across the island and grabbing her hand. "Holy shit, he did good." I study the large princess-cut diamond surrounded by smaller sapphires. It's perfect for her.

"If you like it, then you better put a ring on it." She giggles, and I laugh right along with her.

"You're getting married." Tears fill my eyes, and I move around the island, wrapping her in a hug. No one deserves happy more than she does. No one.

"Will you be my maid of honor?"

"If you even think of asking anyone else, I'll kill you."

"I would never." She rocks me back and forth then pulls away. "I'm pissed I didn't get to be at your wedding."

"I don't even really remember it, honestly." I laugh, and she shakes her head then her eyes widen.

"Does your dad know you got married?"

"No one except Jax knows. I have no idea how I'm going to tell them," I sigh, letting her go.

"Oh, God, I do not envy you right now. Your dad is going to lose his mind when he finds out his baby got married." She's right; my dad will lose his mind. He's always been protective of me and has hated every guy I've ever dated.

"I know," I huff, moving to sit on the stool next to hers. "Dillon told my mom that he and I are dating. I don't know if my mom just hasn't told my dad or what, but he hasn't asked me about it when we've talked."

"Knowing your mom and dad, she's told him and he's trying to figure out how he feels about it. He likes Dillon. They always talk whenever your family invites him to functions. He respects him."

Sheesh, how could I forget that? Since almost the moment Dillon came into my life, he's been at all of my family gatherings, and he and my dad do get along. They are always off chatting when they are together. It used to annoy me, but now I'm wondering if it is something that will work in my favor.

"You're right."

"I'm always right, and once again, I was right about you and Dillon. I told you he had the hot's for you."

She did tell me that all the damn time, and I always ignored it, never even wanting to think it was possibly true. "Whatever. So are you not working today?"

"I have a few showings this afternoon, and a closing at five. Why are you not at work?"

"This." I lift my foot and her face scrunches up. The wound is healed, but the stitches are still in place, and the bruising has turned an ugly shade of yellow.

"What the hell happened?"

"Jax got in a fight with Dillon. They broke my lamp, and when I tried to break them up, I sliced my foot open."

"Have we not spoken in the past week?" She frowns, and I shrug.

"We have, but not much."

"Apparently."

"So I'm guessing what Jenna said about Dillon's ex was true?"

"Yeah, I don't know." I drop my head to the countertop. I completely forgot that a few months ago, Michelle told me Jenna, a mutual friend who works at the airport, helped the she-bitch from hell get on a flight back to New York after Dillon broke up with her. At the time, I didn't believe it since Dillon never mentioned it and Jenna tends to lie about everything.

"It will be okay." She rubs my back, and I turn my forehand on the counter to look at her.

"He told me that he has to explain to me about their relationship."

"What?"

"I don't know. Every time he's tried to bring it up, I've lost my mind. Like, literally… lost my mind. Even the mention of her name pisses me off and makes me see red."

"Jealousy."

"Yeah, and I've never felt that emotion before, so I don't know how to deal with it."

"You'll get used to it."

"It's not something I want to get used to. I don't like feeling like that."

"So talk to him."

Snorting, I lift my head. "Yeah, at some point I'll grow some balls and hear him out. I just don't know when that will be."

"Don't let it go too long. If you want this to work with him, you need to know she's out of his life and hear why she was in it in the first place, when they obviously didn't suit each other."

"You don't think they did?" I question, running my hand over the cold countertop.

"No, he's nice, and she makes the ice queen seem tame. I only saw them together a few times, and I definitely never saw him touch her like I saw him touch you this morning."

"I never saw him touch her either," I mutter, wondering what the hell that's about.

"Just ask him about it."

"I will," I agree.

"I should go." She hops down off the stool. "I need to pick up some groceries and take them home before I have to meet my first client."

"Sure." I follow her down the hall toward the front door.

"We should do dinner with the guys this weekend."

"I'll talk to Dillon," I concur, giving her a hug before stepping back and opening the door.

"Call me. Love you."

"Love you too." I wait, watching her get into her car, then shut the door and head back to living room, where I plop down on the couch and wonder if I will have the guts to talk to Dillon before it's too late.

Chapter 4

Ashlyn

BEING CAREFUL NOT to cut myself, I sing, "Fuzzy Wuzzy was a bear. Fuzzy Wuzzy had no hair. Fuzzy Wuzzy wasn't very fuzzy, was he?" and listen to the sound of my voice bounce off the walls around me. It's been ten days since I was able to enjoy a normal shower, and I'm loving every second of it. Humming the end, I scream as the shower curtain is ripped open and Dillon's eyes scan over me, leaving me frozen in place.

"Babe, seriously?" He laughs, and my brain kicks in as I scramble off the bench I was sitting on while shaving my vagina and attempt to cover myself, smearing shaving cream everywhere in the process.

"Oh, my God! What are you doing? You can't just come in here!" I screech, bending at the waist in an attempt to hide as much of myself as I can.

"I think the real question is why do you have a theme song for shaving your vagina? And"—he holds up his hand, pointing at his finger and the band there—"you're my wife. I can do whatever the fuck I want when it comes to you."

"Get out!" I shout, knowing it's pointless to argue, since every time I do, he goes over the top on me and forces me to admit we are married.

"I need a shower." He lifts his hands behind his head and pulls off his shirt.

Squeezing my eyes closed, I growl, "You are not getting in here with me." Feeling my core tighten at just the thought, I can't take much more of this self-induced torture. Every time he's close to me, it makes it hard not to give in to my body and jump him.

"Why are your eyes closed?" I feel his heat at my back and his teeth nip the skin of my neck as he slides his hands around me, pulling me flush against him.

His arousal bumps against me, and I beg silently for mercy. "Dillon."

"Hmm?" he breathes against my neck, coasting his fingers down my stomach. "Are you smooth now?" God, I don't know. I can't even remember how much shaving I got done before he interrupted me, but I think I at least got myself cleaned up enough so it's no longer a jungle down there. "Are you wet?"

"I'm in the shower, so yes," I state, trying to sound mad, but the moan that escapes proves I'm a liar.

His free hand moves up to tweak my nipple, sending a bolt of pleasure through me. "I guess I'll just have to find out for myself." He nips my earlobe then licks down the column of my throat, biting my shoulder while his fingers slide between my folds and over my clit, causing my hips to jerk forward. I'm lost in him. Completely lost in him—his mouth on my neck, his hand at my breast, his fingers between my legs. I will give him anything he wants right now, as long as he doesn't stop what he's doing.

"Oh, God," I moan as one finger slides inside of me.

"Not God." He nips my neck hard, thrusting two fingers deep. "Your husband."

My head falls back against his shoulder as I ride his fingers. I knew I missed his touch, but didn't know how much until right now. His thumb rolls over my clit and his hand at my breast squeezes.

"You're close."

I am. I don't know how he knows that, but I am… so close. His hips shift and his hard cock slides between my legs from behind, making my legs almost buckle.

"Put your hands on the wall in front of you," he breathes against the shell of my ear.

I don't even think. My hands shoot out in front of me, my palms slapping against the cold tile hard. His hand between my legs slides around my hip and over my ass. I know what's coming and my bottom lip goes between my teeth, biting down in anticipation. It feels like an eternity, and then the head of his cock bumps my entrance.

"Yes." I press my ass back toward him, offering myself up, not caring one iota how desperate I appear right now.

"Fuck." He slides in slowly, wrapping my hip in a firm hold and keeping me in place. "So goddamn tight. So fucking wet." He pulls out an inch and slides back in two.

"Please hurry," I pant. I can't take much more of this. Now that I've felt him again, I need him, all of him. His mouth drops to my shoulder and his tongue glides across and up to my ear as he slides fully inside of me. His breath skims my ear as his hand at my hip moves forward between my legs once more. "Is this good?"

"Yes." I don't even lie. There is no point; I have no doubt he can feel exactly what it is he does to me.

He doesn't move once he's planted deep inside of me. His forehead drops to my shoulder, his chest pressing against my back heaves as his heart beats rapidly against my skin. "You undo me." He slides his hand down my arm and it covers mine against the tile as his mouth drags across my shoulder. His fingers between my legs move, making my core tighten around him. "Mine." That one word spoken against my wet skin makes my legs weak. Sliding out then back in, his fingers lace with mine. "Kiss me."

I turn my head without thinking, and his tongue slides against mine on an inward stroke. Moaning around his tongue, he growls around mine, speeding up his fingers while he strokes in and out of me with precision, hitting that spot deep inside me that sends a jolt of pleasure and pain in a solid tempo of ecstasy.

"I've missed this," I breathe without thinking. His body stills for a moment before he pulls out and thrusts in hard, making me gasp.

"No more keeping this from me." His tone isn't one I've heard from him before and I want to lean back and search his face, but before I can, his fingers circle over my clit faster and faster, making me lose all coherent thought as he sends me hurling over the edge into an orgasm that takes my breath away. Before I've even caught my breath, he spins me around and lifts me to rest against the cool tile. "Legs tight."

My legs around his hips wrap tighter. Taking my hands from his shoulders, he pulls them above my head, pinning them there with one of his. Thrusting hard, he sends me sliding up the wall then dips his head to catch my breast in his mouth, sucking and skimming his teeth over my nipple.

My head falls back against the tile as he moves to my other breast, doing the same after a slide out and a deep slide in. "Dillon," I pant, digging my nails into his hand.

"Love that," he mutters, taking my mouth in a punishing kiss, dropping my hands and grabbing my ass in both his large palms.

"I…"

"I'm with you. Come with me," he breathes against my mouth, cutting me off. Using his hands at my ass, he lifts and drops me along his length, each stroke making me see stars. I know when I fall it's going to kill me. Wrapping my arms and legs tightly around him, I press my forehead to his and come on a shout as he roars his release against my mouth. We stay like that, breathing heavily against each other's mouths, kissing softly and running our hands over each other's wet skin until the water starts to turn cold.

"We need to get out," he grumbles, kissing me once more before releasing his hold on me and forcing me to slide down his wet body. Turning off the shower, he sends me out ahead of him with a tap on my bottom.

Getting out, I grab a towel for myself and one for him, and start to dry off, wanting to just go plop down in bed, but there is nothing worse than the idea of having to sleep on wet sheets later tonight.

"How much time do you need to get ready to go out?" His arms wrap around me from behind, and I tilt my head to the side to look at him.

"About an hour. I have to dry my hair." Tonight, we are having dinner with Michelle, Luka, Jax, and Ellie. I'm still annoyed with Jax, or maybe he's annoyed with me, so we haven't talked much. But Dillon saw him yesterday and told him he and Ellie should come out to dinner with us, and Jax agreed. I just hope tonight is not a huge drama fest. I love my brother; I love his wife and daughter, but I refuse to let anyone ruin this thing between Dillon and me.

Wait, what? I freeze, wondering where that thought came from.

"So we can go nap for a bit?" He nuzzles my neck, making me lose my train of thought as he lifts me into his arms and carries me to the bed.

And for once in my life as he crawls in behind me, I don't care that my hair is soaking my pillow and sheets.

"ASHLYN." ELLIE SMILES, standing from the table when she spots us across the restaurant. As soon as I'm close, she wraps me in a hug, whispering, "I'm so happy for you, and I think everyone else will be too." God, I really hope she's right.

"I hope so," I say aloud, squeezing her back, then I let her go and look at Jax, who is standing behind her.

"Come here." He holds out his arms and I move right to him, giving him a tight hug. "You know I love you, sis," he mutters against my hair, and tears sting my nose.

"I know. I love you too," I agree, letting him go, then turn when Michelle comes sashaying toward the table, followed by Luka.

"Oh, my God. Where did you get that dress? I need one just like it." She whistles and I look down at my dress, ignoring Dillon's grumble behind me, since I heard his annoying dislike of the dress after I put it on at the house. Actually, he totally loved the dress; I think he had me pinned against the wall two seconds after seeing me in it. He just didn't like the idea of me wearing it out of the house, but oh well.

"Nordstrom Rack." I smile. I love my dress, with its V-neck lace halter, deep cut in the back, tight bodice, and pleated skirt.

"You are not getting a dress like that," Luka says from behind her, and she rolls her eyes, wrapping me in a hug as Dillon says something agreeing with him.

"Luka." I smile warmly once Michelle has let me go then launch myself at him, wrapping my arms around his huge, muscular waist, and try to pick him up. I fail miserably, but his grin is enough of a reward as he presses a kiss to the top of my head.

"I'm so happy for you two," I tell him, and his grin broadens.

"It's about time she agreed to marry me." He eyes soften over my head, and I know he's looking at Michelle. Luka was a player before her, but somehow she wrapped him around her tiny little finger within a week of dating, he's been asking her forever to marry him. Laughing, I step back to stand next to Dillon and feel his hand against the exposed skin of my back.

"Luka, Dillon. Dillon, this is Luka," I introduce them, since Dillon knows everyone else at the table.

"I gotta say this and get it out of the way, so we can relax and enjoy dinner. You hurt our girl, and I will personally kill you," he states, completely straight-faced, and I feel my eyes widen. Looking up at

Dillon to see his reaction, I almost fall over when he nods and takes Luka's hand in a firm shake. "Now, that's out of the way. I need a beer." He smiles at Dillon then chucks me under my chin with his fist.

I expect it to be awkward after that, but as soon as we sit and the waiter comes over, the guys each order a beer and us girls order a bottle of wine to share, along with appetizers to munch on while we wait for our food.

"Fuck," Michelle says, and I turn to look at her with my fried mozzarella wedge halfway to my mouth.

"What?"

"Your ex."

"What?" I frown then turn my head and catch my ex, Josh, heading toward our table.

"Oh, great," I grumble, setting my uneaten cheesy wedge of goodness on my plate. Josh and I dated about eight months ago and had approximately two-point-two dates before I ended things with him. He really didn't do anything to me; he was just annoying.

"Ashlyn, I thought that was you," he greets, coming to stand at the table near my side. I tilt my head back to look at him, then squeak when Dillon grabs my chair and slides me so close I may as well be on his lap.

"Hi, Josh."

"How are you?" he asks, tucking his hands into the front pockets of his jeans.

"Really good, and you?"

"Good, good." He nods then looks around the table, smiling at everyone and saying hi. "My mom and I are actually moving to Knoxville next weekend."

Okay, so maybe there were a few reasons why I stopped seeing him besides the fact he was annoying. He also lived with his mom and still had her cooking, doing his laundry, and cleaning up after him. She even filled his car up with gas when it needed it.

"That's great."

"Yeah, it really is." He nods then tucks his hands farther into his pockets, making his shoulders shoot forward. "I was going to call you to see—"

"You're not calling her," Dillon cuts in, and I hear someone, probably Michelle, giggle.

"Uh… what?" Josh frowns, pulling his eyes from me to look at Dillon.

"You're not calling her. There's nothing for you two to talk about. Now, if you could step away from the table, we're in the middle of dinner," Dillon continues, and my shoulders stiffen. I couldn't care less about Josh, but there is no reason for him to be so harsh.

"Oh. Yeah, sorry about that. I didn't think." He looks at me, and I give him a weak smile, because I have no idea what else to do. "See you around."

"You won't," Dillon mutters. "Bye," I say, watching him move back through the restaurant.

"You know Ash has dated a lot, right?" Jax asks, and I turn to look at my brother, wondering where the hell he's going with that statement. "You gonna do that to all of her exes?" He lifts his chin in the direction Josh just left.

"Maybe." Dillon shrugs, and I bite the inside of my cheek. Feeling eyes on me, I turn to look at Michelle, who is sitting next to Ellie, and they both have bright smiles on their faces.

"You're gonna be busy," Jax says quietly, wrapping his arm around Ellie, who rolls her eyes but cuddles into him.

"I know," Dillon says, and my insides twist.

"I've had enough of that to last a lifetime," Luka puts in, and Michelle turns to glare at him. "Just sayin', baby. You and Ash have run the men in this town through the ringer."

"Excuse me?" Michelle voices my question, but he's right. I've dated a lot, probably too much, but what was I supposed to do? How else is a girl supposed to find the man she wants to spend the rest of her life with? I can't help that most every guy is an idiot.

Feeling fingers trail lightly down the skin of my back, I turn my eyes to Dillon, seeing his worried ones looking back at me. I don't know if he's worried I'm pissed, or that Luka is right. Leaning closer, he presses a kiss to my ear and whispers, "Mine," sending a shiver down my spine and making me wonder if it's wrong that the one word turns me on. I don't have time to think about it for too long. Our meals arrive, and I use eating as an excuse to ignore the feeling in my chest.

Standing outside the restaurant saying goodbye to everyone an hour and a half later, I give out hugs then let Dillon lead me to his car and help me inside. Once I'm in, I buckle up and turn to watch him fold his tall, lean frame behind the wheel.

"I need to stop at my house and grab some stuff," he states, starting up the car and putting on his seatbelt without looking at me.

"Okay," I agree softly as we pull out into traffic. I have no idea what to say to him or how I feel. We didn't really talk at dinner after the whole Josh thing. I don't know if I'm mad at him for how he acted, or happy he feels so possessive over me. If you would have asked me three months ago how I'd feel if a guy, any guy, went caveman and basically pissed on my leg, I would have told you I'd hate it, but with Dillon my emotions are totally jumbled.

"What the hell?" I squint through the dark and blink when I see a *For Sale* sign planted in Dillon's yard, close to the road. "You put your house up for sale?" I turn my body and eyes toward him.

"Yep," is all he says as we park out front of his house, near the obnoxious fountain in the middle of the driveway. Shutting down the car, he gets out, slamming the door, then jogs around to my side, taking my hand and helping me out.

"You didn't tell me you were putting your house on the market," I accuse as he takes my hand and leads me up the steps toward the front door.

"You hate this house. Why would I keep it?" He frowns, shoving the realtor key box on the door handle out of the way so he can punch in the code for the lock.

He is going to make me nuts, totally nuts! I think as he pulls me into the house along with him and shuts the door behind us.

"You said this house reminded you of your grandparents' house."

"It does," he agrees, and I follow behind him up one of the staircases and across the second floor landing toward his bedroom.

"I don't get it." I rub the bridge of my nose in frustration. "Then why are you selling it?"

"Why would I keep it?" he grumbles, walking through the door to his room.

Following, I stop in the middle of the room, planting my hands on my hips.

"Because you love it!" I practically shout.

"You don't want to move in here, Ashlyn. There is no point in me keeping it!" he shouts back from the bathroom, where he disappeared, and I immediately feel like shit. I did tell him I hated it, but that was before I knew why he bought it to begin with.

Coming out of the bathroom, he tosses some stuff on the chaise lounge near the bed then heads for the closet, turning on the light in there.

"Take it off the market," I say, sternly, when he walks out with a handful of clothes on hangers, laying them across the back of the chaise.

"Why?"

"Because you are not going to sell it just because I don't want to live here."

"We're married. I'm not going to live in a separate house from you."

God, why do I hate it so much that those reasons are not words of love? Like, "I'm selling it, because I love you and I can't imagine not living the rest of my life with you," or "I love you, and I want us to find a house that we are both happy in."

"You are so frustrating," I growl, feeling a headache coming on, and I squeeze my eyes closed, putting the palms of my hands against my face.

"It's for the best." His arms wrap around me and he pulls me flush against him.

Dropping my hands to my sides, I stare into his handsome face. "I don't want you to get rid of this house because of me."

"I'm getting rid of this house, because I want to," he states, looking sincere, but I'm not sure I believe him. I saw his face when he was talking about the house his grandparents owned. He loved their house; he wanted to raise a family in one like theirs. "Stop stressing about this. It's just a house." He bends down, nuzzling my neck, and my arms slide around his shoulders as his hands move down to my ass and he hoists me up.

"What are you doing?" I question as he puts his knees onto the bed behind me and settles me under him.

"I really do love this dress." He smiles, running his fingers along the edge of lace near my breast.

"I thought you hated it."

"No, I hate that other men get to see so much of you." He places a kiss against my mouth then leans back.

"You've never liked my choice of clothing," I grumble, and he slides his fingers over my temple and into my hair.

"Because I've always considered you mine." He nips the underside of my jaw, and my heart starts to beat wildly against my ribcage. Since almost the first moment we met, he's told me I need to cover more skin. I thought he was just being a dick, but now... now I'm not so sure, and I'm not brave enough to ask him the questions I really need to ask him.

"Dillon," I pant as his fingers slide up the inside of my thigh and over the center of my panties.

"Hmm?"

I don't get to say more. His mouth covers mine, and before I know it, we're both naked using our mouths for better things than talking.

WAKING WITH MY heart pounding, I blink my eyes open, finding it completely dark. Grumbling something I can't make out, Dillon pulls me closer and shoves his face in my hair. As my eyes adjust to the darkness, looking around, realizing we are still in his room at his house.

"Breathe, Ashlyn, it was just a bad dream," I whisper, holding the palm of my hand to my chest and feeling my heart beating hard. I can't recall what happened exactly in my dream, but I remember Isla, Dillon's ex, was there, and I remember feeling raw, powerful fear.

Lifting Dillon's arm from my waist, I get up from the bed quietly, grab his button-down shirt that he wore to dinner off the floor, and head for the bathroom while putting it on. Closing the door silently, I turn on the light and take care of business then head for the closest sink to wash my hands. Turning the water to cold, I splash some on my face letting it wash away the last of the dream.

Feeling better, I turn the light back off and head for the bed, stopping in the middle of the room when I notice the light under the door in the closet. My heart rate speeds right back up as I walk toward the door and place my palm on the handle, opening slowly. Peeking in, I find it empty, except for Dillon's clothes and shoes. Without thinking, I walk in, closing the door behind me, and start snooping around. I have no idea what I'm looking for, but I'm on a mission as I open and close drawers.

"She didn't sleep in here. Her shit was down the hall."

"AHHHHHH!" I scream, coming out of my skin, spinning to find Dillon wearing a pair of loose sleep pants while standing in the doorway with his arms crossed over his chest and his eyes on me. "You scared the crap out of me!" I snap, holding my hand to my chest.

"You scared the shit out of me when I couldn't find you," he snaps right back. "What the hell are you doing hiding in here?"

"Huh?" I play dumb then look around like I just realized where I was.

"Jesus, you are a total fucking nut. C'mere." He holds out his hand, and my eyes drop to it like it's a snake that will strike me at any moment.

"I'm not a nut," I defend, even though I may be, but only because he is making me one.

"C'mere."

"I'm right here."

"Yes, but I want you right here." He points to the ground at his feet and raises a brow.

"Why?"

"Because I do."

"That's not a good reason." I shake my head, and his eyes close briefly like he's annoyed then open and pin me in place, narrowing. Lunging forward, he catches my waist and pulls me into him.

"You're so annoying," I grumble, watching him smile. "What did you want to tell me that you couldn't say with me standing over there?"

"She never stayed in here. We didn't share a room or a bed."

Snorting, I lean my head back, looking at the ceiling, wondering how stupid he thinks I am, and he gives me a squeeze, pulling my gaze back to him.

"I'm serious."

"Yeah, I bet," I huff, trying to pull away.

"You were my first." My body freezes, and I wonder if I heard him right.

"What?"

"You were my first," he repeats, and I swear he's saying he was a virgin. I want to laugh, but the look in his eyes says he isn't joking. Then I remember our first time, and every time since then, and I wonder how much porn he's watched, because moves like the ones he has had to come from somewhere.

"I see that you don't believe me," he mutters, and I shake my head, trying to process his words and exactly what they mean.

"No, actually, I'm just wondering exactly how much porn you've watched," I say, and he gives me a sexy grin then takes a step forward, pressing me into the island in the center of the closet, then lifts me up to sit on top of it.

"Haven't watched any porn, baby." His words vibrate against my ear that he nips, causing my knees to go weak as he uses his hips to spread them open.

"Are you sure?"

"Didn't want to go to hell." I hear the smile in his voice, and I move my hands up to wrap around his shoulders then lean back so I can see his face. "It was you." His fingers trail down my cheek gently. "I knew it was you. At times, it pissed me off that it was you, but that doesn't change the fact it's been only you since the moment we met."

"Dillon." I feel my face soften, and my body presses closer to his.

"I'm no saint. I've had my fair share of close calls, but no one ever felt right." He holds my face in his palms and kisses me softly… so softly I feel that kiss score through every cell in my body. "Until you."

Tears sting my nose, and I drop my forehead to his shoulder and try to get myself under control as his fingers slide back through my hair to wrap around my scalp. His words are not the words of love I so desperately want to hear from him, but they are words that make me hopeful.

"You didn't even like me," I whisper into his skin, and his fingers tense against my scalp.

"You're wrong," his lips whisper back against the top of my head, and I squeeze my eyes closed, wondering what the hell is happening and when I will wake up from this crazy, impossible dream… or if I ever want to.

Chapter 5

Ashlyn

"YOUR MOM AND dad get home today," Dillon reminds me as he leans against the counter opposite me with a cup of coffee in his hands. His broad chest and abs visible for me to drool over.

"I know." I don't need his reminder. I've talked to both my parents a few times since they've been gone, and neither of them has brought up my relationship with Dillon. I'm worried. My dad isn't someone who beats around the bush, so to speak. So I have no idea what to expect from him when he gets back into town.

"I know you're worried."

"I am," I agree, thinking that's the understatement of the century.

Turning, he drops his coffee behind him to the granite then moves to where I'm standing, wrapping his hands around my waist and lifting me up to sit on the counter I was just leaning against. "I won't hide our marriage from anyone else."

"Dillon," I sigh, wishing he understood where I'm coming from. "It's not as easy as just telling them we got married."

His hands rest against my thighs and his fingers begin to rub circles there. "I know, but we are married."

"My parents are going to have concerns, valid concerns." I rest my hands on his shoulders and lean into him. "We didn't date. We jumped right into being married and basically living together."

"There is no 'basically' about it. We *are* living together, and will be until the day we die," he growls, and I fight the urge to roll my eyes at him. He's so damn hardheaded.

"Can you at least try to see where I'm coming from?" I plea.

"You're an adult. You live on your own and make your own money. What you do with your life is your choice."

"It's not as black and white as you see it," I huff, knowing from our previous talks on the matter it's pointless to argue with him. He just doesn't understand, or he really believes what he's saying and thinks it is as easy as just telling them about us.

"You're making this harder than it needs to be."

"No I'm not."

"You are."

"Dillon, please think about it. I mean, we're not even in love," I whisper a half lie. I, at some point over the last two weeks, have accepted I'm in love with him, but that doesn't mean he feels the same as I do.

His hands drop from my thighs like I've burned him and he takes a sudden step back, leaving me feeling cold. Watching, I'm at a loss from his reaction. He runs a hand through his hair, and my heart lodges in my throat. "Jesus, what the fuck?" he barks, looking up at the ceiling, then turns and leaves. I don't know how long I sit there, stunned. But when he comes back, he's dressed in black workout pants, a plain gray tee, and sneakers.

"I'll be back." He grabs his car keys off the counter, barely sparing me a glance as he turns to leave.

"What?" I ask, suddenly panicked. Hopping down from the counter, I follow behind him toward the door. "What the hell just happened?" I shout at his back, and his pain-filled eyes shoot to me over his shoulder with his hand on the knob.

"I just found out the woman I'm in love with isn't in love with me," he states matter-of-factly, then storms out through the front door, slamming it behind himself.

"What?" I ask, but it's too late. He's gone. Plopping down on the sofa, my head drops to my hands and tears of annoyance fill my eyes.

"*Hssss.*" Pulling my hands from my face, I look at Leo as he hisses again and takes a swipe at me.

"How was I supposed to know?" I cry, glaring at my cat when he swipes at me again. "He didn't tell me," I defend myself as his golden eyes meet mine, and then I swear he glares before hissing once more and hopping down off the couch, prancing off.

Seeing my cell phone on the coffee table, I pick it up and dial Dillon's number, but he doesn't answer. I dial again, and still get no answer. I want to toss the stupid thing across the room. I don't understand why he's mad. It's not like I knew he was in love with me; I had no clue. Getting off the couch, I go to my room and straight to my closet, where I put on a pair of my most comfortable jeans that are ripped to shreds, my bra, and a tank top, then slip my feet into my flip-flops. Once I'm dressed, I run a brush through my hair quickly then dial Michelle.

"Hey-yo," she greets on the second ring, and I sigh in relief.

"I need your help with something. Can you meet me?" I ask softly, wondering if I'm making a huge mistake, but I've been thinking about this for a few days and it's now or never.

"Does this meeting involve burying Dillon's body in the woods?"

"No." I laugh, walking back through my house toward the kitchen where my keys are.

"Cool, just wanted to know so I can figure out what to wear," she murmurs, and I hear Luka in the background say something to her that I can't make out.

"Crap, you're home with Luka. I totally forgot it's Sunday."

"I am, but he's topped up. He'll be fine for a few hours. Where are we meeting?" she asks, and I can hear Luka laughing about never being topped up.

"The Coffee Hut, and bring your realtor stuff with you."

"My realtor stuff?" she questions, sounding confused.

"Just bring it!" I cry.

"Okay, but can I ask what the hell is going on and why you sound so freaked?"

"I'll explain when I see you. Meet me in fifteen."

"Fifteen?" she hisses, "Crap, woman, can I have at least thirty minutes? I haven't even showered."

"Fine, thirty." I hang up and head for the door.

"OKAY, SERIOUSLY, WHAT the hell is going on?" Michelle asks as soon as she takes the seat across from me, and I scoot the coffee I got her to her side of the table.

"I want to buy a house."

"Um..." Her brow furrows. "You just bought your house. Are you looking for an investment property?" she asks, taking a sip of her coffee before setting her laptop on the table and turning it on.

"No, I want to buy Dillon's house," I admit, and her head snaps up to me.

"What? Why?"

"You know Dillon put his house on the market. He loves his house, and I don't want him to give that up because of me, so I'm going to buy it."

Leaning back, she crosses her arms over her chest and studies me. "What the hell is really going on? You hate his house."

"I don't hate it, not exactly anyways." I shrug, and her eyes narrow. "It'll grow on me," I gripe, and her eyebrows lower.

"Ashlyn."

"Fine, I think Dillon and I are fighting." I bite the inside of my cheek. I'm pretty sure we're fighting; I just still have no idea why.

"You think you're fighting?"

"Maybe not *fighting*-fighting, but I told him we're not in love and he got pissed and stormed out, but not before tossing a grenade at me. I think his words were, 'I just found out the woman I'm in love with isn't in love with me.'"

"Oh," she sighs, and slouches forward on the chair.

"Yeah."

"Buying his house isn't going to fix this."

"I'm not stupid, Michelle. I know buying his house isn't going to fix anything, but I want him to know I believe in us as much as he does."

"You're in love with him." It's a statement, but I still nod, picking up my coffee.

"Yes, I've also accepted that," I grumble into my cup.

"Don't sound so mad about it." She laughs. She *would* think this is funny.

"I'm not mad, but we just got on a crazy roller-coaster together, and I can't see the top. I'm freaking out, because there could be no more tracks left once we reach the tipping point."

"He's in love with you. That's not going to change just because he's mad. He's kind of intense, and you probably hurt his feelings since he's been lusting after you forever. Maybe even in love with you for that long. And now he thinks you don't feel the same. It's standard Alpha Male Syndrome."

"Alpha Male Syndrome?" I laugh, and she nods.

"Yes, Alpha Male Syndrome, and your man is suffering from the worst case I've ever seen."

"I'm still buying the house," I tell her, and her eyes soften.

"Let me look it up. Do you know the address?"

"Yeah." I tell her, and she types it into her computer then blinks at the screen. "What? Please don't tell me someone has already put an offer on it."

"No, no offer." She spins her laptop around to face me. I scan the screen and the details of the house, and then feel bile rise up the back of my throat when I see the asking price.

"Six hundred thousand?" I whisper in disbelief. My house only cost me a hundred and sixty thousand. Granted, it's much smaller than his, but still. That price is outrageous. "Stupid fountain."

"What?" she questions.

"Nothing," I mutter. "How much would my down payment need to be?"

"One hundred and twenty thousand, give or take, depending on if he's willing to negotiate."

Sitting back, defeated, I sigh. "I don't have that much saved." I have some money, but not a hundred and twenty thousand dollars. If I did, I would have zero school loans and a newer car than the one I have now.

"You should just talk to him. He doesn't need a grand gesture like this." She waves at the computer, and I bite the inside of my cheek.

"I don't really have a choice, do I?"

"Not unless you want to go bankrupt."

"What the hell have I gotten myself into?" I moan.

"It's called a relationship." She smiles, taking a sip of coffee, and I kick her under the table.

"I wish you could have seen the look on his face when he talked about why he bought it. He loves it, and because of me, he's giving it up."

"So move into it with him."

"What?" I frown, and she rolls her eyes.

"If you don't want him to sell it, then just move in with him."

"Why didn't I think of that?"

"Because you're blonde now."

"Shut up." I smile as the wheels in my head start to turn.

"What did you drive?"

"My Suburban, why?" she asks, studying me.

"I need your help."

"Does this help involve carrying heavy shit?"

"Maybe." I shrug, picking up my coffee, taking another sip and hoping this plan of mine works.

"You are so lucky I wore sneakers," she mutters, and I grin.

"WHAT THE FUCK is going on?" is roared, and I look at Michelle with wide eyes and feel my heart lodge itself in my throat.

"Oh shit," I breathe, and my stupid best friend has the audacity to point at me and laugh as the bottles of my shampoo and conditioner in my hand drop and clatter to the bathroom floor.

"Ashlyn?" he calls, and I duck down. Why? I don't know; it's not like he can't see me. But I feel safer hidden behind Michelle, who is now laughing like a hyena.

"Michelle, can I talk to my *wife*? Alone?" he asks, exaggerating the word wife, and I cringe.

"Yep." She turns to look at me, mouthing, *Alpha Male Syndrome,* then smiles. "I'll call you tomorrow, love you," she chirps, disappearing out of the bathroom and leaving me to face my very pissed off husband.

"Do you want to tell me why the fuck all my shit is packed?" he asks, swinging his hand in the direction of the bedroom.

"I…" I freeze. He must not have noticed I packed a lot of my stuff as well.

"Jesus, what the fuck?" he growls before I have a chance to answer. "I'm not moving out, and if you think I am, you have lost your damn mind."

"Dillon," I interject softly, and his eyes narrow.

"I wasn't even gone for three hours, and in that time, you convinced yourself that we're separating?" He leans in. "Think again, baby, 'cause it's not happening. Not now, not ever. We're married, and are staying fucking married." He clips off the last point close to my face.

"Married?"

Oh, fuck me, not again.

My eyes slice past Dillon to my dad standing in the doorway of my room. "Dad."

"What's going on?" my mom questions, coming up behind my dad and putting her hand to his waist so she can see around him.

"Apparently, your daughter is a married woman now," he growls, looking down at her.

"Dad," I repeat, feeling suddenly heartbroken. He only does the whole 'I'm my mom's kid' thing when he's really pissed off at me.

"Married?" Mom whispers, looking at me with wide, hurt-filled eyes.

"Let's go sit down and talk about this," Dillon suggests, sounding much calmer than he did moments ago, and my dad's eyes swing to him and fill with anger.

"Talk? You want to talk to me now? Why the fuck didn't you talk to me before you married my only goddamn daughter?" he barks, and my arms wrap around my waist. I knew this would be bad. I knew it. But still, I secretly hoped it would turn out okay once I told them.

"Honey, calm down," Mom whispers from his side, and I watch him pull in a ragged breath.

"I don't even know what the fuck to say right now." He pulls off his hat and runs his fingers through his hair then looks at me. "I can't believe you kept this from your mom and me."

"I'm sorry," I whisper, thinking those words don't even come close to conveying how horrible I truly feel right now.

"You." He points at Dillon. "I've trusted you."

"He wanted to tell you," I defend without thinking, stepping between them, only to have Dillon put his hand to my waist and pull me to his side.

"Yeah, but he didn't," he mutters, then looks down at my mom. "Come on, let's get home." He wraps his arm around her shoulders, leading her away. I want to say something to stop them from going, but I know right now it's best if I let them go and give them a chance to cool down. I also know I need to come up with a valid reason for keeping them in the dark.

"Shhhh." Dillon's arms engulf me as a sob climbs up the back of my throat and my body jerks forward. "It will be okay. They just need some time for the news to sink in," he whispers, and I cry harder into his chest. Scooping me up into his arms, he carries me out of the room to the living room and settles us on the couch, with me in his lap. "Please calm down. The tears are killing me."

"I… I ha-have nev… never… see-seen… m-my da… dad so mad," I cry, and his hand on my back rubs in soothing circles.

"He'll come around." He will, but when? I've never seen my dad look at me the way he did just now, and I hate the idea of him being mad at me, so mad that he walked away. And let's not even get into my mom's reaction. She didn't say anything, but I know she's hurt and I hate that. "Everything will be okay, but please stop crying. I don't like it."

"You can't make me stop crying!" I sob, and his mouth drops to my ear, placing a kiss there.

"I know," he mutters, sounding annoyed by that fact. I don't know how long we sit there, me in his lap, curled around him, his hands rubbing gently over my back, but my tears eventually dry up and I melt into him, feeling the day start to set in and my eyes and body begin to get heavy. "Can I ask why you were moving me out?" he questions, and my body stiffens. I try to move off him, but his arms hold me tighter, keeping me in place. "Talk to me."

"I wasn't moving you out."

"You packed my shit."

"And mine. I was moving *us* out," I admit quietly, and his body goes rock-solid.

"Pardon?"

"I know you love your house, and I know you don't really want to sell it, so I asked Michelle to tell me how much it was so I could buy it from you, but I don't have enough for the down payment," I complain, and his body tenses further.

"You were going to buy my house?" he asks after a moment, and it's my turn to tense. Pulling my face away from his chest with his hand on my jaw, his eyes search mine. "You were going to buy my house?" he repeats softly, and my teeth go to the inside of my cheek as I shrug. "You hate my house."

"I like the library and the kitchen, I also like your bedroom," I defend quietly, feeling guilty.

"Baby." His eyes move past me as his head shakes from side to side. "I'm selling because I want you to be happy."

"I want the same for you." I've never had to consider anyone else's feelings before, but I do want him to be happy. And I really don't want him to resent me for making him give up something that means so much to him, something that represents a part of his childhood; a childhood that was scarred by the loss of his parents.

"We're not moving into my house," he states after a moment, and I feel my face scrunch up in annoyance.

"Yes we are."

"We're not."

"You are so damn annoying." I push away from him, and since he's not prepared for my sudden shift I almost fall onto my ass, but thankfully he's strong and quick, so he catches me before I do damage to myself.

"Be careful."

He steadies me once I'm on my feet, and I lean closer to him, and shout, "Stop telling me what to do!"

"Fuck me, now you're mad that I won't let you move into a house you hate?"

"No, that's stupid," I hiss, even though it is partly true. "I'm mad, because I'm trying to do something to show you that I love you, and you're being a giant dick about it."

"What did you just say?"

"You're a giant dick," I huff and turn to leave, but before I even make it two steps, he's on me. His arms wrap around me from behind then he spins me around to face him.

"Tell me what you said."

"I did."

"Tell me again."

"You're a dick," I repeat, wondering why the hell he wants me to keep calling him that.

"No, the part about you being in love with me."

"What?" I rear back in a panic, realizing what I admitted to him, not even realizing that I was admitting it.

"You love me," he repeats quietly, and I stare, having no idea what to do now. "We'll try my place out for a few weeks. If you don't like it, we'll put it back on the market and find a place you and I can agree on." He smiles then drops his face and nuzzles my neck. "You love me?"

"I'm rethinking it," I mutter, wrapping my arms around the back of his neck while tilting my head to the side to give him better access to the column of my throat.

"It's too late for that." He leans back, smiling down at me, then places a soft kiss against my lips. "Have you eaten?"

"No."

"Good, me either, let's go." He grabs my hand and starts to lead me away, but I stop him.

"Where are we going?"

"Pizza, I'm starving."

"Where did you go today when you left?" I frown; he was gone three hours, maybe a little more than that.

"I drove around for a bit then went to Jax and Ellie's."

"You did?" I whisper in disbelief, and his face softens.

"He and I are good. He knows how I feel about you, and I needed his advice on how to proceed. You're not exactly an open book."

"Oh, Lord," I groan. "I can only imagine what he said to you."

"Nothing bad. He told me to get over myself, that I'm the first man you have ever been serious about and I need to give you time to adjust to us being an us."

"That's good advice." I nod, and he shakes his head in denial.

"I don't think so," he mutters, dropping his forehead to rest against mine. "I want all of you. Your mind, your soul, and most importantly your heart. I want every breath you take to be for me. I want to imprint myself into your skin so you'll crave me like a drug and never want to be without me."

"I think you may be crazy," I cut in, studying the sincerity in his eyes. He really does want that from me, and the scary thing is, I think I already feel that way about him.

"I'm in love with a woman who has made me crazy."

"You've made me crazy too," I say quietly, and his face moves closer to mine.

"No more fighting about the things that don't matter. We have enough to deal with without fighting each other."

"You need to take your own advice."

"I'll try," he agrees, kissing me once more. "Now let's go eat, I'm starving."

"Okay," I agree, letting him lead me out of the house to his car that is parked in the driveway.

Once we are both in and buckled, he backs out of the drive and heads down one street after another, out of my subdivision, with his hand wrapped around my jean-covered thigh while his fingers stroke my skin through one of the many holes in the material.

"You're going to make that tear enormous if you keep doing that." I place my hand over his, catching him smile out of the corner of my eye. Running my fingers over the top of his hand, I watch the screen on his dash light up, announcing that he has a call, and my body freezes when I see the she-bitch-from-hell's name pop up, catching me off-guard.

"Fuck me," he mutters, pressing deny on the call after the second ring.

"Why is she calling you?"

"Probably because her parents have been calling and I've not answered their calls." I try to take a few breaths before I speak, because I don't want to sound like a crazy woman when I do talk, but seriously, what the hell?

"Why are her parents calling you?" Okay, good, that came out sounding halfway normal and not screeched at the top of my lungs like it did in my head.

"Are you ready to talk about her and me?"

God, am I? I don't think so, but I really need to understand what the hell is going on.

"I'm taking that as a no," he mutters, sounding disappointed.

"Are you close with her family?" I question, figuring that's a safe place to start.

"My brother and I lived with her parents after ours passed away," he says, and my hand over his spasms. Flipping his palm upright, his fingers lace with mine and his thumb rubs gently over the rapid pulse in my wrist.

"What about your grandparents?"

"My grandfather passed the year before my parents, and my grandmother had been in the hospital for a while with dementia and passed away my second year of college."

"I'm sorry."

"It was a long time ago," he says softly, but I still catch the twinge of pain in his tone.

"Maybe, but I'm still sorry." I squeeze his fingers. "How did you end up with her parents?"

"My mom and her mom were sorority sisters in college and opened a law practice after they graduated. They were in our lives since I can remember."

"You didn't have any other family?" I ask softly as he pulls up in front of the pizza place and parks diagonally in one of the empty spots.

"My dad has a brother, but he didn't have the ability to take two teenaged boys on. His plate was full with his wife and three girls, and my mom didn't have any siblings. Her parents were older, much older when they had her, and they weren't in a place where they could take us in either."

"So her family took you and your brother in?"

"Yeah, the Trent's were our saving grace. They lived close, so we didn't have to change schools or make any huge adjustment. They were like family to us."

"And they were okay with you dating their daughter?" That is something I find hard to believe. There is no way my dad would be okay with me dating a boy who lived under the same room as me. No way in hell.

"Are we talking about her now?" he asks, looking at me, and I squirm.

"I don't know," I admit, and he sighs, shutting down the car, opening the door, and getting out. Releasing a deep breath, I open my door and meet him in front of the car before he can make it to me.

"I can see the wheels in your head turning," he says quietly, getting close and taking hold of my face in his large palms. He's right. I have a billion questions, but I feel like it's safer to live with my head buried in a mound of denial. "I know talking about her upsets you, but I'd really like to explain things to you."

"Dillon." I sigh, wishing I was braver.

"I'll give you time, but if you have questions just ask."

"Do you still talk to her?"

His thumb sweeps gently over my cheek and his eyes search mine. "I haven't for a long time."

"Does she know you and I got married?" My heart accelerates at the idea of her knowing about us. I don't care that she knows; I actually want her to know he's mine. But with the things that have happened in the past to my family, I know sometimes information like that can set a person off, and regardless of whatever he thinks their relationship was, I have no doubt she was in love with him.

"I'm sure she knows, since I told her parents about you and me."

"You did?"

"They're like family to me. I wanted them to share in my happiness," he says, but the way his brow has furrowed says more than his words do. Brushing his lips over mine quickly, he takes my hand and leads me into the pizza place before I have a chance to ask him what they said, even though I'm pretty sure I already know the answer to that question.

Chapter 6

Dillon

HITTING THE SNOOZE button on the alarm for thirty minutes, I smile as Ashlyn grumbles something in her sleep and burrows into my side. I wish we didn't have to work today. I should have closed the office and taken her somewhere. We need a honeymoon, and I need an excuse to lock her in a room and keep her naked for at least a week, if not more.

"Time to get up, gorgeous." I sweep the hair off her forehead, and smile again when she bats my hand away and growls. She is not a morning person. I have never met someone who hates waking up as much as she does. Rolling her to her back, I kiss her jaw then down the column of her throat, grinning when she turns her head to the side in an offering, mumbling something I can't make out. I can't get enough of her.

I knew I had it bad before, but now that I can touch her and taste her whenever and however I please, it's different. She's become my addiction. Licking across her shoulder, I cup her breast with my palm and pull her nipple into my mouth, feeling it tighten against my tongue as I pull on her nipple ring. Her back arches and her fingers slide into my hair as I glide my free hand down her stomach.

"Dillon," her sleepy voice calls, and my fingers move farther, finding her already primed and ready for me. I don't wait. I position myself between her legs and wrap them around me before slipping inside of her.

"Jesus." I still and wait. There is always a moment during that first thrust that my balls draw up tight and my conscience leaves my body as her wet heat takes hold of me. Her hands sliding down my back bring me back to life and I pull out, only to thrust back in slowly. Hearing her mewl, I take her mouth and swipe my tongue over her lips, hearing her sharp intake of breath on a downward glide.

"Faster."

I ignore her, keeping my pace slow and steady. Pulling her hands from my back, I drag them above her head. "Tell me you love me." I need to hear her say it. It doesn't seem possible that she does. Her eyes slide closed and I thrust in hard. "Look at me." When her eyes open, I hold her gaze. "Tell me." I thrust in again, feeling her walls tighten around me. I know she's close, and I know in just a few more thrusts she will be coming all over me. "Tell me," I growl on an outward slide, keeping myself from thrusting in hard and giving us what we both need.

"I love you," she cries in desperation, and I thrust deep, wrap my hand around both her wrists, and lean back so I can slide my free hand over her stomach. Finding her clit with my thumb, I circle. Whimpering against my mouth, her back arches off the bed. I love that this is only mine; every moan, every whimper, every time her breath catches, it's only for me.

"You're so close," I grit as her tight walls begin to pulse and spasm around my length, trying to hold me in place as I quicken my tempo. Rolling her clit in quicker circles, I cover her mouth, drinking down her orgasm as mine explodes deep within her. With one last thrust, I plant myself balls-deep, allowing her pulsing core to pull every last drop of my orgasm from me as my forehead drops to her collarbone.

"Good morning," she whispers after a long moment, and I place a kiss against her chest then pull back to look down at her, releasing her hands as I do.

"Morning." I grin, watching her slowly smile and stretch her arms over her head, thrusting her breasts into my face.

"I think I just found the cure for my hate of mornings," she moans as I suck her breast that she offered up into my mouth then let it go with a pop.

"Is that an invention to wake you up like that every morning?" I question, drawing her other breast into my mouth while pulling out just a bit and sliding my still semi-hard cock back in.

"Definitely," she breathes, dragging her nails through my hair as I rock slowly in and out of her.

"We need to get up and shower," I remind her as the heels of her feet dig into my thighs in a silent demand.

"We do," she agrees, swiveling her hips, making me groan and my cock start to slowly come back to life.

"Fuck," I grumble against her mouth as the alarm goes off, breaking into the moment between us. "We need a vacation."

"What time is it?" I don't answer. I'm too caught up in the way her body is reacting to my touch. Arching her back, her head presses into the pillow then her eyes widen. "Oh shit, we have to get ready!" she shouts, catching me off-guard, rolling me to my back, leaving me lying there half-hard and stunned as she quickly rolls off me and out of the bed.

"What the fuck?" I do an ab crunch and try to catch her, but before I can get my arms around her she jumps back a foot, the movement making her breasts bounce enticingly.

"Sorry." She shakes her head then looks at my cock, which is now rock-hard and pointing at the ceiling. "Sorry," she says again, apologizing this time to my cock that twitches in reply.

"Christ," I groan, falling to my back and covering my face with my hands in frustration. "You owe me." I don't even look at her. I can hear her opening her closet, so I know she's close and can hear me loud and clear.

"I swear I'll make it up to you when we get home." Dropping my hands from my face, I turn and glare at her.

"Damn straight you will."

Her eyes roam over me, and she half apologizes through a soft giggle before turning and rushing off to the bathroom, where I hear the shower turn on a minute later. Looking down at my cock I fall back into bed with an aggravated sigh. *It's going to be a long fucking day.*

"COFFEE, BLACK, ONE sugar."

"And you?" the girl behind the counter pulls her eyes from me to ask Ashlyn. She must be new, since everyone else who works here knows Ashlyn by name and knows her coffee order by heart.

"I'll take a large iced coffee with cream and two sugars," she says, and the girl types it into the register before looking at her once more.

"Is that all?"

"No… um…" She scans the display case. "Two chocolate cake pops, one birthday cake pop, and one blueberry muffin. Oh, and one of those chocolate chip cookies." Ashlyn points out each item as the girl smiles, placing the items she asked for in a paper bag.

"Hungry?" I question quietly, tugging her into my side, and her head tips back to look up at me.

"A little." She shrugs, smiling sheepishly, making me laugh. Without a thought, I dip my face and touch my mouth to hers, not able to help myself.

"Will you share?" I ask against her lips, and she shakes her head.

"Probably not."

"Not even with your husband you left high and dry this morning? We could have stayed in bed another twenty minutes. I had no idea this," I jerk my head toward the display, "is why you were in such a rush."

"Okay, since you put it that way, I guess I can share a few bites with you," she grumbles, making me smile and kiss her again. With my hand against her lower back, I lead her to the end of the counter where I pick up our drinks and get straws, watching as Ash opens the bag the girl hands her then pulling out a chocolate cake pop, eating the whole thing in one giant bite.

"So I guess you're not sharing." I laugh, and she shrugs, chewing like crazy then swallowing hard. She then leans over, without taking her cup from me, and takes a huge gulp through the straw.

"There's one chocolate one left." She smiles, and I shake my head.

"You've got chocolate all over your teeth."

"Do I?" She grins, showing off her chocolate-coated mouth, and I toss back my head and laugh.

"You're a nut." I wrap my hand holding her drink around her back and tug her into me.

"I'm not a nut." She leans up, giving me a chocolaty kiss, then freezes when someone whimpers behind us.

Peeking around me, her eyes widen. "Mom," she whispers, pulling from me. "Are you okay?"

"Fine, I'm fine. I have to go." She rushes out of the coffee shop with Ashlyn hot on her heels. I follow close, but not too close, and wait a few feet away, watching Lilly pull her daughter in for a hug, closing her eyes. I can't hear what she says to her, but I can see her mouth move. Then she leans back, kisses Ashlyn's cheek, and sends me a wave before getting into her car. Standing on the curb, Ashlyn wraps her arms around her waist while her mom backs out and drives off.

"Baby," I murmur, seeing tears in her eyes when she starts toward me. Holding my arms out, she comes right to me and drops her face to my chest while wrapping her arms around my middle. "I hate the tears. Please stop crying." I do hate them; they are something I have no control over, something that makes me feel helpless when it comes to her.

"She… she saw us."

"I know," I confirm, and her forehead bobs up and down against my chest.

"Let's get into the office where I can put this shit down and hold you." I kiss the top of her head.

"'Kay," she agrees, taking her drink from my hand in the one still holding the paper bag full of her treats, and twining my fingers with her free ones.

Walking the few feet to the office, I let her go to unlock the door then let her in before me, only stopping briefly to shut off the alarm. "We have patients coming in soon," she reminds me as I wrap my hand around hers and lead her to the back, without doing the normal routine of turning on the lights and starting up the computers.

"Matt can do it when he gets in," I say softly, once we're in my office and the door's closed. Taking her drink and the paper bag from her grasp, I drop both to the top of my desk, along with my coffee. "C'mere." I take a seat in my chair then maneuver her into my lap, with her legs over my thighs, and wrap one arm around her back. "Now tell me what she said," I say as I push a large hunk of hair over her shoulder so I can see her face completely.

"She told me she loves me, that she's still angry." She pulls in a deep breath, and I can see a fresh wave of tears swimming in her eyes. "Then she said she's happy for us." A single tear falls down her cheek, and I catch it with my thumb while my teeth clench shut.

I knew her parents would both be happy for us. I knew if I could ever make Ashlyn see me for more than her boss and a dick we would have something beautiful. Something like what my parents had before they died. Something her parents have now. I know I shouldn't have married her in Vegas. I knew when she suggested we get married as a joke, I should have taken her back to the hotel and put her to bed so she could sober up. I didn't do what I should have done. Instead, I took her directly to the nearest wedding chapel, where I bought us each a ring from a cheep plastic display case, and then stood in front of a guy who looked a lot like the Hulk.

She laughed herself silly up until it was time for us to say our vows to each other. During that part of the ceremony, I would have laid down money she was sober. Her words were clear, her eyes too; she was in that moment with me, completely conscious of what was taking place. I know I took advantage of her, but I regret nothing. I wanted her to admit there was something between us, and I got my way in the end. I just hate that the relationship between her and her parents was collateral damage.

"They'll come around," I assure softly, tucking her head under my chin then wrapping my arms around her middle, holding her tighter against me.

"I hope so." Her quiet, sad voice grates at my skin. I know I need to give her parents time to come to terms with what happened, but with the way she sounds right now, I know I won't give them much. I can't stand seeing her this sad, especially when I know the reason why she's so hurt. "We really should get out front before Matt thinks we're in here having sex." She pulls her head back and smiles a beautiful smile, and I grin back then look at the door.

"Or we could just have sex," I suggest. Dropping her face, her forehead rests against my chin as she laughs, and her hands twiddle with the front of my shirt.

"I didn't think I could ever be this happy," she quietly says after a moment, and I pull in a breath, swallowing down the shards in my throat. I didn't think I could ever be this happy either, not until her. Dipping my chin, I kiss her forehead and help her off my lap, stopping her when she starts to walk away, grabbing her hand.

"You gonna be okay?"

Her face softens as she turns toward me, stepping between my thighs. "I'll be fine." She bends at the waist, resting her palm on my cheek, then touches her mouth to mine, pulling away far too quickly. I want to drag her back into my lap, but I know we don't have time. Letting her go, I stand and watch her pick up the paper bag and pull out a white cake pop covered in sprinkles, shoving the whole thing into her mouth.

"I'm not even going to be mad at you right now," I mutter, then laugh when she shrugs and sashays out of the office with her cup of coffee in her hand and the bag tucked under her arm. Standing there I watch her as she goes, enjoying the view of her ass in a tight pencil skirt that shows off her curves, and the heels on her feet that make her legs look unbelievably long.

Before we were married, I made it a point to put my foot down about her choice of office attire. She's beyond gorgeous, and I fucking hated seeing men check her out. I hated the way their eyes would glaze over when she spoke to them, the way they would watch her come and go from a room. Even more, I hated knowing that if one of them ever built up the courage to ask her out, she could say yes and there was not one goddamn thing I could do about it.

Until now. Now, she's mine. It's my ring sitting on her finger. It's me who she's in love with, and it's my cock that makes her breath catch every time I enter her. Men can look and fantasize all they want, but none of them will ever experience firsthand what it feels like to have her. None of them will ever know what it feels like to have her love, because every part of her is mine.

Chapter 7

Ashlyn

HEARING MY CELL phone ring, I reach my hand out and pat the bedside table until I find the offensive piece of junk, squint one eye open to hit the answer button, and put it to my ear. "'Lo," I breathe, half asleep as Dillon tucks his head into the crook of my neck and wraps his arm tighter around my middle, pulling my back closer to his chest.

"Angel girl."

"Papa?" I bolt upright in bed, accidentally elbowing Dillon in the stomach, making him grunt and mutter something I can't make out. Pushing my hair out of my face, I look at the time, and ask, "Is everything okay?" It's after ten in Alaska, where my mom's parents live, which is late for them to be calling.

"I just got off the phone with your mama." *Oh, God.* I plop myself back down on the bed and squeeze my eyes closed, feeling Dillon move away from me, then see the light turn on through my closed eyelids. "She told me you ran off and got married to your boss. Is that true?"

"Papa," I sigh. I love my mom's parents, but they are a little bit crazy and a whole lot in-your-business, and have been that way since I can remember.

"HOLD ON, WOMAN!" Papa shouts as the phone is jostled on his end. "I'm asking her. No, she hasn't answered yet. I just asked the damn question. Hold your horses. No, I'm talking to her. Dammit, give me the phone back," he barks, and the line goes silent for a moment. Opening my eyes, I sit up, finding Dillon up in bed. His back against the headboard, the sheet down around his waist, and his eyes looking at me intently.

"You better tell me that your mama was pulling my leg and that you did not get married to a man I have not met or approved of!" Memaw shrieks in my ear, making me wince.

"Memaw—"

"You did, didn't you?" she asks before I can answer. "You got married and didn't even think to call me and your papa?"

Staring into Dillon's eyes, I whisper, "I did get married." I watch as his face softens and his eyes darken. Leaning over, he pushes my hair back over my shoulder and kisses my neck, causing my eyes to slide half-mast. Scooting closer to him, I tuck myself into his side, resting my cheek against his chest and listen to Memaw shout.

"I can't believe this! Frank, can you believe this?"

"I AIN'T GOT no choice but to believe it," Papa mutters, and I fight back the laughter I feel bubbling up inside of me.

"What the hell happened to the good old days, when a man would ask a woman's family for consent to date her?" she grumbles, and this time I can't fight the laughter I feel, so I press my face into Dillon's chest and let it go. "Are you laughing?" she asks in disbelief.

I laugh harder, asking, "Would you like him to pay you in cattle for my hand in marriage, Memaw?"

"That would be a start, though, I do think you're worth more than a few head of cattle," she mutters dryly, making me giggle.

"What the hell are you talking about cattle for, woman?" Papa shouts from a distance, and I tilt my head back to look at Dillon, wondering if I should put the phone on speaker so he can hear for himself what *real* crazy people sound like.

"Nothing," she snaps. Then whispers, "When did you get old enough to get married, baby girl?"

My laughter dies in my throat and my eyes fill with tears. "I don't know," I whisper back, listening to her pull in a ragged breath.

"Please tell me that he makes you happy," she pleas quietly, and my eyes close tight.

"I promise you he makes me happy," I say, feeling Dillon's fingers still on my side, where he was drawing lazy patterns, and then his lips at the top of my head press there.

"Well… I guess I got no choice but to be happy for you then, do I?"

"I would like you and Papa to be happy for me. I'm really sorry I didn't tell you, but things have been a little crazy around here."

"I bet." She sighs, then mutters, "Hold on, your granddad is biting at the bit wanting to say something. Darn it, Frank, let me let the darn phone go before you strangle me with the stupid cord!" she shouts, and I laugh once more.

"Angel, is your young man there with you?"

"Yes, Papa."

"Put your phone on speaker so I can say something to him."

"Papa," I sigh, knowing what's coming and not really wanting to subject Dillon to it.

"Now, angel girl," he demands, and I reluctantly put my cell on speaker and hold it out between Dillon and me.

"Okay, he can hear you."

"You there, young man?" he asks, and Dillon smiles, kissing my forehead.

"I'm here."

"Good, now you listen to me, 'cause I'm only going to say this once. If you hurt my girl, I will fly my old ass to Tennessee, kidnap you, bring you back to Alaska, and let the bears have your cold, dead body.

Do you understand what I'm saying to you?"

"I understand," he says with a smile on his handsome face.

"You better take care of her."

"I will," he agrees adamantly while looking straight at me. The soft look in his eyes making my stomach fill with butterflies.

"Good, now I expect to hear that you two are planning a trip out to see us soon."

"I'll make it happen," Dillon agrees, and I lean farther into his side.

"Angel?"

"I'm here, Papa."

"Love you, girl."

"Love you too," I say, then hear the phone go quiet for a brief second.

"Love you, baby."

"Love you, Memaw," I whisper, closing my eyes.

"Call me when your guy isn't around so you can tell me about him, and send me pictures to my e-mail. I hope he's good-looking," she mutters, and I open my eyes, tipping my head back to look at Dillon.

"He's very handsome. You would definitely approve," I confirm, and he rolls his eyes.

"Well, at least there's that," she grumbles, but I can hear in her tone that she's smiling. "We'll talk soon."

"We will," I agree, and the phone goes dead in my hand.

Taking the phone from my grasp, he tosses it to his bedside then rolls me to my back and looks down at me. "Your grandparents are crazy. Now I know where you get it from."

"Whatever, I'm not crazy."

"You are, but I've become addicted to your brand of crazy," he confesses, roaming his hand from my neck down over my breast.

"That's good," I breathe as he dips his head and kisses me in a way that proves he certainly does love my kind of crazy.

"I STILL CANNOT believe you are married to Dillon." July, my cousin, sighs dreamily across the table from me, and I watch her husband, Wes, turn his eyes to her and narrow them.

"I'm sitting right fucking here," he growls, and she smiles, shrugging, then takes a sip of the chocolate shake in front of her.

"Have your parents talked to you?" she asks, and I move my eyes back to her, fighting back laughter as Wes does something to her under the table that makes her eyes widen.

No, they haven't—not about that anyway. My dad still sends me messages daily that simply say "I love you," and my mom does the same. It's been a week since they found out, and I really don't know how much more time I should give them. It's getting old. Yes, I should have told them I got married, but it's not as if I went to a nunnery, got the nuns drunk, and filmed an episode of *Nuns Gone Wild* in the middle of Sunday mass. I got married to a man I love. Okay, so I didn't know I was in love with him when I married him, but I am in love with him, and I know he loves me. We're happy, really fucking happy, and they should be happy for me.

"No." I shrug, and her face softens.

"They'll come around. Just give them time," she murmurs as I take a giant bite of my hamburger and wash it down with some Coke.

"Everyone keeps saying they'll come around, and I know they will, but to be honest, I'm kind of getting pissed off at them."

"You're their only daughter," Wes puts in, and I look at him, with his dark messy hair, blue eyes, stubble-covered jaw, and faded black tee that is molded to the muscles of his arms and chest like a second skin. My cousin might think Dillon is hot, but seriously, her husband is totally gorgeous in that dark and wild kind of way.

"Yes, and that's kind of my point." I point my fry at him. "They can be mad, but really, what is the point? God forbid I walk out into the road and get hit by a car," I state, and he raises a brow. "They'll feel guilty for doing this, for making this into a giant deal, when it is really just semantics." Now that Dillon and I have been together for a while, I know we were supposed to be together. "What would it have mattered if we dated for a week, or a year, before he popped the question?"

"Your dad would have known about it. That's the difference," he says softly, and I nod.

"Yeah, but the outcome would have been the same," I tell him, sitting back and feeling sick. I shouldn't have eaten so much, but then again, I always eat too much when I come here.

"Enough about me. How are things with you guys?" I ask, looking between the two of them. For a while now they have been trying to have a baby with no luck. I know one day it will happen for them, I just hope it's soon. I hate seeing my cousin disappointed each month, and I know Wes hates it even more than I do.

"Good. We leave in three weeks for Barbados. You and Dillon should come along. It'll be fun."

"I wish," I mutter, taking a sip of Coke. "Things have been getting really busy at the office. We're actually looking into hiring another receptionist and two more techs to help out." I sigh. I really do want to take a vacation, but I know I can't right now.

"Dillon really is a big deal in the dental world, isn't he?"

"He is," I agree with a nod. I used to think he was just being pompous, but he really is amazing at what he does. "And since he remolded the office and updated everything, we are constantly getting new patient requests which is great, but with only him and I on staff it doesn't make it easy to get away."

"Even with how great the office looks, I still hate going there." July shakes her head, and I roll my eyes.

"You're a wuss." I giggle, and she kicks me under the table, making me laugh harder.

"I can't help it that I don't have a high pain tolerance."

"I still love you." Wes kisses her cheek, and she turns her head to smile at him, resting her hand against his jaw. Watching the two of them, I wonder if Dillon and I look as sappy as they do right now.

"I really should get back to the office. Thank you guys for stopping by to invite me to lunch."

"Anytime, and seriously, think about Barbados."

"I will," I agree. And I will think about it, but I know there is no way for me to pull a trip like that off. Not right now, unless I went without Dillon, and I'm definitely not going without him. I reach into my bag for money, but Wes slides his card to the waitress as she passes the table. "Next time, my treat," I say, looking at him, only to have him shake his head in denial. "Whatever." I roll my eyes then scoot out of the booth and lean over to kiss each of their cheeks. "Call me. We need to set up a girls' night soon," I tell July.

At the same time, I hear Wes mutter, "Fuck me," which makes me smile.

"I'll call soon," she confirms, and I send them each a wave as I head out of the restaurant. Stopping at the edge of the sidewalk across the street from the office, I watch Dillon standing in the doorway with his hand up high, keeping the door open and his eyes on the patient he's talking to. Smiling at the older woman, he nods, saying something to her before she walks off. Turning to go back inside, his eyes catch mine and he grins, letting the door close behind him, and he jogs across the street to me.

"Hey." I smile once he's in front of me.

"Did you have a good lunch?" he asks, wrapping his arm around my waist, dropping his mouth to mine and kissing me softly before I can answer.

"Yes," I breathe against his lips then turn my head when I hear July shouting.

"Oh, my God! You guys are so cute," she yells as she rushes toward us, out of the café, with Wes following close behind her, shaking his head. "Congratulations, Dillon." She grins, giving him a hug and making me laugh.

"Thanks," Dillon mutters, hugging her back with one arm, since his free hand is still holding mine.

"We should do a double date." She smiles excitedly, looking between the two of us.

"Ignore her. She's crazy," Wes mutters, taking July by the waist and pulling her back to his side, then sticking out his hand. "Congrats, man. Welcome to the land of crazy." He smiles as July smacks his shoulder, and Dillon shakes his hand chuckling.

Rolling my eyes, I see my cousin do the same. "I wish we had time to chat, but I need to get back to the clinic," she grumbles, looking at her watch then me. "Call me soon, so we can set up girls' night. Maybe we should have a bachelorette party for you, since you didn't have one." She smiles, and her eyes light with mischief.

"Not happening," Dillon and Wes say in unison, making us girls laugh.

"We'll see." She grins then leans over, giving me a hug and speaking softly against my ear, "You guys look perfect together, and seriously, I'm so happy for you." Tears sting my nose and I hug her tighter. I may not have any sisters, but who needs them when you have some of the best cousins in the world?

"Love you," I murmur, feeling her arms tighten before she steps back.

"See you two around," Wes says with a flick of his fingers as he takes July's hand, leading her toward his bike that is parked a few feet away, near the curb.

"You are not having a bachelorette party," Dillon mutters, just loud enough for me to hear as he moves us toward the road.

"We shall see." I grin, stepping ahead of him, then hear him roar, "*Nooo!"* as his hand holding mine tugs me back roughly. The sudden impact of a car clipping my hip and thigh sends me spiraling to the concrete, where my head bounces, turning everything black.

"YOU HEARD THE doctor. She's going to be fine. Calm down. You won't do her any good if you're a fucking wreck when she wakes up," my dad's gruff voice says off in the distance. My head feels like I got hit in the skull with a bat, and my eyes are too heavy to open. I feel myself start to panic as I try to fight against whatever the hell has dragged me under, but it seems impossible and eventually I give up, letting the darkness take over.

"Baby, you have got to wake up and let me know you're okay," Dillon whispers against my ear, sounding worried, and I frown. Why wouldn't I be okay? Then the pain in my head and side registers, and I remember getting hit by a car.

"Dillon." Without opening my eyes, I know I'm in the hospital by the smell of disinfectant.

"Finally." His warm hand rests against my cheek, and my body relaxes ever so slightly from his touch. "Open your eyes for me." I try. I really try, but they are so heavy. "Please open your eyes," he murmurs, resting his soft lips against my forehead. I fight against the weight, and my eyes slowly flutter open. It takes a second to focus, but when I do, I find his face looming above me and his worried eyes searching mine. "There you are." His thumb slides down the bridge of my nose, causing my heavy eyelids to drift closed once again. "Look at me, gorgeous." I blink back open and look up at his handsome face.

"Fuck." He bends, touching his mouth to mine. "I love you. Stay awake for me," he demands, leaning back, picking up the remote attached to the bed, and pressing something on it before grabbing a pink cup with a straw in it and placing it against my mouth. "Slow," he instructs as I drink down gulp after gulp of cool water.

Releasing the straw, I shake my head then whisper, "I got hit by a car." I watch his eyes close and his jaw clench.

"Honey?" my mom calls softy, pulling my attention from Dillon. Turning my head, I watch her come toward me through the dimly lit room. "You scared me and your dad," she scolds, stopping at the side of the bed. "We've been worried sick." She bends over the rail and engulfs me in a hug that squeezes the oxygen out of my lungs, making me wince in pain.

"Sorry," I croak out.

"Easy," Dillon grumbles from my side.

"Where's Dad?" I breathe into her neck, and she looks over her shoulder then takes a step back.

"Right here," my dad says, sounding choked up, and I see he's a mess. His eyes are red and his hair is in disarray. "I'll always be right here." He gets close, resting his hand against my cheek then his lips against my forehead before looking down at me.

"I got hit by a car," I repeat, and his eyes slide closed.

"Let's not talk about that right now," Dillon cuts in, and I tilt my head to look at him, noticing his jaw ticking. Something I noticed the first time when I mentioned getting hit.

"How are you feeling?" Mom asks, resting her hand over mine, and I turn my head back toward her, wincing from the movement.

I feel like I've been hit by a car, I think but don't say, since that statement seems to make Dillon mad every time I do. "My head hurts a little," I lie. My head is pounding actually, and my hip is killing me.

"You hit your head pretty hard. You had to get eight stitches," Dad explains, and I lift my hand toward my head, only to have Dillon grab my wrist, stopping me before I can feel for them.

"Ashlyn," Dr. Woods says, coming into the room, and I wonder what she's thinking since she's the doctor who stitched up my foot weeks ago after Dillon and Jax got into it. "I'm so glad to see you awake. How are you feeling?" she asks, looking at me then dropping her eyes to the computer pad in her hand, typing something in while walking toward the bed I'm lying in.

"How long was I out for?" I frown, and she pulls her eyes from the computer to meet my gaze.

"Just about an hour."

"An hour?" I breathe, feeling Dillon's hand squeeze mine. I knew I was out of it, but being unconscious for an hour is bad… really bad.

"You're okay," she says gently, getting closer, forcing my mom and dad to move away. "But you have suffered a small acute subdural hematoma that we need to keep an eye on." At her words, my hand holding Dillon's tightens in distress. "Do you mind if we ask you a few questions?" she continues, not knowing my insides are seizing up with worry.

"Sure," I whisper, and she smiles softly then looks at a man I didn't notice before.

"This is Dr. Desmond," she introduces, and he smiles gently, taking the pad from her as she hands it over. "He's going to be asking you some questions while I check your wound and vitals."

"Okay." I try to relax while Dr. Desmond asks me questions about current events and the people in the room, and Dr. Woods checks my injuries and then my pulse.

"You are going to be okay," Dr. Woods assures, slipping off a pair of latex gloves and tossing them in a trash bin near the bed a few minutes later. "I'm going to release you to go home." She smiles as Dr. Desmond says a quiet goodbye and leaves the room.

"Are you sure it's safe for her to go home?" Dillon asks, cutting her off, and the doctor looks at him.

"I'm sure, but if she becomes nauseous, dizzy, or if her headache continues for more than a few hours, she will need to come back and have a CT scan done."

"Maybe she should stay, just to be safe," he suggests, giving my hand a squeeze.

"Dillon," I sigh. I know he's worried, but there is no way in hell I want to stay at the hospital if I don't have to.

"I think Dillon's right. I think you should stay," my dad mutters, and I huff, closing my eyes.

"There is really no reason for her to stay. She's not suffered any memory loss and her vitals are all perfectly normal. If I thought for one moment it would be better for her to stay, I would insist she do so," Dr. Woods conveys softly, looking between the two overbearing men in my life.

"I want to go home. I want to sleep in my own bed," I say, and Dillon looks down at me. I can tell he's not happy; I can see he's torn between giving me what I want, and having his way and keeping me here until he feels sure I'm okay.

"Someone will need to wake you every four hours tonight. No driving for a few days, and no drinking either."

"We'll take her home with us and make sure to wake her," Dad interjects, and Dillon's jaw tightens, along with his hand still holding mine.

"Over my dead body," he grits out through his teeth, glaring at my dad across the bed from him.

"I can make that happen," Dad growls back, and I feel tears fill my eyes. Apparently, not even getting hit by a car can make this mess better.

"Stop it now, you two. Look at what you're doing," Mom hisses, pointing at me, and both my dad and Dillon's eyes drop to me in the bed and soften. "Both of you follow me, now," she barks, stomping toward the door. Shaking his head, my dad leans over, kissing my cheek before following behind her.

"I'll be right back." Dillon sighs, bending to kiss my forehead as the tears spill over and fall down my cheeks. "Please stop crying. Everything is okay."

"Okay," I agree, trying to fight the tears back.

"Good girl, I'll be right outside the door."

He kisses me softly then follows my parents out of the room, where I hear my mom shout, "Cash Mayson, if someone ever tried to take me from you when I was injured, you would loose your ever-loving mind, so cut Dillon some slack! And Dillon, Ashlyn is Cash's daughter. He, of course, is worried about his little girl, so take that into consideration and stop being a dick."

God, I love my mom.

"You're a lucky girl to have so many people who love you," Dr. Woods says, making me jump. I completely forgot she was still here.

"You would think so, except the people I love hate each other," I mumble, feeling a fresh wave of tears fill my eyes. I hate that my Dad and Dillon are not getting along, and I hate that I'm the cause of the rift between them. They weren't best friends before, but they at least liked each other.

"We don't hate each other," my dad's voice cuts in, and my heart stops. "We love you and are worried about you." Wiping my cheeks with my palms, I hear Dr. Woods whisper that she'll be back with my discharge papers, feeling her squeeze my shoulder before leaving. "I was being hardheaded." Dad gets close, taking my hand. "I didn't want to believe my baby was grown up enough to get married. I should have talked to you days ago, but I didn't know what to say."

"Dad," I whimper, and his hand comes to rest against my cheek.

"I love you. You're my little girl. You will always be my little girl, but I also know you're a smart woman who has never made a bad decision."

"I'm sorry I didn't tell you. I just didn't know how. I knew you would be disappointed in me," I confess as more tears slide down my cheeks.

"You could never disappoint me." Sobbing, I lean up, wrapping my arms around him, not caring that it hurts like hell to do so. "Come on, stop crying before your husband really has a conniption," he says, sounding like he's smiling. I shake my head as he pulls away enough to look down at me. "I love you."

"I love you too," I implore, then look at my mom, who is crying with her hand covering her mouth.

Rushing toward us, she wraps me in a careful hug. "I love you."

"I love you too," I breathe, blinking back the wet in my eyes when I find Dillon's eyes studying each tear. Clearing my throat, I wipe my face and lay back in bed.

"Was the person who hit me okay?" I ask, and my dad steps back, tucking one hand into the front pocket of his jeans, while wrapping his other arm around my mom, tucking her close to his chest.

"We don't know who it was," Dad says quietly, and I study his sudden unease and feel the vibe in the room thicken with tension and anger.

"Didn't they stop?" It's not like they didn't know they hit me. I may be small, but I know they had to feel the impact of their car hitting me.

"The police are looking into it," Dillon states, in a tone that says he doesn't want to talk about it any more.

"They don't know who it was?" I whisper, feeling sick to my stomach. What kind of person hits someone with a car and drives off?

"Let's not talk about that right now," Mom cuts in, stepping away from my dad, coming over and pushing down the rail on the side of the bed. "Let's just focus on getting you better." She smiles, but I can tell it's forced. "Jax dropped off some clothes for you to change into, since yours were ruined. I put them in the bathroom for you."

"Jax didn't stay?" I frown, and she shakes her head.

"No. He wanted to, but something came up with work." She shrugs, and I know then that I'm the something that came up with work. I have no doubt he's searching for the person who hit me right now.

"I'll help you change," Dillon mutters, picking me up off the bed while my mom hovers close to us.

"I can help her," Mom says, and Dillon's jaw tightens.

"I've got her," he states quietly, and I rest my hand against his tense jaw while he carries me across the room to the bathroom, where he shuts the door before my mom has a chance to follow us in. Setting me to my feet, he steadies me with his hands on my waist then searches my eyes. "Are you sure you're okay to go home?" he asks cautiously.

"I'm sure."

"You swear you'll tell me if we need to come back?"

I fight the urge to roll my eyes at his overprotectiveness, and mumble, "I swear," while slipping the hospital gown off my shoulders and letting it drop to the floor at my feet.

"Look at you." His fingers skim softly down my shoulder, which is covered in road rash, then over my black and blue covered hip and thigh.

"I'm okay," I assure him, seeing the unease in his eyes as they scan me over from head to toe.

"You're not okay, so stop saying you are," he growls, looking into my eyes and palming my cheek gently. "You were hit by a car and were unconscious. When we got to the hospital, they thought you were going to need surgery because of the hit you took to the head. No fucking part of that says you're okay."

"Please calm down," I whisper, hating the fear I see in his gaze. "Dr. Woods said I'm okay, and she's right. I'm sore, but I'm all right, and if that changes, I swear I'll tell you and let you bring me back here."

"If something happens to you…" He closes his eyes briefly before opening them back up. "I can't even think about what that would do to me."

"What are you not telling me?" I question gently, knowing in my gut he's keeping something from me. His fear is palpable.

"Nothing." He shakes his head then turns me away from him before I can ask him more.

Catching my reflection in the mirror, my throat closes up. The side of my face, from my cheekbone to my temple, is an ugly shade of yellow-green, and my new blonde hair is copper-colored and matted with blood at the roots. "Oh, my God." I move a chunk of my hair to the side and see a large portion has been shaved clean to my scalp, which is angry-looking with a row of stitches in the center.

"I'm sorry," he whispers behind me, and I catch his gaze in the mirror. "They didn't have any other option."

Swallowing, I nod, knowing now is not a time for me to be vain. "It will grow back," I assure him and me at the same time.

"It will." He kisses my road rash covered shoulder softly then picks up my T-shirt that is sitting on the side of the sink. "Let's get you dressed and then get you home."

"Please." I turn toward him, letting him slip the shirt on over my head and help me feed my arms through the holes in the sleeves. I then watch him get down on his suit-covered knees and hold open a pair of my sweats.

"Put your hands on my shoulder for balance," he instructs, and I rest my hands on his shoulder and lift my foot then do the same with the opposite side. Once I have both feet in, he pulls them up my legs, being careful of my thigh and hip as the material skims over my bruised skin. "There." He kisses my stomach then slides a pair of flip-flops onto my feet.

"Where are my shoes I had on?" I know, of all the things I should be worried about right now, my shoes should not be one of them, but my Louis Vuitton peep-toe, leopard-print heels were one of the first things I ever bought with my own money, and they are one of my prized possessions.

"Your cousin has them," he mutters, dumping the gown I had on in a large red container in the corner of the bathroom.

"Who?"

"July. She and Wes didn't see what happened, they heard my shout and the car…" He stops talking and shakes his head, running his fingers though his hair roughly. "I was going to put you in my car, but July was adamant about not moving you and insisted we call an ambulance. They stayed with me until the ambulance got their then they followed us to the hospital."

"They didn't stay?"

"They stayed for a while, but they weren't allowed to stay in the room, so they went home after the doctor assured them you were okay and Jax took off."

"You should call her and tell her I'm okay."

"Your mom sent out a mass text when we were in the hall earlier. I'm sure the state of Tennessee will be over to see you tomorrow," he says as he carefully picks me up.

"I can walk."

"You may be able to, but I would rather carry you. Open the door for me."

I lean over and turn the nob, and he pushes us out with his shoulder.

As soon as we step out of the bathroom, my mom comes toward us, holding a few papers in her hand and giving them to me. "Dr. Woods dropped those off. She said you need to come back in a few days to have your stitches checked, along with the wound, to make sure it's healing properly and is not infected."

"Okay," I agree, and her face softens as I yawn.

"How is your headache now?"

"Not as bad as it was." I rest my head against Dillon's shoulder, feeling exhausted. "I'm just tired."

"Let Dillon take you home," Dad mutters, taking my mom's hand in his. "We'll come over tomorrow to check on you."

"Sure, but we're staying at Dillon's house, so you'll have to come over there," I inform them, and their eyes widen. "Oh, come on," I sigh. "Was I really that vocal about his house?" I question as Dillon chuckles.

"A little." Mom smiles as Dad shakes his head, grinning.

"It's growing on me," I admit, and Dillon's arms tighten slightly. It's not a lie; it really is growing on me. I love the kitchen and the library, but I really love his bedroom and his closet. I also love that he has a giant tub with jets in it. And really, wherever he is, that's where I want to be.

"And the fountain?" Dad asks with a raised brow. Apparently, I was vocal about that too.

"I still hate it, but I was thinking about buying some gold fish to put in it." I shrug.

"You really are crazy." Dillon laughs along with my parents.

"Come on. We will walk you out," Dad says, and Dillon and I follow behind my parents, out of the hospital. After giving them each a hug and a promise to call if anything changes, they wait with us until Dillon has me buckled in the car before they head for my dad's truck across the lot.

Once Dillon's behind the wheel, I turn my head to look over at him and smile. "I should have gotten hit by a car a week ago," I joke, then wish I didn't when his eyes darken and narrow.

"Do not say shit like that."

"It was a joke," I defend quietly, and he runs his hands roughly down his face.

"It's not funny. I would rather have your parents hate me for the rest of my life than to see you in the hospital ever again."

"Okay." I rest my hand against his cheek. "Please calm down. I'm okay, remember?"

"I know." He turns his head, kissing my palm, then starts up the car. I can tell he's still tense as he drives, but I have no idea what to say to put him at ease. As soon as we get to the house, he parks in the garage without a word and carries me inside and up the stairs to the bedroom, where he helps me brush my teeth and get undressed. Crawling into bed a few minutes later, I roll to my side and watch him strip down to his boxers.

"Are you coming to bed?" I ask when I see he's putting on a pair of sleep pants, and not stripping down like he normally does every night.

"In a few. I just need to make a quick call," he explains, coming over to where I'm lying, then bends to kiss me. "Try to sleep. I'll be right back."

"Sure," I agree, watching him pick up his cell phone off the bed, where he tossed it. I don't know how long I lie there looking at the ceiling, but eventually exhaustion takes over and I fall asleep before he comes back.

"Wake up, baby."

"I swear if you wake me up one more time, I'll divorce you," I growl into my pillow, praying I fall back asleep more quickly this time. All I want is to sleep, but every time I do he's waking me up, which wouldn't be so bad, but it takes longer and longer for unconsciousness to find me again each time.

"We're never getting a divorce." He kisses my shoulder, and I sigh, turning to face him and forcing him to his back. "How's your head?"

"Not too bad. My headache's gone."

"Good," he murmurs, kissing the side of my head. "Sleep, baby," he commands, lightly running his fingers down my bare arm.

"Okay." I close my eyes, but I don't sleep. Instead, I listen to the sound of his breathing even out and his heartbeat thump against my ear as my mind replays the sound of his shout right before the car hit me.

Chapter 8

Ashlyn

LYING IN THE library with my bare feet on the sofa and my head on a pillow, I rest the book I'm reading against my chest and look out the window, watching the sky darken and a tree sway in the breeze. It's been three days since I was released from the hospital, and for the last three days, things between Dillon and I have been tense. I know he's worried and frustrated with everything that has happened, and there is nothing I can do to help put him at ease.

The morning I woke up at Dillon's after the accident, my parents showed up, along with the police, who needed to take my statement. I found out from them that a few witnesses reported seeing a black Nissan Altima with dark-tinted windows double-parked with the driver behind the wheel. They then said the moment I stepped out into the road, the car drove toward me and swerved in my direction. The only thing that prevented me from getting hit head-on was the fact Dillon pulled me back before I took another step into the street.

I could have been killed. That may be a little bit dramatic, but maybe not, since someone wanted to intentionally hurt me. The thing that worries me the most is the police have not been able to find the car, even with the story of the incident appearing in the news the last three days.

"Hey."

Coming out of my head, I find Dillon standing in the doorway with his tired eyes on mine. His hair is rumpled and his face is unshaven, but he still looks as gorgeous as ever in a dark gray suit, and a crisp white shirt that is unbuttoned at his neck.

"You're home early," I murmur, watching him walk toward me. As soon as he's close, he tosses my cell phone onto the coffee table in front of me and lifts my feet. Taking a seat on the couch, he rests my legs over his lap, running his hand up my bare leg then thigh.

"I just came to check on you. I have to go back in a bit."

"You didn't have to do that. I told you earlier, I'm okay," I remind him, covering his hand with mine and lacing our fingers together.

"I actually did, since you haven't answered your phone the last five times I called you, and your mom said she dropped you at home over two hours ago," he mutters, and I move my eyes to my cell phone.

"Oh." I chew the inside of my cheek, feeling guilty that he drove home just to check on me when I know he's been swamped with patients since I've been out of the office.

"It's fine. It gave me an excuse to come see you." He lifts my hand, pressing a kiss to my knuckles, making my belly melt. "You washed your hair," he points out, and I run my fingers down my still damp hair with my free hand while nodding.

"Dr. Woods said it was okay to wash it today, so Mom helped me when I got home from my appointment."

"I would have helped you this evening," he says as he picks up a piece of my damp hair, rolling it between his fingers.

"I know, but I didn't want to wait." I've hated not being able to wash my hair. The first thing I asked Dr. Woods when I saw her today was if I could wash it, and she said yes, as long as I was careful and dried the area after I was done.

"Did Dr. Woods say anything else?"

"Just that if no infection sets in, I should be able to have the stitches removed in ten days. And that I can return to work Monday, as long as

I feel up to it."

Frowning, he shakes his head. "Maybe I should call and speak to her. Monday is only three days away. That doesn't seem like an adequate amount of time to heal properly from a head injury."

"Stop being crazy overprotective. I'm fine, and I'm coming back to work Monday, whether you like it or not."

"We'll see." He shrugs, and my teeth snap together. There are times when I love how protective he is, but there are also times it makes me seriously crazy.

"Have you heard anything from Jax?" As soon as I ask, his eyes shutter and he looks away from me.

"No."

"No, you haven't, or no, you're not going to tell me about it?" I ask, knowing the answer already, since Jax has had the same reaction each time I've talked to him. Meaning, he closes down completely.

"If he tells me something you need to know, I'll tell you."

"Will you, though? You were pissed when the police told me someone tried to run me down on purpose, and I think that is something I definitely needed to know," I say, watching his jaw tighten.

"We don't know they were trying to hit you. And like I've told you, we're dealing with it. Right now, all you need to do is rest and heal," he grits out, and I pull my legs from his lap and sit back against the armrest of the couch, tucking my feet under me while pointing at him.

"They swerved toward me with their car. I think it's obvious they were trying to hit me."

"They could have been trying to hit me," he states, and my blood runs cold.

"What?" I breathe, studying him as his eyes close and his hand runs through his hair in aggravation.

"We're not talking about this."

"Do you think they we're trying to hit you?" I question, feeling panicked. I didn't even think about the fact he was right next to me. That person could have been trying to hit him, but hit me instead.

"Baby, seriously, please fucking drop it. If something comes up that you need to know about, I will tell you. Until then, just focus on getting better."

"You sound like my dad and Jax. I'm really getting sick of you guys telling me what I need." Since I got home, my dad, Jax, and he have all been saying the same thing, and my mom, who is normally the only person who is sane in my family, has been mute on the situation, which isn't like her at all.

"I thought you'd be happy we are all getting along."

"Bonding over annoying me isn't working for me," I grumble, watching his lips tip up in a small smile. Seeing that smile, I realize it's been a while since I've seen him do that or laugh. "I miss seeing you smile," I whisper without thinking, and his face softens as his hand reaches out to wrap around my wrist.

"Come here." He drags me onto his lap to straddle him then slides his hand behind my neck, putting pressure there until we're sharing the same breath. "Stop fighting with me about taking care of you."

"I'm not fighting with you," I disagree, even though I kind of am, but still kind of not.

"I love you," he whispers, running his thumb down the column of my throat, and my body melts further into his.

"I know you do," I whisper back, watching him grin.

Giving my neck a squeeze, his mouth comes closer to mine. "Tell me you love me."

"You know I do."

"Yes, but I want to hear you say it. There is nothing better than hearing you tell me that you love me."

Searching his eyes, I lean even closer, and whisper, "I love you, even though you're annoying," against his lips. Then I watch close up as his eyes darken. Leaning in, he nips my bottom lip before soothing it with his tongue. "Dillon," I gasp, pressing into his erection.

"Right here." His free hand slides around my back and he locks my hips tightly against his as his mouth takes mine in a devastating kiss that leaves me wanting more, and whimpering at the loss of his mouth when he pulls away and rests his forehead against mine.

"Keep your phone close so you can hear it if I call," he demands, sliding his hand from the back of my neck to the underside of my jaw.

"I will," I agree, resting my hands against his chest and my lips against his in a soft touch.

"I wish I didn't have to go back to the office."

I wish that too. I wish we could get away for a few days, just the two of us.

"Me too." I move my hands up his chest and neck, then his jaw, pausing to run my thumb over his bottom lip.

"Kiss me, baby. I gotta go," he murmurs, and I pull my eyes from his mouth to look at him.

"If I don't kiss you, will you stay?" I pout, and he shakes his head, pulling me closer and nipping my bottom lip again, this time hard enough to sting. Gasping, my mouth opens, and his tongue slides in against mine. I've missed this over the last few days. I've missed feeling consumed by him. I've missed having his hands and mouth on me. My body starts to come back to life and I rock against his erection, feeling it rub against my clit. "Don't make me stop," I beg. I don't want him to stop this. He's been so careful with me since I got home, and though, I do love his soft side, I miss the feeling of him owning me. Pulling back slowly, he presses one more kiss against my lips.

"I gotta go, baby," he breathes regretfully, making me sigh in frustration.

"You owe me," I grumble, squirming on his lap, and his erection hits me in just the right spot once more, making my breath catch.

"I'll pay up." He smirks, flipping me gently to my back on the couch. "We'll go out to dinner tonight, your choice, so think about where you want me to take you." He pecks my lips then stands quickly, adjusting himself as he does. "Call me if you need me."

"I need you now," I whine, tossing my arms over my head in defeat.

"Poor baby." His eyes slide over me, and for a brief second, I think he's going to change his mind, but instead, he shakes his head and adjusts himself yet again. "I'll be home by five." He leans over, kissing me once more before grumbling something under his breath as he leaves, shaking his head.

Getting up from the couch, I pick up my cell phone and take it with me, wanting a glass of water. Moving through one of the living rooms and down the long back hall toward the kitchen, I notice the door that leads out to the garage is open and I feel the hairs on the back of my neck rise on end. Dillon is always overly careful about locking up; he's never left any of the doors open or unlocked.

Hearing something, my heart begins to race and my breath freezes in my lungs as panic starts to set in. Leaning back against the wall, I listen carefully, swearing I hear the sound of someone breathing. "Dillon?" I call, feeling my heart in my throat when I get no response. Lifting my cell that is clutched in my hand, I press 9-1-1 then move toward the door with my thumb on the call button. "Dillon," I repeat, then jump and scream when the door is shoved open.

"Dammit, Leo!" I cry, holding my hand over my heart that feels like it's about ready to explode out of my chest. "You scared the crap out of me," I chide, scooping up my cat before he can get away from me. Hissing, he swipes at my chin, but then gives up on being mad and starts to purr when I flip him to his back and rub his tummy. Shutting the door to the garage, I lock it and head for the kitchen with Leo purring loudly in my arms.

Since we've been staying here, he's been laying low. I don't think he knows what to do with so much room to roam, and most days I find him hiding in the top of the towel closet in the hallway upstairs. "Have you been locked in the garage all day?" I ask, kissing his head before dropping him to the top of the island in the middle of the kitchen.

Stretching out, he looks around then looks at me before falling to his bottom. "You didn't even eat breakfast," I say, picking up his still full bowl of food and setting it on the counter near him. Looking at the bowl, he bends to sniff it then looks back at me and blinks. "Is it not to your liking, King Leo?" I smile, rubbing the top of his head. Seeing he's not going to eat it, I dump the contents down the disposal and rinse the dish before grabbing him a new container of food. As soon as the dish is on the counter near him, he sniffs it again. Obviously finding it to his liking, he shoves his face in the bowl and begins to eat.

Taking a seat on one of the stools, I watch him lick the bowl clean, and then watch as he wanders around the top of the island for a moment before hopping across to another counter and up to the top of the fridge. "Are you going to hide up there for the rest of the day?" I ask him as he walks in a circle before lying down. "I guess that is a yes," I mutter, taking a sip of water, and then jump as my cell phone rings. Seeing it's my cousin June, I pick it up and put it to my ear, smiling. "Hey, you."

"Hey, are you home?" she asks as the sound of the doorbell rings through the quiet house.

"Yes." I snort, sliding off the stool. "But I think you're supposed to call to make sure I'm home *before* showing up. Not call as you ring the bell." I laugh, heading for the front door.

"I'm not there yet. I just left work. I should be there in five."

"Oh, someone's at the door. I thought it was you," I say, and hear the sound of a horn through the phone then listen as she shouts.

"Put your cell phone down before you kill someone, asshole!"

Shaking my head, I mutter, "One day, someone is going to follow you home."

"Please, if someone ever followed me, they would have to deal with Evan. You and I both know they would run for the hills the second they saw him.

"True." I grin at my feet as I walk across the marble entryway toward the door, knowing she's right. Evan would lose his mind if someone even looked at her in a way he didn't like, especially now that she's pregnant.

"But seriously, is checking Facebook so damn important that you can't wait until you get home?" she grumbles.

"I wouldn't know. After MySpace went up in smoke, I gave up on social media." I smile, hearing her laugh. "Hold on a sec. Let me see who's here." I pull my cell from my ear and lean up on my tiptoes to look through the peephole. "Fuck me." I close my eyes when I see none other than the she-bitch-from-hell standing on the front porch.

"Who's there?" June asks, and I grit my teeth.

"Take a wild guess."

"Please tell me that bitch is not at your house."

"I won't tell you then." I sigh, wondering if I should just ignore her and pray that she goes away.

"Don't answer it. I'll be there in less than two."

"I can hear you in there," Isla calls, and I lean my head back.

"God, even her voice is annoying," June gripes, and I groan as Isla pounds on the door.

"I just want to talk," she yells, and my hand balls into a fist at my side.

"Do you want me to call Dillon?" June questions softly, and I think about it for a second, but the idea of him dealing with her doesn't sit well with me… or the ugly green monster that lives in my head.

"No."

"Well, I'm pulling down the drive now."

"What does she even want?" I whisper, more to myself than my cousin.

"Who knows, but you're not dealing with her alone," she mutters as I hear the sound of her car getting closer then the crunch of gravel, and a moment later, I hear her car door slam. "Is there something I can help you with?" she asks loud enough for me to hear through the door. Hanging up my cell phone, I turn the knob and swing the door open.

"I just want to talk," Isla says softly, turning to face me, looking remorseful.

"I don't think we have anything to talk about." I cross my arms over my chest as a chill from the wind slides over my skin.

"I know you hate me." Snorting, I shake my head as June steps up onto the porch and comes to stand next to me, resting her hands on her very pregnant, very round stomach. "Dillon and I—"

"There is no Dillon and you," June puts in. Isla's attention slides to her, and I see the icy look in her eyes before she hides it behind a look of sadness.

"My family has been his only family since his parents passed away. I don't want your hate for me to take him away from my parents."

"I would never stop him from having a relationship with anyone. He's his own person. He can do what he likes."

"Then why hasn't he returned any of our calls? Why wouldn't he see me when I went by the office today?"

Shrugging, I answer silently while wondering if she went to the office before or after he came home, and why he didn't tell me that she was in town, even if he didn't meet with her. Really, I haven't thought much about her over the last few weeks, but seeing her standing in front of me now, I wonder if she hates me enough to try and hurt me.

"Where were you three days ago?" I ask, and she frowns, making a wrinkle pop out between her perfectly plucked brows.

"What?"

"Where were you three days ago?" I repeat, studying her.

"I don't know, home." She shrugs, smoothing her hands down her waist and hips.

"So you weren't in Tennessee?" June asks, seeing what I'm getting at with my questions.

"No, I just flew in this morning. Why?"

"Just curious," I mutter, waving my hand out, and her eyes move to it and narrow.

"Is that your wedding ring?" My eyes drop to the band on my finger and I ball my hand into a fist to keep it on, as if her seeing it will cause it to disappear. "He didn't give you his mom's ring?" she whispers, and even though I know she's not talking to me and it's just an observation, her words are a direct shot to my gut and I feel my legs get weak.

"Are you done?" June asks, and her head turns toward my cousin.

"I—"

"You're done," June states, not giving her a chance to finish her reply as she crowds me back into the house behind her.

"Please talk to him," Isla cries, looking at me as June starts to close the door. "My mom is worried about him. She just wants to make sure he's okay."

"I'll tell him to call her," I agree quietly as June shuts the door in her stunned face.

"God, I hate her," June hisses, getting up on her tiptoes to look through the peephole.

"Me too." Dropping my eyes to my hand, I look at my wedding ring. Shaking my head, I close my eyes.

"You okay?"

"No." I sigh, feeling her hand on my shoulder. "I need a drink," I murmur as I head for the kitchen.

"Can you drink right now?"

"Unfortunately, no." I really wish I could have a glass of wine, but I can't.

"Do you want to talk about what you're thinking?" she asks, taking a seat on one of the stools at the island in the middle of the kitchen.

Grabbing a bottle of water from the fridge, I pass it to her, pick up mine I left earlier, and take a gulp before dropping my eyes to the marble whispering, "He has his mom's wedding ring."

Looking up at my cousin, I wonder what it means that he didn't give it to me. I know I shouldn't be thinking it, but I can't understand why I'm wearing a band from a wedding chapel, while he has his mom's wedding ring. A ring I know means something to him. A ring I didn't know about until now. A ring he has talked to the she-bitch about, even though he obviously didn't give it to her either.

"You have him. Don't let that crazy bitch get to you or get into your head."

"I'm not," I lie shakily. I don't know why this is bothering me so much, but it feels like I just got to the top of the roller coaster and found out there are no more tracks for my ride down.

"Get that look off your face right now," she snaps, and my eyes focus on hers. "Dillon is in love with you." She points at me. "You don't know his reasoning for not giving you his mom's ring, or if there is even a ring to be given. For all you know, he could have lost it years ago, or he could be waiting until the right moment to slide it on your finger." Her eyes soften and I hold my breath. "In the end, it's just a piece of metal that means nothing. Marriage isn't based on the size of the rock on your finger. It's based on what you feel for the person you are sharing your life with."

Feeling properly scolded, I set my water bottle down and rub my forehead. She's right. One minute with Isla has me questioning everything and doubting Dillon's feelings for me. "I'm an idiot."

"You are not an idiot. You're in love. Love makes you feel vulnerable and unsure, and it also makes you doubt and question everything.

It's normal to feel like you feel right now." She waves me off as I take a seat next to her.

"I don't know what I would have done if you weren't here," I mutter, and she grins, bumping my shoulder.

"My guess is you would have probably run away."

"Probably." I laugh, knowing she's right. I don't like questioning his feelings for me, and I don't like the feeling of jealousy and envy I get every time I think about his relationship with Isla, or the fact she probably knows more about him than I do.

"You, my beautiful cousin, have a lot to learn about love and relationships. Dillon is the first guy you've ever been serious about. This is all new to you and—"

"I've dated," I cut her off, and she raises a brow. "Okay, fine, I've skimmed through a selection of men." I sigh, and she laughs.

"The point is you will figure it all out. Just don't overthink things, and always talk to him if you have doubts about anything." She nudges my shoulder then takes a sip of water before moving her eyes over my face, letting them linger on the bruise at my temple. "How are you feeling?"

"Thankfully, better. I go back to work Monday, and get my stitches out in ten days," I reply as I absently rub my fingers over the side of my head where my stitches are.

"Have the police said if they caught the person or gotten any leads?"

"They still don't know. No one saw a license plate, only the make of the car. Even with the story being in the news the last few days, they still haven't gotten anything."

"It's scary that something like that can happen in the middle of the day and no one knows anything."

"I know. I just…" I pause, taking a breath. "I don't even want to think about it any more. Every time I think about it, I start to panic," I admit, which is something I haven't told anyone until now, but it's true. There is a constant fear in my stomach. Even today, when I went to the hospital with my mom, I was scared to death about having to walk through the parking lot.

"It may have just been a freak accident."

"Maybe," I agree, but something in my gut tells me it was intentional, and even though Dillon said the person may have been after him and not me, the more I think about it, the harder I'm finding it to believe. He was at the office. There is no way they could have known he would be standing in the door, talking to a patient when I walked out of the restaurant, or that he would have come across to meet me. And not only that, but if they were after him, they could have aimed for him when he jogged across the street toward me. They had a clear shot of him then, if he was who they wanted to hurt.

"Earth to Ashlyn." She snaps her fingers in front of my face, and I blink.

"Sorry, I spaced."

"It's fine." She studies me thoughtfully for a moment then smiles. "In better news, I was talking to July yesterday, and we were going over ideas for your bachelorette party next Saturday. There were a few things I wanted to run by you."

Frowning at her, I shake my head. "I'm not having a bachelorette party next Saturday," I deny, and her smile turns into a grin.

"You definitely are having a party. Everyone is coming. Even the moms are going to come out for a drink or two."

"Oh, Lord," I murmur, seeing that she's serious. "Dillon is not going to be happy about this."

"What am I not going to be happy about?" Dillon asks, startling me, and I squeak, turning on my stool and coming face-to-face with him. I didn't even hear the garage door open like I normally do when he comes home.

"I thought you said you would be home at five." His eyes narrow then move to June, and he lifts his chin in a silent hello before crossing his arms over his chest and turning his eyes back to me.

"What is it that I'm not going to be happy about?" he repeats, and I pray June can once again know what I'm thinking without me having to say a word.

"We're throwing Ash a bachelorette party." She smiles.

Apparently not.

"Seriously, did you have to just come out and say it like that?" I snip, glaring at her, and she shrugs at me then smiles brighter at Dillon.

"Don't worry. We're not going to have strippers. April mentioned getting strippers, and Evan overheard then proceeded to lose his mind." She rolls her eyes, and Dillon's jaw begins to twitch.

"Oh, God," I whisper, and she looks at me.

"I know. Then Evan told Wes, and Wes freaked on July." She shakes her head. "I didn't really want strippers there anyway. I mean, guys with nice bodies are fun to look at, but I have my own hot guy and I really don't like polyester-covered sausage flung in my face, and I can't imagine you would want to have a ding-a-ling in your face either," she mutters. I shake my head, and my eyes widen at her in a silent plea for her to shut up before she causes Dillon to have a stroke. "Anyway, the plan is to have dinner with everyone before as a congratulations dinner, and then go to my house, change, and meet the party bus."

"Um..." I mumble, taking a chance to look at Dillon out of the corner of my eye and see his jaw is still ticking away.

"Also, April mentioned that maybe we should just rent a hotel room downtown and make a night of it."

"I..." I look from her to Dillon and can tell he is barely keeping it together.

"Dinner sounds good, but I don't think I want to stay out overnight." And that's the truth. I haven't spent a night away from Dillon since Vegas, and I don't really want to start now.

"I figured." She smiles then looks between Dillon and me as she hops off her stool, causing her belly to bounce. "I should go. Evan will be home soon, and I told him I would make dinner tonight."

As she wraps her arms around me in a tight hug, I whisper, "I'm so going to get you back for this."

"You'll be fine." She grins at me, leaning back.

"Uh huh." I roll my eyes, listening to her laugh as she lets me go before walking across the kitchen to Dillon, who leans down to kiss her cheek and grumble a goodbye.

"I'll call and let you know what time I get a reservation for."

"Sure," I agree, sliding off my stool to follow her to the door.

"Don't worry. I can see myself out." She winks over her shoulder, and I narrow my eyes. She knows Dillon is pissed and thinks it's funny. "Love you," she singsongs, leaving the kitchen, and a few seconds later, I hear the front door shut. Keeping my eyes off my man, who's pissed-off energy is pulsing through the room, I move to the fridge, open it, close it, and then move to one of the cupboards, doing the same. I'm hoping there is portal hidden somewhere that will teleport me into another dimension, where Dillon is the kind of guy who would be okay with me having a bachelorette party.

"How are you feeling?" The rough edge of his voice slides over my skin, making me shiver. Turning my head, my eyes connect with his and my core pulses.

"Fine," I whisper, and he nods then takes off his suit jacket as he starts toward me. Instinctively taking a step back from the predatory look in his eyes, I bump into the counter then look left, debating if I should run.

"I wouldn't do that if I were you." My head swings back toward him, and I realize it's too late. He's too close for me to run now.

"Wh-what are you doing?" I stutter out, feeling my nipples harden and the space between my legs flood with heat as his hands rest against my hips and slide up under my shirt along my sides.

"I'm going to fuck you." He nips my neck before my shirt is ripped over my head and tossed to the floor at our feet. "I'm going to remind myself that you are mine." His hands span my waist then slide softly down, pushing my shorts and panties off my hips, and they fall to the floor. "And that no one else will ever get to touch you." Grabbing onto his shoulders, I start to pant as he lifts me to the top of the island and pushes my legs roughly apart with his hands on my knees. "Take off your bra," he commands, then groans as his fingers slide between my spread legs and over my clit.

"So fucking wet for me. Does making me crazy jealous turn you on?" he asks, pinching my clit. My head shakes side-to-side as my bra slides from my shoulders. "I think it does. You're drenched and I've barely touched you." His fingers that were between my legs raise, and I watch him slide them into his mouth and close his eyes. "Lay back, heels to the counter, and spread your legs."

"Dil—" His name gets lodged in my throat as he presses his hand against my chest and forces me back against the cold marble.

"Now spread your legs," he growls. Moaning, my legs fall apart and my eyes snap closed as his fingers begin to toy with me. "You're so perfect," he praises, palming my breast while his fingers fuck into me, leaving me breathless and my body begging for him. Forcing my eyes open when he stops, I watch him free himself from his slacks then take a deep breath as he pulls my ass to the edge off the counter and lines himself up with my entrance. "Who do you belong to?"

"You," I breathe, wrapping my legs around his waist, using my heels to pull him closer to where I need him.

"Only me." He thrusts forward hard, and my mind screams with pleasure as his hands wrap around my hips to keep me in place. "You're mine."

"Yes," I cry out, arching my back, feeling heat spread from my core throughout my entire body.

Sliding one hand up my stomach then between my breasts, he wraps it around the back of my neck and lifts me forward, gently, until we are sharing the same breath. Leaning up, I nip his bottom lip then whimper when he takes my mouth like he owns it, thrusting his tongue against mine in sync with each hard blow as he pounds into me ruthlessly. "Fuck," he snarls down my throat while slamming into me over and over, sending me closer to the edge. Overheating, every inch of me starts to sing with pleasure and my core begins to clamp down around him.

"I'm so close," I breathe into his mouth, then wrap my arms around his back, pull my mouth from his, and bite down on his shoulder as my body ignites and fireworks explode behind my closed eyelids.

"Again."

"Dillon," I whimper, locking my legs tighter around his hips as my orgasm starts to come back to life.

"This time, you wait for me," he groans as my nails dig into his skin and my core tightens.

"I don't…" The words end as he thrusts hard, making my breath catch.

"You will wait for me." He thrusts hard again and again, and my body begins to shake as I tighten my limbs around him and fight back my release. "God, fucking dammit," he roars, then growls, "Come." And just like that, I let go and fly over the edge, clinging to him with every single inch of me as I do. "You will always be mine," he whispers, and my eyes fill with tears. Isla may know more about him than I do, but she will never have this. She will never know what it feels like to have all of him.

Chapter 9

Ashlyn

SITTING ACROSS FROM Dillon, I use my chopsticks to pick up a piece of sushi then dip it in my wasabi and soy sauce mixture before shoving the whole thing into my mouth, moaning in happiness as the taste explodes on my tongue.

"I can't believe of all the places you could have picked, this is the place you chose." He shakes his head, looking around, and I follow his eyes around the restaurant. I'm not surprised by his reaction. The place isn't all that great to look at, but they have an all-you-can-eat sushi bar that makes the cheesy décor and questionable environment worth the risk of food poisoning.

"I love this place." I shrug, picking up another piece of sushi, dunking it in my perfected mixture.

"I could have taken you to an actual sushi restaurant instead of a all-you-can-eat Chinese buffet."

"And what? Pay fifteen dollars for a California roll, I think not." Smiling, he shakes his head as I shove another piece of sushi into my mouth.

"Nut." His face softens, and I feel mine do the same then shift in my seat and lower my voice.

"Isla came by the house this afternoon."

Sitting forward, his eyes narrow, and he rumbles, "Why didn't you tell me?" sounding pissed, and I feel my temper spark due to his reaction.

"Why didn't you tell me?" I challenge him back immediately. "She told me she stopped by the office but you wouldn't see her, so I know you knew she was in town." I raise a brow, and his eyes narrow further.

"What did she say to you?"

"Nothing, she just wants you to call her mom. She said you haven't been returning any of their calls. Why aren't you talking to them?" I question, watching him closely, surprised by how angry he looks.

"You—" I know what he's going to say before he speaks, and I point my chopsticks at him.

"If you tell me it's not something I need to worry about, I will stab you with these," I cut him off, snapping my chopsticks at him, and he grins then runs his hand through his hair.

"They were not happy about me marrying you."

"So," I shrug. "My family wasn't happy either but they are slowly coming to terms with it. You have to admit they have a reason to be upset. You dated their daughter and were supposed to marry her. Instead, you married me in Vegas, and I doubt they even knew my name, any parent would be worried," I mutter, picking up another piece of sushi.

"Isla's gay. I was never going to fucking marry her," he growls and I blink, staring at him in disbelief with a piece of sushi frozen an inch from my mouth.

"Pardon?" I finally get out, not sure if I want to laugh or scream at the ridiculousness of the words he just uttered in one sentence.

"She's gay," he repeats, and I point my chopsticks at him, flinging the piece of sushi across the room as I do, not even checking to see if it hit anyone.

"She is not," I hiss, jabbing the wooden sticks in his direction then snap, "Dammit, give them back," when he snatches them from me.

"She is, but she did not want to hurt her family or risk anyone finding out about her sexuality, so she asked me to help her when people started to get suspicious."

"You can not honestly expect me to believe this garbage," I mutter, looking into his eyes.

"It's the truth.

"She told you she was a lesbian?" I ask, looking around to see if anyone is listening.

"Yes." He nods, and I shake my head.

"Wow." I rub my forehead, really wishing I could have a drink. "So what was your plan when you put a ring on her finger?" I grit my teeth, feeling anger swell inside my chest at the idea of them together.

"I didn't put a ring on her finger." His frown deepens as his jaw clenches tight.

"I'm sure. Let me guess, she proposed to herself?" I roll my eyes and his narrow.

"I didn't know what she had planned. We were at her parents' house for dinner and she announced our engagement to them, she already had the ring on her hand."

"Seriously?"

"I didn't want to hurt her parents, and I knew I could put an end to all of it as soon as I moved here."

"You didn't end things with her when you got here," I point out, and his jaw clenches tighter.

"She needed more time."

"I bet." I nod in agreement, having no doubt that she needed more time to try and convince him that she was just confused, and not actually a lesbian. More time to make him see that they were perfect together and should really try to make it work. "I'm in love with you." He reaches over and attempts to take my hand, but I pull back before he can grasp it.

His eyes fill with distress, and his nostrils flare as he growls low,

"Do not fucking pull away from me."

"You…" I close my eyes, trying to get my thoughts in order, but my mind is a complete mess. "I don't even know what to say to you right now."

"Isla and her parents do not factor into our life."

"But they do." For the rest of our lives, he is going to be connected to that conniving bitch through her parents who took him in after he lost his mom and dad. "I want to go home," I say quietly, pushing my still full plate away from me while standing. Without looking back at the table or him, I head toward the front of the restaurant then push through the door that leads to outside and take in a huge gulp of cool night air, while wrapping my arms around my middle. This is crazy, absolutely crazy. I've thought about what he may be wanting to tell me about him and Isla's relationship, but not once did I ever think he would tell me she is a lesbian.

Feeling him come up behind me, I tense when his hand rests against the small of my back. I want to go to my house and crawl into my own bed, but I know with him that option isn't available. "Come on," he mutters, leading me toward his car where he helps me in before shutting the door. Buckling up, I watch him walk around to the driver's side then watch him lower his eyes to his feet, shaking his head before opening the door and sliding in behind the wheel. Starting up the car, without a word, he pulls out of the parking lot and heads toward home while I stare absently out the window.

"What the fuck is going on?" His voice pulls me from my head a few minutes later, and I notice a mass of news trucks and people gathered along the side of the road near the entrance to one of the parks I jog through on occasion.

Slowing, he merges into a line of cars that are all driving about five miles an hour. "I wonder what happened?" I mutter as a police officer directs the line of cars were in to move into the on coming traffic lane, past the group of news trucks.

"Maybe an accident," he murmurs back, and I turn to look over my shoulder to see if I can see anything. There are no cars that have been in a collision, but just inside the park large floodlights are lit up around a blue tarp that is angled toward the road, with a van that is marked CSI parked off to the side with the side door open wide.

"I don't think it was an accident." I turn to face forward as a chill creeps down my spine, then feel his hand cover mine on my lap. "There was a crime scene van and a lot of police," I say quietly while he laces our fingers together.

"The story will be on the news." He gives my hand a squeeze and I nod, resting my hand over our locked fingers, hearing him inhale at my touch. "You know I love you, right?" he asks after a few quiet minutes, and my eyes slide closed.

"I know."

"Don't ever doubt that you are the most important thing to me." I hear the sincerity in his tone and know deep in my gut that he's speaking truthfully, but that still doesn't put my mind at ease.

"She played you," I state, gaining no response. He doesn't see it or doesn't want to, and there is obviously nothing I can say to make him. "I know you don't think so, but it's true," I mutter as he turns onto our street, then turns again down the drive. As we get closer to the house I notice a black car parked in front near the fountain and I sit up, leaning closer to the windshield. "Whose car is that?"

"Don't know." He presses the button for the garage as we drive by the car, and I see that it's empty.

"There was no one inside of it," I point out, feeling unease run through me as he puts the car in park and shuts it off inside the garage.

"Stay here."

"Stay here? I'm not going to stay here!" I yell at him as opens his door. "There could be a killer in the house, call the police." I try to grab him, but he is already out of the car. "Dillon!" I shout, and he bends at the waist to look at me.

"Do you really think a killer would park out front of the house in plain sight?" Okay, that just sounded stupid, but I still don't want him to go into the house alone. For all I know, Isla could be inside.

"I'm coming with you." I unhook my belt and his eyes narrow on mine.

"No, you are going to stay put until I come back to get you."

"Have you lost your mind? I'm not going to let you face a possible killer by yourself," I growl, and he opens his mouth to say something, but a deep voice asks,

"Who's a killer?" Screaming at the top of my lungs, a large guy with shaggy hair and a beard walks up behind Dillon, wrapping his arm around his shoulder.

"Jesus, Parker," Dillon growls, and I look at the guy standing next to Dillon and feel my stomach twist when I realize the guy is not an ax murder, but Dillon's brother, Parker. "What the fuck are you doing here, man?" Dillon asks, and his body turns toward his brother. Opening the door, I get out of the car and watch them over the roof, a little taken back by how much they look alike.

"Did you really think you could tell me you got married and I wouldn't make time to come out and meet your wife?" Parker asks, tugging Dillon into a hug that rocks him back and forth roughly.

"Where are Cara and the kids?" Dillon asks him once he pulls away.

"Inside, wandering around the monstrosity you call a house," he mutters dryly, and I giggle then freeze as two sets of blue eyes turn toward me.

"Baby, meet Parker. Parker, my wife, Ashlyn," Dillon says, and his face softens as he speaks, making butterflies take flight in my stomach.

"She is pretty." Parker smiles at me over the roof and I smile back.

"I know she's pretty," Dillon grumbles then palms the side of his head. "Stop staring at her."

"I cant." He grins, then heads around the back of the car toward me. As soon as he's standing in front of me, his arms wrap around me and he forces me into his chest so tight that I cant breathe. "Nice to meet you Ashlyn."

"You too." My words come out muffled against his shirt and I pat his back, trying to make him understand that he's cut off my supply of oxygen.

"She can't breathe, idiot," Dillon grumbles, tugging me from his brother and tucking me under his arm. I take a gulp of air as Parker's eyes jump between the two of us with a thoughtful look on his face.

"There you are," a woman says, and I look behind me at the door that leads into the house and watch an African American woman with rich dark skin, and short cropped hair that accentuates her almond shaped eyes, high cheekbones, and full lips step down the two steps into the garage. Even though she's dressed casual, in a pair of white Converse, dark jeans, and a plain gray V-neck, she screams elegance.

"Cara." Dillon lets me go, and her face lights up as he moves toward her and pulls her into a hug.

"I told your brother that we should call to make sure you would be home, but he insisted we surprise you," she murmurs, hugging him back.

"You never have to call," Dillon says softly, letting her go as she smiles studying him, then leans up touching his cheek.

"You cut your hair."

"I did." He grins, wrapping his hand around mine and pulling me back to his side.

"Maybe you could have a talk with that one," she nods toward Parker, "about chopping his off."

"Never gonna happen, baby," Parker says, dropping his arm around her shoulder, and she rolls her eyes skyward then moves them to me for a brief second before going back to Dillon.

"Is this your wife?" she asks him quietly, and I don't see his reaction, I just watch her face soften before she looks at me once more.

"Cara this is Ashlyn, Ashlyn this is Cara, Parkers wife," Dillon introduces us as she steps away from Parker.

"Nice to finally meet you." I stick out my hand and she shakes her head, wrapping her slim arms around me.

"I've heard so much about you, I'm so happy to finally meet you." She leans back enough to see my face and shakes her head again before hugging me once more, this time tighter.

"Dad, Uncle Dillon has like five bathrooms!" is shouted a second later, and she pulls away just in time for me to watch two adorable little boys in matching outfits bound down the steps into the garage.

"Did you use all of them?" Dillon asks, and the boys each look at him, grinning widely. "Uncle Dillon!" they shout, launching themselves at him. Stepping back, I smile as he scoops up both boys into his arms and swings them around. I've seen Dillon numerous times with my niece, Hope, but now it's different. I can actually picture him holding a little boy who looks like him and me in my head. My heart does a little flip inside my chest at the idea and my breath catches when his eyes meet mine and soften, like he knows what I'm thinking.

"Jordan," he lifts his right arm holding one little boy, "Kenyon," he lifts his left holding the other, "I want you to meet your aunt Ashlyn."

"Hi," they chime in unison, studying me with curious looks on their faces.

"It's nice to finally meet you both, your uncle talks about you guys all the time," I say, wondering how long it will take before I can tell them apart, since they look identical and are dressed exactly the same.

"You do?" Jordan asks, and Dillon turns his eyes to him and smiles.

"Of course I talk about two of my favorite guys."

"But you haven't come to visit us in forever." He pouts and Dillon's smile fades away.

"I came to visit you guys three months ago."

"Yeah, and that was forever ago," Kenyon says, making me smile. I'm sure that at five, three months does seem like forever.

"Well, you're here now."

"Yeah, and we brought cupcakes from Mimi's," Kenyon says as Parker takes him from Dillon, tickling him.

"Did you really?" Dillon asks and Jordan nods.

"Yeah, we got your favorite strawberry ones," he says proudly and Dillon smiles, lifting him high above his head.

"Too bad it's your bedtime, now I get to eat all of them."

"It's not my bed time," Jordan shouts, laughing as Dillon drops him to his feet and turns to look at Cara.

"How many cupcakes did you bring?"

"A dozen." She smiles.

"So just enough for me." He grins, looking between the boys.

"Not if we eat them all first," Kenyon yells, wiggling himself free from his father then tugging his brother along with him, and they run back into the house.

"I should leave them with you tonight after they've eaten those cupcakes," Cara mutters, and Dillon smiles.

"How long are you guys staying for?" he asks, and Parker answers.

"We're here until next week. The boys are on fall break, so we figured it was the perfect time for a visit."

"So you guys will be here Saturday?" I question and Cara nods.

"Yes, but if you have plans or need us to find a hotel, that's totally okay with us. I know us showing up is unexpected."

"No, that's not necessary. You guys are welcome here anytime." I wave her off. "Really, your timing is perfect. My family is throwing us a kind of after-the-fact reception type dinner Saturday, then my cousins are taking me out for a bachelorette party afterwards, in Nashville."

"I'm in." Cara grins, and Parker frowns at her.

"You are not in."

"Oh yes, I'm totally in." She smiles. "It's been far too long since I've been out, and I've always wanted to experience Nashville's nightlife."

"Perfect." I smile at her and she wiggles her brows, leaning closer.

"Are there going to be male dancers at your party?"

"No!" Dillon barks, and Parker's frown turns into narrowed eyes on his wife.

"No, no strippers." I smile. "I'm actually not sure what my cousins have planed but it will be fun, and there will be a party bus so we can drink."

"Drinking and a girls night out works for me." She grins as Parker grumbles,

"I don't like your wife anymore," to Dillon, making me laugh.

Wrapping her arm around mine Cara starts to lead me inside, mumbling, "Ignore him, he's crazy."

"Dillon is the same way," I mumble back, listening to her laugh as we head toward the sound of the boys and find them in the kitchen sitting on top of the island, each with a cupcake and icing covered faces.

"After you eat those it's time to shower then bed," Cara says in a motherly tone, and both boys pout and look at their dad and uncle.

"Do we really have to go to bed, we just got here."

"Sorry boys." Parker shrugs as Dillon walks to where they are sitting and picks up a cupcake out the box on the counter and takes a huge bite. Going to the fridge, I grab the gallon of milk and take it over to them then head across the kitchen for glasses.

"Uncle Dillon, isn't it your house and your rules?" I think Jordan asks, but I could be wrong, it could be Kenyon.

"Yep, my house, my rules. And the number one rule is listening to your mom and dad."

"That will be a change," Cara mutters as Parker pulls her into his side, kissing her temple.

"Bite." Dillon instructs, holding his half eaten cupcake out toward me as I set the glasses down on the island. Leaning forward, I place my hand on the back of his and take as much cupcake as I can into my mouth, listening to him laugh as I close my eyes, chew, and swallow the delicious cake.

"It seems I've been missing out my whole life," I say, opening my eyes. He grins down at me then leans forward, kissing me softly.

"Gross!" the boys shout, making me giggle.

Stepping away from him, I pour milk for the boys then lean against the counter and watch them talk animatedly with Dillon about what they have been up to for the last couple of months, and what they want to do during their visit. They are so adorable and so full of energy; I forgot how different little boys and little girls are.

"OKAY, BOYS, TIME to shower then bed," Cara instructs a few minutes later while grabbing a paper towel, and they each turn to pout at her.

"Do we really have to, Mom?" Jordan asks, pulling his jaw from her grasp as she attempts to clean off the cake and icing that has been smeared across his face.

"You really have to, honey," she murmurs, wiping Kenyon's face before helping him down off the counter. "If you guys want to go to the zoo tomorrow, you need to get to bed."

"Oh, all right," Jordan grumbles, scooting to the edge of the island before jumping down and running toward his dad, who Kenyon is already standing next to.

"Say goodnight to Uncle Dillon and Aunt Ashlyn," Parker instructs, using the palms of his hands on the top of the boys' heads to turn them to face Dillon and me.

"Night." They grin, and then duck their heads and run off, shouting and laughing.

"I'll be back," Parker mutters before looking at Cara. "Are you coming?"

"It depends." She turns to look at me. "Do you have wine?"

"I've got wine." I smile, feeling Dillon's body shake with silent laughter against my back.

"I guess I'm coming," she sighs, and I laugh out loud watching them leave, then lean into Dillon and look up at him.

"Are you happy?"

"My favorite people are all under one roof," he replies without answering, and I press farther into him.

"So you're happy?" I surmise, but instead of answering again, he kisses me until I'm breathless.

TAKING A SIP of soda, I lean back against Dillon, who pulled me down onto his lap as soon as we got outside, and look across the gas-lit fire at Cara and Parker, who are sitting exactly like we are, and smile. I could hear Cara and Parker arguing with the boys the whole time they were upstairs and knew they would both need a drink by the time they were done, so I had Dillon start up the outdoor fireplace and open a bottle of wine. As soon as they came downstairs, I handed Cara a glass and Parker a beer and lead them to the backyard to relax.

"So tell me, how did Dillon finally convince you to go out with him?" Cara asks, and I bite my lip, trying to figure out how much I should tell her. She told me earlier that Dillon mentioned me to her and Parker during their last visit, but was convinced I wasn't interested in him.

"I didn't convince her," he says, running his fingers along my hip under my sweater, and she frowns. Seeing the confused look on her face, I open my mouth to speak, but then snap it shut when Dillon continues. "When we went to Vegas for the dental convention, I canceled her room so she had to share mine. She got pissed at me and got drunk, so I took advantage of her inebriated state and dragged her to the nearest wedding chapel, where I married her. And the next morning, when she woke up asking for a divorce, I refused," he finishes, and I know my eyes are as wide as Cara's, which are staring back at me.

"Wow," she whispers after a moment, and looks at Parker. "And I thought you were crazy." Smiling, he tugs her head down toward his and says something I can't hear, and her face softens before he pulls her even closer to kiss her.

Dragging my eyes from them, I look at Dillon. "What do you mean you canceled my room?" I ask, and he grins.

"I canceled my extra room the day I told you I needed you to come with me."

"You did?" I breathe, and he runs his fingers across my stomach. "Were you planning on seducing me?"

"You refused to see there was something between us, so I was going to convince you there was, one way or another."

"And you think *I'm* a nut." I run my fingers along his jaw, watching his grin turn into a soft smile.

"It worked out in the end."

"Yeah, but you still could have asked me out like a normal guy," I mutter, and he wraps the front of my sweater in his fist and forces me closer.

"If I was normal, we wouldn't be together."

"You don't know that." I frown, and he pulls me even closer.

"Don't forget, I've seen what you've done to normal men, baby."

"Whatever." I narrow my eyes on his when he chuckles.

"We're gonna go on in and get to bed early," Parker says suddenly. I turn to look at him, and then hide my smile when Cara ducks her head.

"Sure. Night, guys."

"Night," Cara replies quickly as Parker propels her into the house in front of him.

"I'm surprised he didn't just pick her up and throw her over his shoulder like a caveman," I mutter, feeling Dillon laugh, and my eyes drop to his. "I like them."

"I'm glad."

"I like the boys too. They're adorable."

"They are." He nods, turning me in his lap to straddle him.

"I'm going to see if Hope wants to go to the zoo with us tomorrow."

"That would be nice," he agrees absently as one of his hands slides up my back under my sweater then around, cupping my breast. "Are you ready for bed?"

I press my chest into his while wrapping my arms around the back of his neck. "Yes." I nip his ear, and he stands, keeping me against him with his hands under my ass. Twining my legs around his waist, I let him carry me into the house and up to bed, where we do not go to sleep until much later.

"THAT'S OUR POINT, not yours," I hear a little boy's voice shout through my sleep-fogged brain, and my eyes blink open.

"No, it's our point," is rumbled back, and I roll my head to the side, finding Dillon gone and the bed cold.

Scooting across the cool sheets, I look at the clock on the bedside table and groan when I see it's just five after seven. I want to go back to sleep, but know I won't be able to now that I'm awake. Throwing my legs over the side, I stand, stretching my arms over my head as I walk across the room toward the closet. As soon as I open the door, I blink in confusion. The clothes that were in my suitcases are now scattered across the floor. Shaking my head, I wonder why Dillon couldn't just tell me to unpack. "This is Dillon we're talking about," I mutter to myself as I go about hanging stuff up and shoving some into drawers.

After finally putting away the last piece of clothing, I grab the jeans and shirt I picked out to wear and head for the bathroom. Tying my hair into a bun on top of my head, I turn on the shower and hop in, making quick work of getting cleaned up since cleaning the closet took over an hour. I know the boys will want to get to the zoo early, and I still need to call Ellie to see about Hope coming along with us.

Once I'm showered and dressed, I put on some mascara and bronzer then grab my cell phone and leave the room, feeling my heart melt as I head down the steps. Taking a seat at the bottom of the stairs, I watch the boys, including Parker and Dillon, play hockey across the marble floors using brooms and mops as hockey sticks and a wadded up piece of paper as a puck.

"We win, you lose!" Jordan yells, giving Kenyon a high-five when he scores a point in the imaginary goal.

"I call a rematch." Dillon smiles, picking up a laughing Jordan under one arm and a giggling Kenyon under his other, before spinning them in circles, making their laughter echo through the foyer.

"Morning," Parker says, and I smile as he takes a seat next to me on the step.

"Morning." I nudge my shoulder with his, listening to the boys giggle and yell for Dillon to go faster.

"When are you guys going to take the dive into parenthood?" he asks, and I feel my face soften when Dillon's smiling eyes come to me.

"I don't know," I say honestly, staring into Dillon's eyes. Seeing him with his nephews makes me want to see him with our kids. I have no doubt he will be an amazing dad. "Maybe a few years. We're still trying to get to know each other, and as you know, we didn't start out like most married couples."

"Do you love him?" he asks softly, and I pull my eyes from Dillon and the boys to look at him before I answer.

"Yes."

"That's all that matters. The rest will fall into place with time."

"I guess you're right."

"I'm always right." He grins, and I roll my eyes, seeing he's just as cocky as his brother.

"You sound just like Dillon."

"Dillon sounds just like me. I'm older." He smiles then looks at the door when the bell rings. Dropping the boys to their feet, Dillon pulls it open, and as soon as I see who is waiting there, I feel my temper flare. Then I hear Parker mutter, "You've got to be shitting me." I'm staring at Isla who is standing on the front porch.

"Dillon, please." She holds up her hand when it looks like he's about to shut the door in her face, and he shakes his head then looks over his shoulder at us.

Standing, I start down the last two steps, but then drop my eyes to my wrist when Parker takes hold of it, stopping me. "Boys, go hang with your mom," he orders, and the boys look at him and frown, probably confused by his change in demeanor. "Now," he urges, and they take off toward the kitchen.

"Can we please talk?" she pleads, looking up at Dillon, and my stomach fills with all the anger I've been holding back.

"Why are you here?" he asks as Parker releases me and goes to stand next to him, crossing his arms over his chest.

"I… I tried to see you yesterday. Did Ashley give you my message?" she prompts, and I grit my teeth, knowing for a fact she's very aware my name is not Ashley.

"Are you serious? Are you so desperate to see him that you came all the way to Tennessee?" I question as I shoulder my way between the two guys blocking the door, and she looks at me.

"I don't want to be rude, but this is family business," she murmurs, looking contrite, and my hands ball into fists so I don't reach out and strangle her.

"Baby," Dillon says gently, wrapping his arm around my waist.

I turn my glare on him, daring him to say something, and then move my eyes back to her and narrow them further. "I'm his wife. That makes me the definition of family." I point at myself, and her eyes fill with spite before she hides it with pity.

"He didn't even give you his mom's ring," she says. Dillon and Parker growl, "What the fuck?" at the same time.

"You're right. He didn't, but I don't see it on your finger, either," I hiss, lunging for her, but Dillon's arms band around my waist before I can reach her.

"Baby, calm down," he rumbles, but I ignore him and attempt to pull myself from his grasp to get my hands on her.

"Get her the fuck out of here," Dillon barks at Parker, who quickly ushers Isla down the steps to her car as I fight against his hold. So pissed that my vision has turned red and no amount of self-control will be able to change it. "Calm the fuck down."

"No!" I buck against him, pissed at myself for acting like a deranged, jealous wife, and pissed at him for having anything to do with her. I'm not this person. I'm not someone who gets jealous and acts crazy… or I *wasn't* until him. Sagging against his chest, I close my eyes, feeling defeated and humiliated. "Let me go." His arms tighten and his mouth drops to my ear.

"I'm not ever fucking letting you go."

"Please," I whisper, feeling tears burn the back of my eyes. I'm not this woman, and I don't want to be her. "Please, just let me go," I murmur, and he must hear the desperation in my tone, because his arms loosen enough for me to get away.

Stepping back from him, I pull in a breath then turn to face him. "Baby." He reaches for me, but I take another step away from him.

"I…" I shake my head as tears sting my nose. Shutting my eyes tightly, I only open them back up once I know I've fought them back.

"What the fuck was that?" Parker slams the door, making me jump, and I look at him, feeling my cheeks heat in embarrassment. I can't believe I acted the way I did in front of him. I can't believe he just saw me at my worst.

"I'll talk to you about it in a minute. Go check on Cara and the boys. I need to talk to Ash."

"Fine, but you better tell me what the fuck is going on," he warns before storming off toward the kitchen, and my eyes follow his retreating back.

"Come here," Dillon calls, and my eyes go to his and I jerk my head from left to right.

I… I need some ti—" I begin quietly, and his jaw clenches as he cuts me off.

"I'm not letting you go."

"You guys go to the zoo. I just need some time alone."

"You don't need time alone," he denies, and my stomach twists.

"I do. This… you… God! I don't even know the person I just was," I cry, and he takes a step closer to me, but I move before he can touch me. "Please, I'm begging you. Just give me some time to think." I hold up my hand to ward him off, and his eyes drop to my outstretched palm.

"Goddammit. Let me hold you!" he roars, and I cringe, feeling my shoulders sag.

"I think we both need some time to think. Some time to calm down," I whisper, and his eyes close then open and pin me in place.

"If you're not here when I get back and I have to come find you, I'm going to be pissed," he snarls, then turns and storms off, leaving me shaken.

Chapter 10

Dillon

"TALK TO ME."

Looking at my brother, I feel my teeth grind together. "I don't even know where to fucking start," I mutter, leaning against the fence in front of me, not seeing the boys and Cara feeding the animals inside the pen. My mind is consumed with Ashlyn and the look I saw on her face before I left her standing in the foyer.

"You can start by telling me why the hell Isla is still around. I thought you cut her out of your life after you ended your bullshit engagement to her."

"I did," I grit out, and he shakes his head, leaning his elbows on the rail.

"I told you it was stupid to even pretend to be with her. I told you that shit was whack and was going to blow up in your face."

"I don't need to hear 'I told you so' right now. You know how it was growing up in that house. Her parents were around, but were never really there. And when you left, it was just me and her. It's not an excuse, but I'd always just taken on the job of looking out for her, so I missed it. I didn't see her bullshit for what it was. I had no idea she was in to me like that."

"I could have told you she was in love with you. She's been standing under your tree for years, trying to get you to give her an apple."

"What the fuck does that even mean?" I ask, feeling my brows pull sharply together.

"I've been reading *The Giving Tree* to the boys at night." He shrugs and smiles.

"I would be better off talking to Cara right now."

"Probably not. You know how she feels about Isla," he mutters, and I cringe, remembering the first time Parker brought Cara to New York to meet everyone. Isla tried during that visit to hook him up with one of her friends, right in front of Cara, and Cara lost her mind. After that, she refused to have anything to do with Isla—or her parents, because they acted like it wasn't a big deal and laughed it off. "I'm just glad Cara didn't see Isla. You and I both know she would have helped Ashlyn kick her ass." He laughs, and my jaw ticks.

"This shit's not funny," I growl, and he pulls his eyes from the kids and Cara to look at me.

"You need to calm the fuck down. It will all be okay," he mutters, but the feeling in my chest won't go away, and I know it won't until I see her.

"Fuck, I can't do this. I can't stay here. I need to go home and check on her." I pull my car keys from my pocket and shove them at him. "Take my car. I'll get a cab to take me back to the house."

"Do you want us to find a hotel for the night?" he asks quietly, and I shake my head.

"No, I just need some time. Take Cara and the boys out to dinner."

"Sure, whatever you need." He nods, putting my keys in his front pocket.

"I'll see you later," I tell him, leaving without saying goodbye to Cara and the boys.

Making my way out of the zoo, I call Tim and see if he's available to pick me up. Luckily, he's close, and is waiting out front for me as soon as I leave the front gate.

"Did your car break down?" he asks, opening the back door.

"No, my brother's using it. He's staying here with his wife and kids."

"Is everything okay?"

"Yeah, something came up that I need to take care of at home."

"I'll get you there quickly," he mutters, shutting the door.

Rolling up the divider between us, I pull out my cell phone to call Ashlyn, and then grit my teeth when she doesn't answer. The drive to the house seems to take forever, even though I know it's only fifteen minutes. As soon as we pull up out front, I hand Tim enough money to cover the trip and extra for a tip before I get out, slamming the door. Entering the house, I head toward the library, knowing that's where I will find her if she didn't take off on me. As soon as I enter the room, I find her curled up on the couch with a blanket pulled up to her shoulders and her eyes closed.

Taking a seat in the crook of her lap, I rest my palm against her cheek and her eyes flutter open. "You didn't leave," I murmur, and she attempts to sit up, but I keep her where she is by leaning my body into hers.

"I told you I wouldn't."

"I'm sorry, baby."

Frowning, she shakes her head and tries to sit up once more. "Why are you sorry? You're not the one who acted like a crazy person."

"You didn't act like a crazy person. You reacted when you felt someone was a threat. Your reaction was completely normal."

"You think trying to attack someone is normal?" She closes her eyes, and I rest my hand over her heart.

"Baby." Her eyes open, and I feel my heart beat against my ribcage in sync with hers against my palm. "I would kill someone if I thought they were a threat, and I would go to war with any person that tried to come between us. That is not crazy. That's me protecting the most vital part of me, because it lives inside of you."

"Dillon." She closes her eyes, resting her hand over mine on her chest. "I… I don't like the person I was."

"That's okay, because I love her," I say gently as I run my thumb over her pouted bottom lip. "I hate what happened, but I loved seeing that your feelings for me are just as strong as mine are for you." I dip my head and kiss her softly then pull back.

"I told you that Isla and her family do not factor into our lives, and I meant that. They do not matter to me. You are my priority. Our future and your happiness are the most important things to me. I cut Isla out of my life when I told her that I was done going along with her lie, and she tried to convince me that she needed more time. I knew then that she was a liar, but my sense of loyalty to her parents made it hard for me to admit it to myself. I wish I never agreed to do what I did, but I can't change that. I can only promise you today was the last time you will see her. If she tries to contact me again, I'll file a restraining order against her."

"But her parents?"

"They will have to understand, and if they don't, I will have to make a decision about what role they will play in my life. Your wellbeing is all that matters."

"How mad is Parker at me?"

"What?" I frown, and she tries to sit up once more, but I hold her down then smile when she growls and blows out a frustrated breath. "Why would Parker be mad at you?"

"Um… because he found out his brother's new wife is a lunatic."

"Baby, Cara hates Isla and has refused to have anything to do with her or her family. If anyone understands what happened to today, it would be Parker."

"What, was Isla fake-engaged to Parker too?"

"No, smartass. Isla tried to hook Parker up with one of her friends right in front of Cara. That did not go over well."

"I bet not," she murmurs, and I grin, running my finger across her brow that is no longer holding the tension it was earlier.

"Are you feeling better?"

"I think so. I still don't like the way I let Isla get to me."

"I understand that, but please don't pull away from me. I hate seeing you upset, and I really don't like when you hold yourself away from me when you are."

"I just needed some time alone to think."

"I get that, which is why I left, but I won't always be able to do that. Leaving you goes against everything I believe in."

"You weren't gone long."

"I didn't tell you I would be able to stay away," I mutter, and her lips twitch as she sits up. "Are we good now?"

"Yes." She ducks her head and drops her eyes to her hands. Seeing her spin the simple gold band around her finger, I shake my head, wondering why the fuck Isla brought up Mom's wedding ring.

"Parker gave Mom's ring to Cara," I explain softly, and her eyes meet mine as she swallows. "My mom wasn't big on jewelry, so that was the only thing of hers that she left us, and Parker, being the oldest, got it."

"Dillon—"

"I know I should get you something that you can show off, something that everyone can see. But this ring"—I grab her hand, rubbing my thumb over it—"this ring represents the moment we started, the moment you became mine, and that makes it more valuable than anything I could ever afford." Tears fill her eyes as she throws herself against me, wrapping her body around mine. Holding her, I let out a breath and feel a weight lift off my chest.

"Tell me you love me," she whispers, and I bury my face in her neck, absorbing her scent of vanilla into my lungs.

"I love you, baby. Don't ever doubt it."

"I love you too." Her soft words seep into my skin and fill in the parts of me that have been missing since I lost my parents. I always knew I would find someone to share my life with, but I never even dreamed she would be perfect for me in every way.

"Did you eat breakfast?" I ask her after a few minutes of just holding her, knowing she wasn't up this morning when we all ate. She has a tendency to forget about food unless it's right in front of her.

"No, I came in here to think after you left, and fell asleep."

"Come on, I'll make you something." I pick her up and carry her into the kitchen, where I set her on the island. "How about peanut butter and jelly?"

"I don't think I've had one of those since I was ten." She grins, and I lean in, wrapping my hand around her jaw and kissing her softly before pulling away.

"Well, let me remind you how good they are." I reluctantly step away from her and go about making her a sandwich then hear her phone ring. Watching her hop of the counter and walk across the kitchen, I see her pick up her cell and put it to her ear.

"I was going to call you," she says with a smile. Then frowns and asks, "No, what happened?" Resting her palm against the counter, her head drops between her shoulders as she speaks softly. "We drove by there last night. I saw the police and news trucks." She shakes her head, and I move toward her. "Yes, at first I thought it was an accident until I saw a CSI van. Do they know who it was?" she questions, looking at me. She replies, "I won't be anymore" to whatever the person on the phone said.

"What's going on?"

"It's Michelle. They found a woman stabbed to death in Oaks Park last night."

"Jesus." With Parker, Cara, and the kids showing up last night, and Isla showing up this morning, I completely forgot about driving by there and seeing the news vans and police. "Do they know who it is?"

"Michelle said no. She just saw the story on the news and thought of me, since she knows I run there on occasion."

"Not anymore," I growl, thinking of her running there alone with her ear buds in, oblivious to any threat, and someone attacking her.

"Definitely not anymore," she agrees, shaking her head then dropping her eyes, and I know Michelle is saying something to her.

"Yes, next Saturday, and no, there will not be strippers," she mutters, and I use my hand under her jaw to pull her face up to gain her eyes.

"I swear to Christ if naked men show up at your bachelorette party, I will spank the shit out of you when you get home." Her eyes widen and her pink tongue comes out to touch her bottom lip as she nods. Seeing the flare of desire in her eyes mixed with trepidation, I wonder if I shouldn't just spank her the next time I have her naked in front of me to see what her reaction is.

"Shut up, Michelle," she grumbles. Then she whispers, "Yeah, bye." Before I can grab her, she pulls the cell phone from her ear, tossing it onto the counter, and scoots past me. "This sandwich is delicious." She grins around a mouthful, and I shake my head while walking toward her.

As soon as I'm close enough to touch her, I bend, placing a kiss to her forehead. "Do you want some milk before you choke on it?"

"Yes, please." She smiles, picking the crust off the bread, then hops up on one of the stools as I walk across the kitchen to grab the gallon of milk from the fridge. Filling a glass for her and one for myself, I take them over to the island and take a seat next to her. "Do you need to go back to pick up your brother?" she asks as I open the box of cupcakes, smiling when I see there are six left.

"No, I left my car with him."

"How did you get home?" she asks after taking a bite of her sandwich and a sip of milk.

"Tim was in the area, so he was able to drive me," I explain before sinking my teeth into the cupcake.

"You must really like those. I never see you eat sweets, and that has to be the third one you've had."

"Fourth," I correct, hearing her laughter ring through the kitchen, making me smile. It's been far too long since I've heard her carefree laughter, and I miss it. "We need a vacation, baby," I say softly, and she nods, ripping a few more pieces of the crust off her sandwich.

"I would love to get away with you, but I know things have only gotten busier since you've taken over the office, and I don't see it slowing down anytime soon."

"More patients equal more money, which means I can afford to hire another dentist. I'll figure it out this coming week."

"You don't think it's too soon to hire another dentist?"

"No, not at the rate we're growing. And really, I want to have a third person on to help cover things if you and I need to be out of the office for an extended period of time."

"Why would we need to be out of the office for an extended period of time?" She frowns, and I study her for a moment before speaking.

"When we have kids, I'll want to be home with you as often as I can. Right now, it would be difficult to do that, and I would most likely have to close the practice and work somewhere else that would allow me to make my own hours."

"Have you been talking to Parker about having kids?" she asks quietly, and I frown.

"No, why?"

"He mentioned us having kids this morning, and asked when we are going to start."

"What did you say when he asked you?"

"I said a few years." She shrugs, taking a large bite of her sandwich, and I stare at her in disbelief.

"We are not waiting a few years," I deny, feeling my lip curl at the idea alone.

"Really, and what was your plan?" she asks sarcastically, raising a brow.

"Now. The sooner the better. We haven't been using protection, so it could happen anytime."

Staring at me with her eyes wide, she shakes her head and mutters, "I'm on birth control."

"No you're not."

"Yes, I am. I'm on the shot. My next appointment is in…" She looks at the ceiling, wiggling her head back and forth, then drops her eyes back to me. "Just about eight weeks away."

"Cancel it. You don't need to get it again."

"Pardon?" She sets her sandwich down on her plate and crosses her arms over her chest while narrowing her eyes on mine.

"You don't need to be on the shot, and why didn't you tell me you were?"

"Have you been trying all this time to get me pregnant?" she questions, sounding pissed off, and I know by her tone I should probably tread lightly.

"I didn't know you were on anything."

"So you have been," she mutters, looking away from me. "Wow, just when I think you can't get any crazier, you go and do something that makes me wonder just how much crazier you're gonna get."

"I want a family with you. There is nothing crazy about that. I want to see you holding our kids the way I've seen you holding Hope, and I want to see that smile you only give her directed at *our* babies."

"We're just getting to know each other as a married couple. I want kids, but I don't think right now is the time to have them. I want us to have time, just the two of us, before we bring a baby into our family.

And I just graduated! I just started my career." She waves her hand around. "I want to enjoy all of this stuff for a while."

"One year, I'll give you that long," I compromise, and she leans close, placing her hand against my jaw.

"At least two. You won't change my mind. It's me who will have to carry our babies, and it's me that us starting a family will affect the most. It should be my decision when it happens," she says then lowers her voice, hitting me right in the gut. "I love you, and I want you to have everything you want, but I also need you to love me enough to understand this is you and me. This is our future. We should be making these big decisions together."

"You're not giving me the opportunity to make these decisions with you."

"If I wasn't on birth control, we would probably be pregnant right now, and that would have been all your choice. So don't try to make me feel bad about telling you what I need."

"Fine," I grumble. "I'll wait until you tell me you're ready, but just so you know, I'm not happy about it."

"Trust me. You're making that very obvious." She laughs, closing the distance between us and touching her mouth to mine.

"I'M GUESSING BY the make-out session we walked in on when we got back here that you and Ashlyn are okay," Parker says, and I hear the smile in his voice but I don't turn to see it. My eyes are glued on where my wife is standing in the kitchen at the island with my nephews, showing them how to make monkey melt—whatever the fuck that is.

"We're good," I mutter back, then smile as I watch her throw her head back, laughing at something one of the boys said. Pulling my eyes from her, I turn to face my brother, catching his smirk and a look on his face I can't read.

"What?"

Taking a pull from his beer, his eyes go to the backyard. "I honestly never thought I'd see you settled down." He shakes his head, returning his gaze to mine. "And I sure as fuck never thought I'd see you in love."

"Why?"

"You've always been obsessively focused on your career. I didn't think you would ever find someone you'd care about more than that."

He's right; I've always been focused on my career, because I wanted to be someone our parents would have been proud to call their son. Everything has, in some way, been about them and keeping their memory alive. *Until her.* She changed my focus and brought me back to life. She made me realize there are more important things than money and work.

"She changed everything," I say quietly, more to myself than him. I hadn't realized it until now how much she's changed me.

"I can see that." He pats my shoulder. "I'm happy for you, and Mom and Dad would be happy for you too."

"Do you think so?" I question, feeling a pain hit my chest. The same pain I get every time I think about them.

"All they ever wanted was for us to be happy, so I know, without a doubt, they would be happy for you."

"I still miss them," I sigh, taking a seat, dropping my elbows to my knees, and watching him take a seat in the chair next to mine.

"Me too, every damn day. And since we had the boys, it's only gotten worse. They would have loved being grandparents, and they missed out on that, while I missed out on seeing them with my kids. That shit sucks and does not go away."

"How do you deal with it?" I ask, realizing this is the first time we've talked about our parents in years.

"Having Cara's parents helps. Having you does, too. But really, having the memories I had with Mom and Dad, and being able to share those with my sons, is what gets me by. There will always be an empty place from their loss, but I hope that in someway I'm keeping their memory alive through my boys."

"You are, and Mom and Dad would have been proud of you," I assure, holding his gaze, and his eyes flash with both sadness and gratitude.

Hearing the sliding door open, both our heads turn toward it as Jordan sticks his head out of the crack, and yells, "Monkey melt's ready! Come on, hurry up!" before sliding the door closed.

"What the hell is monkey melt?" Parker asks, and I shrug while standing.

"Don't know, but I guess we're going to find out."

Taking my empty beer with me, I head inside where I'm immediately struck by the scent of baked cinnamon rolls. Dumping my empty bottle in the trash, I grab a fresh one for me and another for Parker before heading across the kitchen to where Ashlyn is standing. Leaning against the island at her side, I watch her scoop out vanilla ice cream on top of a large pan of baked cinnamon rolls and sliced bananas.

"Will you get me the caramel out of the microwave?" she asks, tilting her head back to look at me, and I nod, placing a kiss to her temple, then get the caramel she's heated in the jar to take over to her.

"This is a communal dessert." She smiles, tipping the jar of caramel over, letting it run across the top of the ice cream, and finishing with a handful of crushed pecans. "Everyone grab a spoon and dig in," she murmurs, pushing the hot pan into the middle of the island we are all gathered around.

"Oh, my God. This is what Heaven must taste like," Cara groans, digging her spoon into the pan for another bite before she's even swallowed her first one.

"Holy shit, this is good," Parker says a second later, and I hear Ash laugh as Cara hits his chest and nods at the boys, who are not paying attention to him. They are both now belly-down on the island, with their faces hovering over the pan, shoveling the monkey melt into their mouths like it's going to disappear, which it kind of is.

"Are you going to have any?" Ash asks, looking at me after she's swallowed her bite.

"I'm trying to come up with a plan of attack, so I don't get my hand bitten off," I mutter dryly.

Laughing, she takes the spoon from me and digs into the dish before holding it in front of my mouth. Leaning in, I close my lips around the spoon and hold her eyes as I pull back, watching them flare and darken.

"So," she tips her head to the side once I've chewed and swallowed, "what do you think?"

"I think you've been holding out on me," I mutter, digging in for another bite, stealing a scoop right off Jordan's spoon. I hear him whine, "Uncle Dillon, that was mine!" which makes me laugh.

"I couldn't make it before now. There has to be enough people to eat it," she explains, scooping out a bite for herself.

"I could eat a whole pan of it by myself," I tell her truthfully around a mouthful, and she grins.

"You would be sick. Trust me, I know from experience."

"You have to give me the recipe for this," Cara says, not even ten minutes later, as the boys scrape the bottom of the pan for the remnants of the dessert.

"It's easy. Just a can of cinnamon rolls cut up and baked. Once they're done, you top them with sliced bananas, ice cream, caramel, and pecans. Sometimes, I melt peanut butter into the caramel and dump that on there, but this is really the best way to make it."

"That seems easy enough," Cara agrees, and Parker smiles.

"Easy enough for even you to make, babe," he teases.

Placing her hands on her hips, she glares at him. "I can cook."

"Baby, I love you. You are a master at many things, but cooking is not one of them."

"I took that cooking class last month, and the instructor told me he thought I was talented."

"That instructor lied to you."

"No, he didn't."

"He did, babe." He chuckles.

"You told me when I got home and gave you the leftovers that it was the best thing you've ever eaten."

"I wanted a blow job." He shrugs, and her eyes narrow even further.

"What's a blow job?" Kenyon breaks in, and Parker's eyes widen while Cara's go to the ceiling.

"Uhh… it's uhh…" He looks around for help. "I-it's kind of like a reward," he stutters out, and I feel Ashlyn's body next to mine shaking uncontrollably then hear her snort.

"Why—" Kenyon starts, but Cara cuts him off, shouting, "Boys. Shower. Now," before he can finish whatever it was he was about to say.

"Do we have to?" both Jordan and Kenyon ask at the same time, looking between their parents.

"Yes, now go on up. I'll be there in a minute."

"Oh, all right," Jordan grumbles as they both hop down off the island and run out of the kitchen. As soon as they're gone, Cara turns on Parker and pokes him in the chest with her finger.

"I swear to God, the first time they say the words *blow job* and *reward* in the same sentence, I'm filing for a divorce," she hisses, poking him one last time before turning on her heels and storming away.

"You're an idiot," I mutter to my brother, hearing Ashlyn snort again then cough.

"Sorry." She giggles, covering her mouth. "I…" She snorts again, shaking her head while her face turns red. "I'll be back." She runs off, and I hear her laughing and snorting as she goes, making me grin.

"I totally forgot they were here," Parker grumbles, watching Ashlyn run off, and then turns to look at me and grins. "I hope they never say that shit around Cara's mom. She will drag my ass to church and drown me in the baptism pool."

"If that happens, call me. I want to come watch."

"Shut up." He smiles, then looks at the door. "I better go help her get the boys to bed."

"That would probably be wise," I agree, watching him go, then pick up the empty pan and spoons and take them to the sink before filling the pan with water and dumping the spoons in.

"Did Parker go up?" Ash asks as I flip off the water and turn to face her.

"Yeah."

"I know it's wrong, but that was really funny." She laughs as she hops up on the counter. "It's like the time Hope couldn't pronounce popcorn and kept calling it cockporn." She giggles, and I grin, walking to where she's sitting and making room for my hips between her legs, then pulling her flush against me.

"You look happy," I state, touching her smiling mouth with my fingertips.

Her face softens, and her hands come up to rest on the underside of my jaw. "I am. Seeing you happy, makes me happy. I wish Parker and Cara lived closer with the boys."

"Me too," I agree, kissing her softly before pulling back. "Tomorrow, I want to take them out to pan for gold. Do you want to see if Hope can come?"

"Yeah, I'll call Jax in a few and see what's going on."

"Good."

"Friday, after I get off work, I have an appointment with Kim to do my hair. I'm going to ask Cara if she wants to come, so if she says yes, you and the boys are on your own."

"That's fine. I'm sure we can find something to do."

"Awesome," she breathes as I run my thumb over her bottom lip, dragging it down before nipping it lightly, listening to her breath catch. I thrust my tongue between her parted lips, swallowing her moan as she clings to me.

Hearing a horrified scream come from upstairs, she shoves me back, hops off the counter, and runs out of the kitchen before I can catch her.

"Dammit Ash," I growl, following her up to the second floor, and then almost plow her over as she stops suddenly.

"What—?"

"There's a rat in the closet!" Cara screeches, holding a towel to her chest as both boys run into the hall naked, dripping water everywhere, with Parker behind them soaking wet.

"A rat?" I frown, and her eyes fill with fear as she looks at the closet and nods.

"Yes, a huge rat. I… I was getting a towel, and it… it—"

"Oh, my God." Ash doubles over laughing.

"This isn't funny!" Cara shouts, and Ash laughs harder. Realizing why she's laughing like a madwoman, I walk toward the closet and place my hand on the knob.

"Don't open it, you idiot!" Cara shrieks, trying to climb up Parker's back while the boys jump around behind her. Ignoring the craziness going on around me, I swing the linen closet door open then reach up and pull Leo down from his hiding place.

"It's a monster!" Jordan screams, running off as Ashlyn drops to her knees, holding her stomach.

"It's Leo." I hold him out toward Cara and Parker. "He's not a rat or a monster. He's a cat," I inform everyone, and Cara glares at me from behind her husband's back.

"That is not a cat."

"He is a cat." I chuckle as Leo hisses and swipes at me to be put down.

"What's wrong with him?" Kenyon asks, studying Leo as Ash finally pulls herself together enough to stand and take him from me.

"He's hairless. There's nothing wrong with him. It's just the way he is."

"Do you think you could have warned me that you have a hairless cat living in the closet?" Cara asks haughtily, and I laugh.

"Sorry, I didn't think about it. Leo isn't very social, so I forget he's even here most of the time."

"I swear, I thought I was going to die when it poked its head out at me." She laughs, holding her chest, walking toward Ash so she can get a better look at Leo, who is fighting to get free.

"Is it safe?" Jordan yells, and I look down the end of the hall and see him sticking his head around the corner.

"It's safe, bud. It's not a monster. It's just a cat," Parker says. Then mutters, "An ugly cat, but a cat."

"He's not ugly!" Ashlyn cries in denial, holding a hissing Leo closer to her chest.

"Sure he's not." Parker smiles at her as Jordan and Kenyon both cautiously come over to pet Leo, but then shriek and jump away when he finally gets his way, breaks free from Ashlyn's hold, and runs off.

"Do you have any other weird animals I should know about?" Cara asks as Parker ushers the still naked boys back toward the bathroom.

"Nope."

I smile, and she shakes her head, muttering, "That took ten years off my life," before turning and following Parker and the boys down the hall.

"Okay, so the blowjob thing was funny, but that was hilarious." Ash giggles.

"Nut." I kiss her head then tuck her under my arm to lead her back downstairs, this time to the library, where I proceed to make out with her until Parker and Cara come down after putting the boys in bed.

Chapter 11

Ashlyn

WALKING TOWARD THE door in the coffee shop, juggling my iced coffee, purse, and bag of treats, I stop dead in my tracks and stare at the rack of newspaper set up near the entrance. Gaping at the picture of police gathered around a white tent on the front page, I feel the color drain from my face as I read the caption.

Another woman found murdered. Police still have no leads.

"Sad, isn't it?" Startled, I turn my head to look at the well-groomed man standing next to me, but then take a step back when I realize how close he is. "Sorry I scared you." He smiles softly, tucking his hands into the front pockets of his dark jeans, causing his button-down shirt to pull tight across his chest.

"Umm… it's fine," I murmur, and he nods, scanning my face.

"Hopefully the police catch the killer before long," he mutters, then turns away and walks toward the counter. Shaking off the weird feeling slithering over my skin, I leave the coffee shop and rush down the street to the office. Once inside, I lock the door behind me, dump everything in my hands onto the reception desk, and head down the hall to Dillon's office. His head comes up from his computer, and he frowns.

"What's wrong?" Without answering, I walk to where he's sitting and climb onto his lap, curling myself against him, pressing my forehead into his neck, and breathing in his comforting scent. "Talk to me," he says gently, rubbing my back, and my eyes slide closed. I know

I shouldn't be freaked out like I am, but the paper I just saw means there have been two women found dead in just a week.

"They found another woman murdered," I whisper as his body under mine turns to stone.

"Pardon?" His hand stills and his fingers move under my jaw, forcing my eyes to meet his.

"I was getting coffee and—"

"How were you getting coffee?" he cuts me off with a growl and I try to sit up, but he keeps me in place, holding me tightly against him with an arm banned around my waist. "I thought you were shutting everything down out front."

"I was, but I wanted a coffee," I explain softly as his jaw begins to twitch like crazy.

"Why didn't you come get me so I could go with you?"

"I didn't think about it, and I knew I would be quick."

"Baby," he sighs, leaning his head back. "The police still haven't caught the person who hit you, so we need to be cautious until they do."

"I'm sorry. I really didn't even think about it."

His eyes drop to meet mine once more, and he mutters something I can't make out, tucking my face into his neck. "We may have nothing to worry about, but until we know for sure that what happened was an accident, I need to know you're safe."

"I know. I'll be more careful."

"Good," he states, placing a kiss to the top of my head.

"Maybe I should call off the party," I say quietly after a moment, and I feel his chest expand. I know my cousins would understand, but I'd still hate disappointing them.

"As much as I would love for you to call it off, it's not necessary. I spoke with Jax and Evan a few days ago and asked them about hiring security. They said they knew a couple guys who would be willing to keep an eye on you girls while you're out."

"So we're going to have babysitters." I shake my head, knowing the girls won't like that at all and will probably do something stupid, just to spite whoever is watching us.

"Not babysitters, just a couple men looking out for you girls. You probably won't even notice them."

"Do you know who they are?"

"Harlen and a guy named Zee, who I haven't met yet."

"Harlen's cool, so that won't be too bad, but Zee is married to July's best friend, Kayan, who is coming to the party, so that could be weird."

"Why would it be weird?" he asks, searching my face, and I shrug.

"You can't exactly let loose when your husband is watching your every move."

"You shouldn't be doing anything you wouldn't do in front of your husband anyways," he growls back.

I roll my eyes then see the time and stand suddenly, muttering, "Crap," as I adjust my skirt. "Cara's meeting me in ten minutes. If we don't go now, I'm going to be late," I remind him as he pulls me right back down onto his lap.

"You have time." He kisses my bottom lip then takes my jaw in his hands, running his gaze over my face. "Are you gonna be okay?"

My body melts against his and I nod. "Yeah. The whole thing about the murdered women just has me freaked out a bit, especially after what happened to me," I admit, and his jaw tightens.

"Nothing is going to happen to you."

"I know. It's just scary. There have been two murders in one week."

"This isn't the small town you grew up in anymore. It's now an extension of the big city that is getting closer by the day. Unfortunately, with that comes crime, baby."

"I guess you're right," I murmur, and his face softens before he places a kiss to my forehead. Standing us both, I watch him turn off his computer and ask, "Did you decide where you guys are going to dinner tonight?"

He tugs off his tie and rolls up the sleeves of his dress shirt. "Your parents' house," he mutters absently, grabbing his wallet from the top drawer of his desk and shoving it in his back pocket.

I stare at him in disbelief. "What? I think I just heard you say you're having dinner at my parents' house."

Grinning, he pulls me against his chest, dipping his face closer to mine. "I did, and we are."

"We haven't even had dinner at my parents' house together yet." I frown, wondering what the hell my mom is up to. She never mentioned inviting Dillon to dinner when I talked to her this afternoon, and that is something she would have brought up.

"Don't pout." He kisses my pouted out lips then turns me toward the door with a pat to my ass.

Spinning back around, I place my hands on my hips when I see his lips twitch. "What if it's a set up?"

"It's not a set up." He laughs, resting his hand against my lower back and leading me out of his office. "It's just dinner. Your parents know Parker and the boys are coming with me."

"Your brother would probably laugh his ass of if my dad or Jax decided to chase you with a shotgun. Maybe I should cancel my appointment and come with you, just to be sure you're safe."

"Stop being a nut. It's going to fine."

"Said every man, before his father-in-law shot him," I grumble under my breath, listening to his booming laughter as he picks up my stuff and leads me out the door.

"I SWEAR IT'S been forever since I've seen you," Kim says, rushing toward me as soon as we step foot in the salon, and I smile as her arms wrap around me tightly.

"It's been way too long," I agree, rocking her from side to side before letting her go to look at Cara, who is standing next to me.

"Kim, this is my sister-in-law, Cara. Cara, this is Kim, my amazing hair stylist and friend," I introduce.

"I still cannot believe you're married to The Dick," Kim says, then her eyes widen and her face pales as she looks from me to Cara. "I'm so sorry." She covers her mouth.

"Don't be sorry." Cara grins. "I used to call Dillon's brother Parker The Prick before we got together, so being an asshole must be a family trait," she confides, making us laugh. Then her eyes glaze over and she breathes, "Holy cow." Turning to see what's caught her attention, I watch my cousin Sage push open the door with one hand while holding Hope's tiny hand with the other.

"Yep, holy cow," Kim grumbles, while Sage lifts his chin toward Cara smiles softly at Kim then grins at me.

"Hey, cuz," he greets as Hope runs toward me and wraps her tiny arms around my thighs.

"Hey."

I smile then look down as Hope shouts, "Auntie Ashlyn, you're here!" while tilting her body back awkwardly to look up at me.

"Hey, princess." I smile, picking her up, even though she is way past the stage of being carted around, and resting her on my hip. "What are you up to?"

"Just hanging with Uncle Sage. Doin' detective stuff." She shrugs, like it's no big deal, and I fight back my smile.

"That sounds fun."

"It was only kind of fun, since we didn't get any bad guys," she huffs, and I laugh then look at Sage, who is smiling at her.

"Sage, this is Dillon's brother's wife, Cara. Cara, my cousin, Sage, and you already know Hope," I say.

"Hello, Cara," Hope breathes in little girl happiness. When we went panning for gold with the boys, we took Hope along with us, and she fell in love with my sister-in-law immediately and convinced herself that Cara is one of the Disney princesses.

"Nice to meet you." Cara smiles at Sage before running her hand down Hope's hair. "Hey, beautiful girl."

"Hi." She wiggles herself to be put down, and then looks between Cara and me. "Are you guys here to get ready for the ball?" she asks. Then she spins when Ellie yells, "Hope!" loud enough to make me jump.

"What ball?" I ask Ellie, and she rolls her eyes.

"Dinner tomorrow. Hope's convinced herself it's going to be a ball." She shakes her head, giving me a side hug, before saying hello to Cara, who she also met last weekend when we picked her daughter up to go with us.

"I thought it was just a family dinner." I raise a brow, seeing she has Hope's mouth covered, and she drops her hand away quickly then spins Hope to face her.

"Why don't you go pick a nail polish. We got some new colors in today."

"Yay!" Hope shouts, shooting her arms in the air while running off.

Planting my hands on my hips, I glare at my brother's wife. "What's going on? First, Dillon tells me that he's having dinner with my parents tonight, and now this. Something is up, and you better spill it."

"There's nothing to spill." She shrugs, and I narrow my eyes, knowing she's lying, since she is the worst liar ever. "Seriously, there is nothing to spill," she repeats, then looks past me and smirks.

"No, I'm working right now," Kim hisses behind me, and I pull my eyes from Ellie and turn to find Sage standing in Kim's space, with his face dipped close to hers.

"We can talk now, or I can stop by your place tonight. You choose."

"That's not exactly a choice." She glares at him, balling her hands into fists, and his lips twitch ever so slightly.

"Your choice, sweetheart. I'm good either way, but we both know what will happen if I have to come to your house," he mutters, and her eyes widen.

"God, you are… you are… I don't even know what you are," she growls, then looks at me.

"I'm so sorry about this. I'll be right back,"

"It's fine," I assure her, watching Sage open the door, allowing her to stomp out past him.

"See you tomorrow." He smiles, looking at Cara, Ellie, and me.

"See you tomorrow," I agree as he let's the door go and walks toward Kim, who is now standing at the edge of the sidewalk with her arms crossed over her chest looking annoyed.

"What's that about?" I question Ellie, who has moved closer to the front window.

"Last week, Sage found out Kim's boyfriend isn't exactly the kind of 'boyfriend' he thought he was. Since then, that"—she points her finger toward Kim and Sage, who are standing close together—"has been happening almost everyday."

"So he finally figured it out?" I ask, staring at Ellie in disbelief, and she laughs.

"He didn't exactly figure it out. He was out with Jax having a drink, and found Chris making out with a guy."

"Oh no," I whisper, and she smiles.

"Oh yeah. Then he punched Chris in the face and gave him a black eye."

"Shut up?" I breathe, looking back out the front window just in time to see Sage grab Kim's waist and tug her hips into his.

"Swear," Ellie whispers while we watch Kim try to push him away, only to have him take her by the back of her neck with his free hand and hold her in place. I knew Kim's plan was stupid when she told me what she did. I told her that claiming her gay best friend was her boyfriend was the wrong way to go about keeping Sage at bay, but she refused to listen to reason. Not that I can blame her. What my cousin did hurt her, and a woman who has been hurt will do whatever's necessary to protect herself from it ever happening again.

"Jax said Sage hasn't been with anyone since her," Ellie says quietly, and I pull my eyes from the window, feeling like a voyeur all of a sudden, and look at her.

"Really?" My cousin was a bit of a manwhore, like my brother was before Ellie, so I find it hard to believe he hasn't been with anyone since what happened between him and Kim went down a long time ago.

"Really," she mutters, and then shrugs. "I hope they figure their stuff out. They would be good together, if they could just get past all the crap between them."

"They would make some beautiful babies," Cara adds, and I look at her, raising a brow. "What? They would."

"They really would," Ellie agrees, then studies me. "But then again, you and Dillon would also have some beautiful babies."

"Yes, they would," Cara puts in, smiling, and I shake my head at both of them then move my eyes to the door when it chimes and Kim stomps back in, looking flustered.

"Are you ready?" she asks, moving toward the back of the shop without stopping to look at us.

"Are you okay?"

Her shoulders slump and she spins to face me, plastering what I know is a fake smile on her face. "Absolutely fabulous."

"You're as bad of a liar as Ellie." I smile, and she presses her lips together.

"He's annoying." She waves me off then narrows her eyes past my shoulder, and I turn to look out the window to find Sage standing in front of his truck, pointing at his watch while looking at her.

"Oh my, what does that mean?" Cara asks, sounding breathless while she stares at my cousin.

"My guess is Kim's time is just about up." Ellie giggles, and Kim growls something under her breath before turning and stomping to the back of the salon.

"That man is seriously hot," Cara mutters behind me as I follow Kim to her station and take a seat in the chair she's turned around for me.

"You're not so pissed that you'll accidentally chop all of my hair off, right?" I joke, and her eyes meet mine in the mirror.

"I'm good." She smiles, pulling in a breath. "I may end up killing your cousin, but I swear I won't mess up your hair."

"Good."

"And you didn't hear me say I may kill Sage out loud, since then it would be premeditated, and I can only get off if it looks like it was a spontaneous decision."

"I didn't hear anything." I smile back then pull my eyes from hers in the mirror to look up at her. "Do you want me to tell him to back off?" I ask quietly, and her face softens.

"I don't know what I want anymore." She shrugs. "Everyday, he asks me out. And everyday, I say no, but…" She shakes her head, tucking a chunk of hair behind her ear. "I just… He's making it really hard to keep saying no."

"You liked him and he hurt you. I get that, but maybe you should give him a chance to apologize, and then go from there."

"He has apologized." She shrugs. "I just haven't forgiven him."

"Maybe you can find a way to do that so you can move on," I say, giving her hand a squeeze. "I'm not saying you need to move on with him, but I think you need to let whatever happened go so you can figure out what you want for yourself."

"You're right," she agrees and I lean up, giving her a hug, and then sit back to look at her in the mirror.

"Now, please tell me that you know something about tomorrow's supposed family dinner."

"I don't know what you're talking about," she replies, and just like Ellie, I can tell she's lying.

Dammit.

"HEY, DO YOU want to get a drink after we're done here?" Ellie asks, and I pull my eyes from the mirror, where I have been watching Kim curl my hair, and look at Cara, who is sitting in front of the nail dryer.

"Do you want to go?" I ask, when her eyes meet mine.

"I'm always down for a drink." She grins, and I smile back then look at Ellie.

"We're down. I just need to send Dillon a text to let him know what's going on."

"I'll send Jax a text too and let him know to come pick up Hope."

"You're coming, right?" I ask, looking at Kim, and she shrugs.

"Sure, sounds good to me."

"Awesome," I mutter, pulling out my cell phone so I can send a quick text to Dillon and let him know what the plan is. Getting his reply text, less than a minute later, I smile.

No doing anything you wouldn't do with me watching!!! Call when you get there, and then when you need to be picked up. Jax has someone keeping an eye on you guys, and he'll follow you to the bar.

"Who does Jax have watching us?" I ask Ellie, and she shrugs.

"I have no idea. He never mentioned it to me. Did Dillon say someone is watching us?"

"Yes."

"Hmm, no clue," she mutters, putting on lip-gloss.

"Why do we need someone watching us?" Cara questions, and I inwardly groan. I don't want her to think she has anything to worry about or that I'm crazy.

"My brother is overprotective of Ellie and Hope, and you know Dillon's crazy," I answer, and she nods like 'Oh yeah, I totally get it my mans the same way,' then pulls her hands out from under the nail dryer and dangles them before Hope, who smiles brightly.

"What do you think?"

"They're beautiful, and now we match." Hope claps, holding her hands out next to Cara's, giggling, and I grin at them.

"Go get your bag from the back, baby girl. Daddy will be here to get you in a few minutes," Ellie says, and Hope pouts.

"Can't I come with you?"

"Sorry, no, but I bet Daddy will take you out for ice cream if you ask him."

"Yay! Ice cream!" she yells happily before skipping to the back of the salon, then coming out a few minutes later with a bright pink glitter backpack.

"You're done," Kim says, and I turn my head to look at myself in the mirror and smile.

"Like always, it's perfect. I wish you could be with me everyday when I get ready for work."

"Oh please, you always look perfect." She waves me off while putting away her curlers and things. "I didn't spray it, since you have the stitches, but with the serum the curls should hold through tomorrow, and before you know it, your hair they had to shave off will grow back. But for now, I blended it in so it will grow a little better."

"Thank you." I stand and give her a hug. She didn't do my color, but she did trim my ends and wash my hair for me, which is what I really wanted since I'm scared to wash it myself after seeing a video of a person with infected stitches.

"Now, lets go have a drink." She takes off her smock and tucks it away then grabs her purse. Once we are outside, Ellie hands Hope off to Jax then proceeds to make out with him—*barf*—before taking my hand and leading me down the street to the bar at the end of the block.

As soon as we get inside, I freeze. "What the hell?" I breathe, seeing my cousins and friends all gathered around two long tables in the back of the bar.

"Surprise!" July smiles, giving me a hug. "I know tomorrow is your party, but since we are all in town, we decided to get together tonight."

"Do not fricking cry," Michelle mutters, pulling me in for a hug. "I so wanted to call and warn you, but June said she'd kick my ass, and it would look really bad if a pregnant woman beat me up," she whispers.

"Whatever." June grins, giving me a hug before stepping away to allow April, December, and May to come forward and hug me too.

"I didn't know you were in town," I choke, fighting back tears as Nalia steps toward me.

"Did you really think I would miss this?" She grins, wrapping her arms around me tightly.

"I've missed you."

"I've missed you too," she whispers, and then Willow and Harmony both tackle us at the same time, rocking us from side to side.

"We are so happy for you."

"Thank you." I smile at both of them, and then feel my jaw drop when I look past them.

"Hanna." I stare at my cousin, who I haven't seen in forever, in disbelief.

"The one and only." She holds out her arms, and I run toward her, throwing my arms around her and then leaning back to look at her.

"I thought you were in Paris."

"I was, but I couldn't miss this. So I took a flight last night and got in this morning."

"God." I lean back and look around the space that is packed full of some of my favorite women, and tears start to burn the back of my throat.

"No fucking crying. It's time to celebrate," April says, handing me a shot, and I laugh then shoot it back, holding the glass up. Hearing the girls all shout and clap. Finding Cara in the crowd standing next to Kim, I quickly introduce her to everyone before doing exactly what April suggested.

Seeing Harmony suddenly disappear under the table, I frown, tilting my head under the ledge to look at her.

"What are you doing?" I ask, feeling a little dizzy from the five lemon drop shots I've had and my awkward, almost upside down position.

"Um… I lost an earring."

"Oh, I'll help you find it," I mumble, scooting my chair back so I can get under the table along with her. Crawling on my hands and knees across the floor, I realize I have no idea exactly what I'm looking for. "What does it look like?" I question, lifting my head to look at her, and her face turns red.

"I didn't really lose an earring," she whispers, crawling toward me, and I fall to my bottom and raise a brow.

"Then why are you under the table?"

"Harlen's here."

"What?"

"Harlen's here," she repeats.

"I thought you two were friends?"

"We were…"

"So why are you hiding from him?"

"I kissed him." She says after a long moment and I blink.

"Oh, my God! You are a damn liar," Willow snaps, and I watch her fall to her ass under the table then crawl toward us, shaking her head and pointing at Harmony. "You told me when I asked why you haven't been hanging out with him anymore that nothing happened between you two."

"So, is the party under the table now?" April asks, suddenly appearing at my side, handing me another shot that I take immediately. "I kind of like it. It's cozy," she mutters, looking around, and I giggle.

"Oh my God," Harmony groans, covering her face with her hands. "You all need to get out of here before you blow my cover."

"What's going on?" July asks a second later, appearing out of thin air.

"God help me," Harmony growls, glaring at everyone.

"What's her problem?" July asks, nodding toward Harmony.

"She kissed Harlen." Willow shrugs as Harmony narrows her eyes on her. "What? I don't understand what the big deal is. So what you kissed people kiss everyday."

"It was bad."

"How was it bad?" I ask, seeing the unease in her eyes.

"I." She shakes her head frantically. "Jeez, this is so embarrassing. Can you guys just go and forget I ever said anything?"

"No," Willow snaps, getting closer to her sister. "Spill."

"I kissed him and he didn't like it.... Okay?" She huffs.

"Oh," I breathe in understanding. "Have you talked to him about it?" I ask softly.

"No." She closes her eyes, whispering, "We were out when it happened and I didn't wait around. He went to the bathroom, and I took off."

"I'm going to kick his ass," July growls already half drunk, and Harmony grabs on to her ankle as she tries to crawl out from under the table.

"Please don't," she pleas, and July's eyes narrow on her over her shoulder.

"You're not going to sit under this table and feel sorry for yourself," she snaps. "You are going to go out there and let him see exactly what he's missing out on."

"Has he tried to talk to you since then?" April asks suddenly, and Harmony pulls her wide eyes from July to look at her.

"No." She shakes her head.

"So he hasn't called you at all?" April's eyes narrow and Harmony looks away shrugging.

"He's called a few times, but I haven't answered."

"Hmm," she hums, then smiles her smile that screams trouble and grabs Harmony's hand, tugging her toward her. "Like July said, you are not going to sit under the table like a weirdo. You are going to go out there and have fun."

"July didn't call me a weirdo." Harmony mutters under her breath as she's dragged out behind April.

"I don't think tonight is going to end well for her," Willow whispers, watching July, April, and Harmony crawl out from under the table before looking at me, smiling. "I'm so happy for you." Wrapping her arms around me quickly, she leans back, bonking her head and grumbling something I can't understand before crawling out behind everyone else. Looking around the now empty space, I shake my head and feel a smile spread across my face. Only in my family would a serious conversation be had under a table at a packed bar.

"GET THE FUCK down now."

Pulling my gaze from Harmony, who is singing along with me to "Keep Your Hands to Yourself," I look down and see a red-faced Harlen glaring up at her, and then notice Dillon standing next to him with his arms crossed over his chest and his lips twitching into a smile.

"You're here," I shout, jumping from the top of the bar and into his arms, hearing him grunt as I wrap myself around him.

"I don't think dancing on bars is something you'd do with me watching," he mutters, and I giggle, tucking my face into his neck.

"I wasn't dancing. I was singing." I lift my head to look at him then grin over his shoulder as I watch Harlen pull a reluctant Harmony off the bar, throw her over his shoulder, and smack her ass when she kicks her feet to be put down. My cousin may think he didn't like the kiss but I know for sure she's wrong. Since the moment Harlen's eyes landed on Harmony tonight he's been watching her like a hawk.

"How drunk are you?"

My eyes focus back on Dillon's and I shrug. "Drunk, but not so drunk I'll end up married again." I smile, and he mouths the word *nut* while carrying me toward the back table, taking a seat. "Where's Parker?" I ask, finding Cara sitting with June and Evan, chatting.

"Home with the boys, who are currently passed out after having too much fun at your parents' house."

"I didn't even think to search you for bullet wounds," I joke, and he smiles.

"Not necessary. It wasn't a setup, just dinner."

"Did you have a good time?" I ask, and he nods.

"It was good," he says, and I yawn, covering my mouth. "We should go soon."

"Oh, I'm not ready to leave," I inform him with a shake of my head, trying to pull away, and he laughs, holding me closer.

"You may not be ready to leave, but the bar is closing in about thirty minutes, which means you'll be kicked out if you don't."

"Is it really that late already?" I ask, and he nods again.

"It's really that late."

"Tonight was fun," I inform him, resting my head on his shoulder, and his hand moves to the back of my neck.

"I'm glad, baby," I hear him murmur, right before I fall asleep smiling.

TAKING A SIP of coffee, I rest the cup on my knees tucked close to my chest and stare out at the backyard. It's still early enough that the sun hasn't quite warmed the earth, and the dew covering the ground is making the grass look like it's been sprinkled with glitter as the light shines down on it. Thankfully, I don't have a headache this morning, but I do feel a little bit out of it after staying out so late.

Tilting my head back when the sliding door opens, I watch Dillon step out onto the back patio, wearing loose sweats and a T-shirt with his hair a mess, like he's ran his hand through it a million times this morning. "I've been looking for you. I thought you'd be in bed. It's still early," he mutters, bending to kiss my forehead, and my eyes slide closed.

"I couldn't get back to sleep after I woke up." Taking my cup of coffee from me, he sets it on the ledge of the gas fireplace then pulls me up out of the chair. Taking the seat I was just in, he tugs me down onto him then leans forward, grabbing the mug and handing it back to me.

"Why couldn't you go back to sleep?" he asks, kissing the side of my head once he's adjusted us both.

"You weren't there," I admit, resting my head on his shoulder. "The bed always feels too big when you're not in it with me."

"Sorry, baby." His lips touch my neck, making me shiver. "I got a phone call and didn't want to wake you."

"It's Saturday." I frown, and his arms around me tighten briefly.

"I know, which is why I was hoping you'd still be in bed when I got back to you."

"Sorry," I murmur, taking a sip of coffee.

"It's okay. I just know I'm going to have to share you with everyone later, so I wanted some time with just you."

"You're alone with me right now," I point out, and his mouth moves to my ear.

"Yeah, but I'm not in you right now. And that's where I really want to be."

"Oh," I breathe as a shiver drifts through my body, and my thighs tighten together to ease the sudden ache there.

Coasting his hand from my knee to my thigh, his hand around my waist glides forward to rest on the underside of my breast, and his words vibrate against my ear. "If we were home alone right now, I'd be fucking you, bent over the back of this chair we're sitting on." Squirming on his lap, feeling the hard ridge of his cock press into my ass, I bite my lip to keep from moaning out loud. "Fuck." His eyes go to the window behind us briefly then come back to me, dark with lust. "Are you wet for me?" His deeply spoken words slide over my skin as his hand slides under my shirt and down the front of my shorts.

"Yes." My eyes flare, and I try to turn my head to see if anyone is in the kitchen, but his free hand grabs my jaw, stopping me.

"Spread your legs a little. Let me feel how wet you are for myself."

"Someone—"

"Now," he cuts me off, and my legs open ever so slightly. I am instantly rewarded with a flick to my swollen clit, making me gasp.

"You have no idea how badly I want to eat you right now," he groans, plunging one thick finger inside of me, and my breath gets trapped in my lungs. "I can practically taste your hot little cunt on my tongue." His dirty words vibrate against my ear as one finger becomes two and his thumb begins to circle my clit. "Does that feel good?"

"Yes." I hold my coffee cup tighter, afraid I'll spill the contents all over us, as my hips instinctively rock against his magical fingers.

"You're so fucking wet. If you were laid out in front of me, your juices would be soaking the bed and my face," he growls, nipping my neck hard enough to sting. Closing my eyes, my core clenches around his fingers and my body starts to tie itself up into a tight knot. "As soon as I finish making you come, I want you to get up, go upstairs, then get undressed and spread your legs for me on the bed. Do you understand?" he questions, licking up the column of my throat.

"Yes," I pant, riding his fingers that are plunging in and out of me.

"First, I'm going to clean you up with my mouth," he groans as my pussy spasms. "Then, I'm going to fuck you on your hands and knees until you come.

"Dillon."

"I know, baby." His fingers speed up, and I pray no one is watching us. There is no way they won't know what we are doing. "Once you come on my cock, I want you on your knees in front of me, sucking me off until I come down your throat."

"Yes," I cry out as the knot inside of me suddenly unravels, and I fly apart in his arms. My teeth clench, my body shakes, and my mind empties of everything as one of the most spectacular orgasms I've ever had in my life rocks through me, leaving me with nothing but the feeling of him and me together.

"You're always so fucking beautiful when you come." Turning my head, I find his lips with mine and kiss him as his fingers move from between my legs. Pulling his mouth away, I watch his fingers disappear between his lips and his eyes slide closed, only to snap back open. "Up."

"What?"

"Up. Get your ass upstairs and do what I told you to do."

"You were serious?" I breathe as my legs start to shake.

"I never joke when it comes to you."

Blood rushes to the surface of my skin, and I quickly get off his lap and drop my coffee cup to the edge of the fireplace.

"See you upstairs," I murmur, rushing inside, catching his smile as I go.

"FUCK, BABY."

Lifting my eyes to Dillon's gorgeous face looking down at me, I moan around his cock. Watching his muscles flex and his jaw tighten, I feel my core convulse. He may be the one fucking into my mouth, but I'm the one with the power right now. Dropping my hand from his thigh, I slide it between my legs. My clit is so sensitive and swollen; not only did he eat me like he promised to do, he did it until I came three times, without giving me a chance to recover.

"Jesus fucking Christ. Beautiful, so fucking beautiful," he growls, raking his hands carefully through my hair and pulling the heavy strands back away from my face. "Are you wet again?" he asks, and I nod, keeping the rhythm of my mouth around his length and my fingers between my legs. "Give me your fingers. Let me taste you."

With a whine, I reluctantly pull my fingers away from my clit and raise my hand. Grabbing my wrist, he lifts my fingers to his mouth and sucks them clean.

"I should make you stop touching yourself. This should be about me getting off, not you. But I fucking love how you look with my cock in your mouth and your fingers between your legs." Gliding my tongue around the tip of his cock, I suck hard, and he releases my wrist with a snarled, "Fuck."

Sliding his fingers softly through my hair once more, his head drops back, face toward the ceiling, and his stomach muscles contract. Working him faster, I suck and lick, using my hand and mouth in sync to bring him close to the edge, and then squeak as he suddenly pulls away from me and jerks me up off the ground with his hands under my arms.

As he lifts me up, my legs automatically swing around his hips and my ankles lock behind his back as he impales me on his hard length. Walking the three steps to the closet, he opens the door, closes it behind us, and then shoves me up against the wall. "You. Make me crazy," he growls, finding my clit with his thumb before pulling out and thrusting in hard. His thumb working me over and his cock thrusting in and out so hard sends me spiraling closer to the edge once more. I know this time when I come there will be no way for me to recover. As I dig my nails into his back, he buries his face in my neck.

"Come with me," he commands, and I do. My body tightens around his, my legs and arms holding him as tightly as I can as I fall over the edge, moaning his name and hearing him groan mine against my skin as he plants himself deep inside of me. Sliding us to the ground, I keep myself attached to him, not even a little ready to let him go.

"I love having your family here, but I can't wait until we have the house to ourselves again," I whisper once our breathing has returned to normal and my heartbeat has slowed down.

"Me too," he agrees, then pulls me back and searches my face. "How are you feeling?"

"Tired." I laugh, dropping my forehead to his chest. "I feel like I could sleep for the rest of the day."

"I wish I could let you sleep, but people will be here in about an hour, so you need to shower and dress before then," he murmurs, kissing my forehead, and I pull back and frown at him.

"Who's coming over?" I ask, and he sighs.

"Please don't ask a million quest—"

"What the heck is going on, Dillon?" I interrupt, glaring at him, and his hands slide up my waist.

"Do you love me?" Knowing that's a trick question, I press my lips tightly together in refusal then feel his hand slide up to cup my breast. "You better answer that with a yes." He pinches my nipples, and I jerk back, covering my chest, glaring at him even harder. "Tell me you love me," he repeats on a growl, pulling me tightly against him.

I hiss, "You know I love you. Now tell me what's going on."

"I'm not telling you, so stop asking."

"D—"

"Quiet," he barks, taking my mouth in a deep kiss, cutting me off.

Forty minutes later, my body and mind are so lost in a state of euphoria that I don't even care that he told me to be quiet, remember about people coming over, or question him again about dinner as he puts me in the shower.

Chapter 12

Dillon

I CAN'T BELIEVE I thought this was a fucking good idea. Shaking my head to myself, I walk across the open second floor landing to the bedroom where I hear the sound of women talking and laughing. It kills me to share Ashlyn, so I don't know why I thought today would be a good idea, or why I let her mom talk me into having all the girls over to hang out and help her get ready, when I knew it would mean I'd get zero time alone with her. Looking around our room as I enter, I scan until my eyes land on my wife sitting on a chair in front of the bed with her feet tucked under her, and Kim standing behind her, putting her hair up in some kind of elaborate style.

I head across the wood floors toward her, and she pulls her attention from her cousins that are sitting on the bed as her eyes come to me. "Hey." Her face softens as our gazes connect. Seeing the happiness in her eyes, the annoyance I've been feeling all day washes away instantly.

"Hey, baby." I get down on my haunches at her side, rest my hand on the side of her neck, and lower my voice, "I'm going to ride with Parker and the boys over to the restaurant, and your mom is going to drive you over once you're done getting ready."

"Oh, I thought I'd be riding with you." She pouts, making me smile.

"I know, but you're gonna be a bit, and the boys are getting antsy," I lie, running my thumb along her jaw before tugging her chin toward me so I can kiss her. "I want you to wear this." I pull out a blindfold and she opens her mouth, but I cut her off before she can ask why or protest. "Please."

Staring at me, she nods, but I can tell it's killing her not to ask the million questions swirling around in her head. "I'll see you soon."

"Okay, we shouldn't be much longer," she murmurs, taking ahold of the edge of my suit jacket and pulling me back toward her. I fight myself, knowing there are people watching us and pull away before I'm ready, when her lips hit mine. Fuck, but today cannot be over soon enough.

Saying a quick goodbye to everyone in the room, I head back downstairs, meeting Lilly in the kitchen. "Tim sent a text a few minutes ago. They'll be at the house soon," I tell her as soon as I'm close, and her eyes fill with tears as she nods then rests her hand on my bicep.

"Thank you for doing this. This means everything to Cash and me."

"I want her happy," I say, trying to shrug off the feeling in my chest and gut as she looks at me with her chin wobbling.

"You are a good man, Dillon. We're lucky to have you as a part of our family," she murmurs, getting up on her tiptoes and placing a kiss on my cheek. "I'll have one of the girls send a text when we are on our way. Hopefully, we can pull this off."

"She knows something's up, so don't be surprised if it doesn't work." I give her a small smile then watch Parker and the twins come into the kitchen, dressed and ready to go.

"It will work. She may think something is going on, but I guarantee you she's not thinking she's about to get married."

"We're already married," I mutter, and she grins, patting my chest.

"Yes, you are. Now go, and we'll see you there," she says, giving Parker and the boys a wave before leaving the room.

"Ready?"

Looking at my brother, I nod. I was ready the first time I married her, and I'm more than ready this time.

"SHE'S OUT FRONT," Cash mumbles, looking from his cell phone to me before tucking it into the front pocket of his suit pants.

"I'll head out back and let them know."

Lifting his chin, he heads toward the front of the house while I make my way to the backyard where everyone is now waiting.

Opening the door, I step out into the grass and take in the people mulling around, the white chairs lined up in rows, and the large gazebo decorated with colorful flowers and white tulle. "She's here," I inform the DJ as I pass him, and he nods then turns down the music, which causes a hush to fall over the crowd and people to immediately take their seats like planned. With the sun sitting high in the sky, I step up the two steps into the gazebo as Parker joins me.

"I love you, man. I wish Mom and Dad could be here for this." He pats my back, and I close my eyes briefly and turn to hug him. "Don't get mushy and start crying," he grumbles, hugging me back, and I grin, patting him once more before letting him go.

As I turn to face the yard and the people sitting in chairs below, my lungs tighten as my eyes land on my beautiful wife standing at the end of the aisle with her eyes covered. Watching Lilly untie the blindfold, my breath comes out in a rush as her gaze moves over the yard and her mouth forms a small "O" before our eyes lock for one brief moment that seems to last a lifetime.

Hearing "Thinking Out Loud" begin to play softly in the background, I watch Michelle come forward carrying a bouquet of white roses, placing them in Ashlyn's shaking hands before kissing her cheek. It takes everything in me not to rush toward her as the tears filling her eyes spill over when her dad takes her hand and wraps it around his bicep with a pat.

I thought nothing would ever be more beautiful than the moment she became mine in Vegas, but watching her walk down the aisle toward me with her face soft, love shining in her eyes, and a cream-colored dress that skims the curves of her body, I know I was wrong. Once she's a few feet away, I step down from the gazebo and meet her and her dad, taking her hand he offers me.

"Take care of her," Cash says, looking at me before dropping his gaze to his daughter and leaning down, kissing her cheek, whispering something there for only her to hear, and letting her go. Leading her back up the steps, I take her hands in mine and direct her to stand in front of me as the officiate begins to speak.

"As I've been reminded on numerous occasions by Mr. Keck over the last few days, Mrs. Keck is already his wife, so this is not a wedding," he jokes, and the crowd laughs as Ashlyn smiles a watery smile up at me. "When Dillon came to me, he asked that today be a show of his devotion to his wife. And a moment for him and Mrs. Keck to share with all of you." He pats my shoulder. "I believe you have a few things you'd like to say to your wife."

Nodding at him, I drop my gaze and look into Ashlyn's eyes.

"I stand before you, our family, and our friends and ask you, Ashlyn Keck, to be mine always," I say, looking into her gorgeous face, feeling her pulse beat against my fingers wrapped around her wrists and I pull her closer, resting my forehead against hers. "For the rest of our lives, I will work at making you happy. In sickness, I will nurse you back to health. In health, I will encourage you to follow your dreams. In sadness, I will find a way to make you happy. And in happiness, I will be there to share your joy. There will never come a time when you are alone, because for the rest of our days, I will be by your side as your anchor, your strength, and the carrier of your heart, like you are the keeper of mine," I whisper the last part, and watch tears fall from her eyes.

"Oh, God, there is no way I can top that," she sobs, and I grin, swiping away the tears that have trekked down her cheeks.

"You don't need to top it. All I ask is that you love me, baby," I say softly, watching her eyes slide half-mast and her face soften even more.

"Forever," she whispers, dropping her forehead to my chest before tilting her face up to look at me. "There will never be a day I don't love you. There will never be a time I don't choose you. Thank you for giving me this." She rests her hand over my heart and my jaw clenches. "It's the most beautiful gift I've ever received, and I'm honored you trust me with protecting it."

"Christ." I blink back the wetness in my eyes and take her left hand in both of mine. "This was a symbol of our start," I state, toying with the plain white gold band around her finger. A band I put there on a wish that came true, a band I had no idea would mean everything to me. Then I reach into my pocket and take out the ring I've been carrying around since the moment I picked it up. "And this is a symbol of our forever," I murmur, sliding the four carat diamond solitaire ring on her finger then lifting it to my lips, resting it there.

Her eyes move from mine to her hand and she covers her mouth, shaking her head. "I… I can't believe you did all of this."

Holding her against me, I move my mouth to her ear and speak only for her to hear, "I know we didn't have the most traditional start, but I wanted you to have this moment to look back on. I wanted you to have a story to tell our kids one day, and I need you to know how important you are to me." Leaning back, I swipe away the tears that are falling steadily from her eyes and watch her pull in a deep breath and look around.

"I didn't need this moment." She smiles softly, throwing her hand out before resting both hands against my chest, and my heart trips over itself. "Since the moment I woke up as your wife, I've had thousands of moments that have shown me how important me and my happiness are to you." She pauses, pulling in another deep breath. "I didn't need this ring." She holds up her hand then grins. "I love it, and I'm totally keeping it." I chuckle at that, and then watch her face soften. "But I didn't need it. In the end, it's just a ring. My devotion to you lives in here."

She holds her hand over her heart then rests her hands back against my chest and leans closer. "I can't wait to tell our kids how I married their dad in Vegas, and how the craziest thing I have ever done in my life was also the best and most beautiful thing I ever did," she breathes, wrapping her arms around the back of my neck. "I love you more than I ever thought possible, and I wouldn't change our story, even if I could."

Clearing my throat that has suddenly closed up, I slide my hands around the curve of her waist, pull her up my body, and take her mouth like no one is watching, hearing a loud roar move through the crowd below.

LEANING BACK AGAINST the bar, I watch Ashlyn on the dance floor toss back her head and laugh, "Papa!" as her mom's dad swings her around in circles. Since the moment dinner finished and the music started up, she has danced with one person after another, and the smile on her face hasn't faltered once.

"I suppose my granddaughter did all right in marrying you." Looking down, I smile at Ashlyn's Memaw. The woman is a tiny thing, maybe four-eight, with long gray hair on her head, and a face I know I will one day see on her granddaughter.

"Thanks."

"Don't thank me." She rolls her eyes, and I fight the urge to laugh. "I'm just glad to see my girl happy," she mutters, pushing in next to me then motioning for the bartender to come over. Once he's close, she asks him for a vodka and cranberry with extra vodka, and then smiles as he hands it to her.

"Gran, you're not supposed to be drinking." Jax takes the drink from her just as she puts it to her lips, and her nose scrunches up in disgust.

"If no one knows I'm drinking it, I can drink it," she informs him, resting her hands on her hips.

"It doesn't work like that, Gran, and *I* saw you order it and know you're drinking, so your point is moot."

"You sound like your mom," she grumbles, then huffs before stomping off in the direction of Lilly, who is standing with Cash and Trevor.

"I'm not quite sure she likes me," I say, watching her go, hearing Jax laugh.

"You could commit a murder in front of all of these people, and none of them would bat an eyelash. Trust me, you've won everyone over without even trying," he tells me, then looks out at the dance floor to where his sister is now dancing with her cousin Bax, who flew in yesterday with her other cousin Cobi, from Montana, where they have been working. "How's she doing?"

"Good, she's been preoccupied with my brother, his wife, and our nephews in town, so she hasn't had much time to dwell. Have you heard anything new?" I ask as he motions for the bartender to come back over.

"No, nothing. And normally with a story like hers being on the news, there would at least be a couple solid leads, but no one has come forward with any new information."

"Did you look into Isla?" I know right now isn't exactly the time to be talking about this shit, but with everything going on we haven't had a second to touch base in over a week.

"I did. She was in New York and didn't step foot back into Tennessee until days after the incident," he says, then pauses, asking the bartender for a beer when he finally makes his way down the bar toward us.

"I have to be honest with you. The more time that goes by without anything else occurring, the more my gut is telling me it was just an accident," he mutters under his breath, smiling at someone who passes.

"I want to believe that, but I'm not going to let my guard down. I'd rather be overly cautions than pissed at myself if something happened again."

"We're on the same page with that, especially with the women who've turned up dead."

"Have you heard anything about that?"

"Not much. The cops I know are keeping a tight lid on the cases since they seem to have been committed by the same person," he explains, taking a pull from the beer the bartender hands him.

"What about the women?"

"I only know what I've read in the papers, and I imagine you've read the same things I have."

I had read the papers. One woman was a known prostitute, and the other was a college student. The only thing they had in common, as far as I could tell, was the fact their bodies were found in town and they were both from Nashville.

"Did you ever think about the rest of the men in the world when you planned this shit?" Parker asks, breaking into our conversation, and I raise a brow at him as he leans across the bar and asks the bartender for a shot of whiskey.

"Cara is currently talking to a group of women about wanting us to renew our vows. First, I didn't know that was an actual thing. And second, there's no damn way I could ever pull off something like this," he waves his hand around, "without asking her mom to help me, and that shit will never happen since I still remember what it was like when she took over our first wedding," he grumbles, picking up the drink the bartender sets down in front of him, shooting half the glass back before looking at me once more with narrowed eyes.

Shaking my head, I open my mouth to speak, but then look out toward the middle of the room when the DJ calls my name and requests me to meet my wife on the dance floor.

"Christ, and now you're going to dance. I'm never going to live this down," Parker mutters with a disbelieving huff, which I ignore as I set my glass of bourbon on top of the bar.

Walking toward my wife, I watch her hold out her hand and her face light up as "A Thousand Years" begins to play through the speakers. "Will you dance with me?" she asks, and without answering I pull her against me as soon as I'm close enough to do so, and then rest one hand on her waist and the other on the back of her neck. "This day has been amazing. Thank you," she whispers, tilting her head back to look up at me.

"You're welcome, baby," I whisper back, placing a kiss to her forehead then lips.

"I can't believe you got all of my family here."

"That was your mom. She knew you'd want to have everyone at your wedding if you had one, so we made it happen."

"You even got Memaw and Papa on a plane," she says in awe, looking up at me, and I smile. That was not easy, seeing how they hadn't flown in years and are set in their ways, but Lilly finally talked them around after I insisted on getting them first class tickets to make the trip a little easier on both of them.

"I'd do anything for you," I state simply, and her eyes close. Tucking her back against me, I sway her from side to side until the song comes to an end, and then dance with her through three more songs before the music changes to an upbeat song, and Hope comes over, shouting it's her turn to dance with her aunt. Leaving her with a hot, wet, and very deep kiss, I head back to the bar where I spend most of the evening watching her with a smile on my face, until it's time for her to leave with the girls to go out.

HEARING THE FRONT door open and close then the sound of giggling and stumbling around, I make my way out of the library toward the foyer then stand back with my arms across my chest, watching Cara and Ashlyn try to shush each other as they laugh drunkenly, holding on to one another to stay standing. Jax told me he was dropping them off; I just had no idea they were as wasted as they are.

"Did you guys have fun?" I ask, and both women look at me with wide, guilty eyes.

"Dillon's awake, act slobber," Ashlyn slurs, looking at Cara, who giggles then stumbles into her, almost knocking her down.

"You texted and told 'im you were coming home to have sess. Of course he's awake."

Cara laughs and I chuckle.

"Oh yeah, I forgot," Ashlyn mumbles while kicking off one heel, letting it fly across the foyer before doing the same with the other. Going to her before she can remove her jeans she is trying to take off, I pick her up. When she texted, I couldn't make out one word of it, so it's good to know what the hell she was trying to say.

"I'm going to bed," Cara announces, and I turn us around just in time to find her crawling up the stairs on her hands and knees.

"Babe, seriously." My eyes move to Parker, shaking his head from side to side, looking down the steps at his wife, who has now crawled halfway up the staircase. "You're wasted."

"I'm not wasted," she huffs, attempting to stand, only to catch herself on the railing before she falls over. "Okay, maybe a little." She giggles, and Parker laughs, heading down the stairs toward her.

"Come on, lush. Let's get you to bed." He scoops her up, giving me a smile and a shake of his head as he carries her the rest of the way.

"I take it you guys had fun?" I ask, kissing the top of Ashlyn's head, and her head tips back to look up at me.

"So mush fun, but I missed you." She smiles drunkenly, rubbing my chest then flicking my nipple through the thin cotton of my tee.

"Let's get you some water." I carry her down the hall toward the kitchen then feel her mouth and hot breath against my neck.

"I want sex, not water," she murmurs, licking my throat, and my cock hardens to the point of pain.

"I'll tell you what. If you can stay awake after I've gotten you some water and aspirin, I'll give you whatever you want."

"Okay," she agrees immediately, but before I've even gotten her up to the room, she's asleep in my arms.

Waking on a groan, my back comes off the bed when my cock slides deeper into Ashlyn's wet heat as she rocks against me. "Christ, baby." My hands cup her breasts and she moans, rolling her hips. Sliding my hands from her breasts to her back, I skim them down over her ass and push her harder against my length, and demand, "Faster." Ignoring me, she lifts and falls, slowly rolling her hips on each downward glide. "Faster," I repeat.

Her only response is to scrape her nails down my chest and abs then move her hands between her legs to roll her clit. Watching her on top of me, her breasts swaying from side to side, her fingers playing between her legs, I know that if I don't do something, I'm going to come long before she does. "*Fuck*," I snarl, flipping her to her belly, lifting her hips, and impaling her in one deep thrust that bumps against her cervix.

Smacking her ass hard enough to leave a mark, I watch her head fly back and listen to a loud, breathy, "Yes!" leave her mouth. Doing the same to her other ass cheek, her walls spasm and more wetness spreads over my shaft.

"How the fuck did I get so goddamn lucky?" I growl, lifting her with a hand around her chest, holding her impaled on my length as I turn her head and take her mouth, kissing her deep and rocking my hips. "Touch yourself."

Whimpering against my lips, her hand moves to between her parted thighs and I pull her nipple, making her gasp and writhe against me as I begin to slowly thrust into her.

"Dillon, I'm going to come." Her breathy words and her pussy milking my cock send me into a frenzy, and without thinking, I push her face-down on the bed, smack her ass hard once more, and come as she does, feeling lightheaded as my hips jerk when her silken walls pull every last bit of energy I have from my body. Collapsing next to her on the bed, I tug her against my chest and listen to us both breathe heavily.

"I fell asleep last night," she whispers, and I kiss the back of her head, smiling.

"You did," I agree, cupping her breast.

"I wanted to make up for it."

"You did that and more." I laugh into her hair then see her smile as she turns to face me. "How are you feeling this morning?" I ask, running my fingers down her cheek.

"Good, hungry." She grins, and I smile, leaning in to kiss her.

"What do you want to eat?"

"I really want a glazed doughnut… or a dozen of them." She laughs, tucking her head under my chin.

"I can make that happen."

"Really?" she asks, looking at me, and I tuck a piece of hair behind her ear and study her beautiful face for a moment.

"When will you realize I'd do anything for you?" I question, watching her lips part and her face soften.

"I hope I never get used to the idea," she murmurs, kissing my chin, and I roll her to her back and loom over her. "Rest. I'll be back with doughnuts and coffee." I kiss her once more then roll out of bed. Coming out of the bathroom, dressed and ready to go ten minutes later,

I find her asleep wrapped around my pillow.

Studying her for a moment, I wonder how I ended up here, how I found my way to her, and then wonder if by some strange chance my parents had something to do with it. They would have loved Ashlyn for me, and if it were possible, I know they would have lead me to her. With a quick kiss to her hair and a shake of my head, I leave the room and head down to my car.

"WHAT'S UP?" I question as soon as the phone is against my ear.

"Where are you?" Jax barks, causing my spine to stiffen as I drive through a green light in the middle of town.

"On my way home. Why?" I bark back, reacting to the fear I hear in his tone.

"How long 'til you're home?"

"Ten minutes, why? What's going on?"

"I'll see you then." He hangs up, and my hand squeezes the phone. Christ, what the fuck is going on? I just left the house. What the fuck could have happened? Pressing Ashlyn's number, I listen to the phone ring then go to voicemail.

"Fuck!" I roar, pressing down harder on the gas. As soon I pull down the drive that leads to the house, I feel bile crawl up the back of my throat. "What the fuck?" I watch the house get closer and see there are three police cruisers parked outside, along with Ashlyn's parents' SUV and Jax's truck.

Putting the car in park, I open the door and jump out. Running up the steps into the house, I roar, "Ashlyn!" feeling fear lodge in my throat.

"Dillon," Lilly says softly, walking toward me down the hall with her arms wrapped around her waist, and a look on her face that causes the doughnut I had on the way home to crawl up the back of my throat.

"What's going on?"

"There's…" She shakes her head and a sob rips from her chest as she buries her face in her hands.

Feeling my knees go weak, I look behind her when Cash approaches. "Tell me she's okay."

"She's okay, but I need you to be calm for her," he says quietly, and I nod, not having the ability to speak or the first fucking clue about what's going on. As soon as we enter the kitchen, I spot Nico and two officers dressed in uniform near the door that leads to the patio talking to Jax, and my heart speeds up. Scanning for Ash, I notice two men wearing suits standing at the island side-by-side, and then feel my lungs tighten when my eyes finally find Ashlyn sitting on the stool she always sits on. Her head is hanging and her hands are balled into fists on the marble island in front of her.

"Baby." Her head comes up and tears fill her eyes as she stares at me. "Ash." Standing abruptly, she rushes toward me, throwing herself violently against my chest as the stool she was sitting on crashes to the ground behind her. Stunned from the impact, I think she's trying to hurt me, then realize she's clawing at me like she wants me to absorb her into my skin. "What's going on?" I ask, feeling her body shake as I wrap my arms around her and hold her against me.

"Sir," one of the suit-wearing men says, and I look at him. "I'm Special Agent Torres, and this is Special Agent Kace. We're with the FBI." He motions to the man standing like a pit bull next to him, and I lift my chin in acknowledgment. "We need to speak with you, but I think it would be better if you and Mrs. Keck got comfortable," he tells me gently as his eyes soften on Ashlyn, who is silently crying against my chest.

Without a word, I scoop her up into my arms and carry her out of the kitchen and down the hall to the library, somewhere I always find her when we're home together and she's disappeared. Taking a seat on the large sectional in the middle of the room, I adjust her on my lap, feeling anger swell inside of me as her tears wet my neck. Looking around the library, I watch Lilly and Cash take a seat on the loveseat across from us, and then watch the two agents place themselves on the chairs next to the couch.

"Does someone want to tell me what the fuck is going on, and why the fuck my wife is crying?" I ask through my teeth, trying to control the fury I feel building with every single one of her tears.

"As you may know, two weeks ago, a woman was found murdered in Oaks Park," he begins, and the hairs on the back of my neck stand on end. "During the police department's investigation, they found evidence that led them to Mrs. Keck."

"She didn't fucking murder anyone," I bite out, cutting him off, and his face softens.

"No, she didn't," he agrees then sits forward, resting his elbows to his knees, and asks, "Do you know the website Dominate Me?"

What the fuck?

"No," I deny truthfully, rubbing my hand down Ashlyn's back when she buries her face farther into my neck.

"It's a fetish website where men and women create profiles with their fantasies, and someone looking for the same thing will get in contact with them through the site to—"

"What does this have to do with my wife and the women murdered?" I cut him off again, while wrapping one hand around the base of Ashlyn's neck and the other around her back, holding her as close to me as I can, needing the contact as much as she does.

"The police found information leading them to the site last night, after one of the victim's friends was questioned and explained that her friend was meeting up with a man she met off the website."

"Jesus." My body tenses in preparation. I know what's coming, and I know I'm not going to like it.

"During the investigation into the site, we found Mrs. Keck also has a profile on that site, and the same man that we believe met with the murdered women was corresponding with who he believed was your wife."

"Tell me this is a fucking joke," I hiss, and he shakes his head, rubbing his hands together.

"I wish I could tell you this is all a misunderstanding, but unfortunately, that is not the case. Over the last two months, there have been four murdered women found in the Nashville area. The detectives working the cases believed they were somehow linked together, but until last night, they didn't know how."

"So this guy is a serial killer," I bite out, and he looks at the agent sitting next to him, gaining his nod before returning his eyes to mine.

"Yes, we believe so, which is why the FBI is now involved."

"Who put up the profile for my wife on the website?" I grit out, feeling my teeth grind together at the thought of her information being on a site like that.

"We do not know at this time. The person used a disposable e-mail and only explained what their fantasy was before shutting off contact with the assailant."

"What was the fantasy?" I ask without thinking, feeling my nostrils flare and Ashlyn tense.

"The request was to be stalked and raped," he says quietly, and Ashlyn's body bucks against mine as I hear her mom's muffled scream. Fighting myself from going ballistic, I hold Ashlyn tighter against me and attempt to soothe her.

"Please tell me you know who the fuck you're looking for?"

"We don't at this time. Right now, we are working the case backward, trying to find out who he is."

"Jesus fucking Christ!" I close my eyes. How the fuck can this be happening, and who the fuck would do this to Ashlyn? "Does this have anything to do with someone trying to run my wife down?" I ask, opening my eyes to look at them.

"We're not aware of that situation." He frowns, looking at Agent Kace then me. "We haven't had a chance to be fully briefed by the investigators working the case. Our priority this morning was getting to your wife, making sure she was okay, and letting you know you need to take precautions until we apprehended the assailant."

"What do you suggest we do? Do we need to leave town until you find this guy?"

"We don't know at this point if he's after your wife, but—"

"But he could be," I fill in the blank, and he nods.

"Yes, he could be, which is why we're here."

"Who is he?" I question, feeling fire course through my veins. "What does he look like? Where is he from? What the hell do you know about him?"

"We promise you that as soon as we have a suspect, we will contact you. Until then, we ask that you stay vigilant."

"So basically, you know not one goddamn thing besides the fact he's already murdered four women and could be after my wife?"

"We understand this situation is a difficult one—"

"*Do* you understand that?" I cut him off, seeing Cash stand and Jax come into the room with Nico. "Fuck me. I'm so fucking thrilled you understand how difficult it is having you tell me women have been murdered after being on a website, where a person pretending to be my wife set up a fake profile asking that she be raped. And now you are telling me you have no fucking suspects and are working the case backward."

"Dillon." Feeling a hand on my shoulder, I look up and see my brother standing over me with worry in his eyes. "Calm, man," he says quietly, looking at Ashlyn, who has curled herself into a tight ball against me. "You need to take care of your wife and trust these men do their job."

Fuck, he's right. Me raging isn't going to help Ashlyn, who is freaking the fuck out and crying so hard my shirt is now soaked through, but the panic sweeping over me is making it hard to think rationally. Swallowing, I nod once at him then look at the agents sitting in front of me.

"If I were you, I'd be reacting the same way you are right now," Agent Kace assures, speaking for the first time then stands, and Agent Torres does the same. "Get a gun if you have to. Put in extra security if you think you need it, but trust me when I tell you that we will find this guy and bury him so deep he won't breathe for years." Lifting my chin at him, he pulls out a card from his pocket and hands it to me. "If you see anything out of the ordinary, get weird vibes from someone, or just have a question, call. My cell is on there."

"Thanks."

"Save the thanks for when I find this guy," he mutters, walking out of the room with Nico following behind him.

"Like he said, get a gun," Agent Torres inserts, lifting his chin before leaving the library. Meeting Cash's gaze, I hold his stare then watch his eyes close as he tucks Lilly against his chest. Seeing the look of devastation on both their faces, my stomach tightens and anger sweeps through me once more.

"I won't let anything happen to you," I vow against Ashlyn's ear, feeling her nod against my chest, making me more determined than ever to keep her safe.

Chapter 13

Ashlyn

"I REALLY WISH you guys could stay longer," I murmur with my arms wrapped around Cara, and my face tucked into her neck.

"Me too." She leans back smiling, and then pulls me close once more to rock me from side to side. "Christmas will be here before we know it." She hugs me tighter, reminding me of the plans we made yesterday evening.

"I'll be counting down the days." I pull away from her and look at Parker as he holds his arms out to me. Walking straight to him, his arms envelop me and I tuck my face into his chest. "Thank you for everything," I whisper as tears sting my nose, and his hold on me tightens. Without him the last few days, I have no doubt Dillon would still be in a rage. And without the distraction of Cara, him, and the boys, I don't know what I would have done. "I love you guys," I blubber against his shirt, then step back and wipe my face and eyes.

"Ah, shit, stop crying. I can't handle tears. Ask my wife," he grumbles, pulling me back against him as Cara laughs.

"It's true. Tears are his kryptonite." She smiles at me as he lets me go with an awkward pat on my back. "Anytime he doesn't want to give me my way, I let a few tears fall then boom—he's putty in my hands."

"I'm going to ignore everything you just said." He glares at her, and I press my lips together to keep from laughing at them. They bicker as much as my grandparents, but also love each other with the same ferocity.

"Aunt Ashlyn." Turning, I watch the boys run toward me, followed by Dillon.

"When we come back, can we make monkey melt?" Jordan asks, wrapping his small arms around my waist, and I rest my hand on the top of his head and look down at him.

"Absolutely."

"Can Hope come over for a sleepover when we make monkey melt?" Kenyon asks, and I laugh, pulling him against me.

"I'm sure she would love that," I agree, and he grins.

"Give your uncle a hug, boys. We need to hit the road if we want to make our flight," Parker urges, and both boys turn to Dillon and attack him at the same time. Watching him swing Jordan and Kenyon up into his arms, new tears fill my eyes. I'm going to miss this over the next few months. I'm going to miss the sound of kids in the house, and miss seeing Dillon looking so content from having his family around.

"We'll see you guys soon." He hugs them both before setting them on the ground then turns to Cara, giving her a hug that lifts her off her feet and makes her laugh. "Take care of my brother."

"You know I will," she says as he sets her on her feet and looks at Parker.

"If you need anything, call me and I'll be here," Parker assures as he and Dillon embrace, pounding each other's backs so hard the sound bounces off the walls in the foyer.

"I'll call," he agrees, letting him go.

Opening the door, he takes my hand in his and leads me to the edge of the porch, tucking me under his arm as we watch the boys climb into the back seat and Parker and Cara into the front. Giving them a wave as the car starts up, I watch Cara blow me a kiss then the boys wave frantically out the back window as the car drives away.

"I'm going to miss them," I whisper, dropping my head to Dillon's shoulder, hearing him sigh as his arm tightens around my shoulders.

"Me too, baby."

"Maybe we should go to Chicago for Thanksgiving," I suggest hopefully, looking up at him.

"That's definitely something to think about," he agrees, kissing my forehead before leading me back into the house, which suddenly feels cold and unwelcoming without other people around to fill the massive space.

"Can we go stay at the townhouse?" I ask once we're in the kitchen, and his eyes come to me and fill with worry. We haven't stayed at my old place once since we've moved in here, and the only time we've talked about it is when I mentioned putting it on the market in a few months, so I know my request has caught him off guard.

Coming to stand before me, he rests his hands on my hips then lifts me to the island, settling himself between my thighs. "Is that what you want?"

"Yes… I don't know." I look around, wondering why I feel so out of place all of a sudden. Nothing has changed since I was sitting here an hour ago with Cara and the boys, but looking around, it feels different.

"What's going on?" he asks, gently touching my chin, and my eyes go back to his.

"The house just feels too big again," I admit, and he nods, chewing the inside of his cheek and studying me for a moment. "Ignore me. I'm being crazy."

"Find Leo and pack a few things."

"Are you sure?" I question, and his hands rest against my thighs as his face drops closer to mine.

"I want you to feel safe, so if staying at your old place makes you feel that way, then yes, I'm sure."

"Thank you," I whisper, and he nods, holding his lips to my forehead.

"Go find Leo. I'll get our bags and take them up to the room." He tilts my head back with his fingers under my chin, touches his lips to mine softly, and then helps me down off the island. Heading upstairs, I go to the linen closet Leo has been hiding out in and search it from top to bottom, coming up empty-handed, then move to his other favorite places to hide. I don't find him anywhere, but then again, the boys have made a game out of finding him the last few days, so he may have found a new place to hole-up away from them.

"Are you looking for this?" Pulling my head out from underneath the bed, I smile as Dillon holds Leo out to me.

"Where was he? I've been searching everywhere for him."

"In the kitchen, on top of the fridge." He grins as Leo hisses and attempts to jump out of his arms.

"It must be warm up there." I laugh, tucking him against my chest so he can't take a swipe at me as he hisses. "You're getting grumpier by the day, sir," I tell him, and he hisses in response.

"That cat's the devil," he mutters, watching Leo try to escape my hold.

"He just doesn't love everyone."

"Baby, he doesn't like anyone, not even you."

"He loves me." I laugh as he gets his leg free and paws my chin.

"Sure he does." He shakes his head, resting his hand against my lower back. "His kennel's in our room. Come on before you lose an eye."

"So dramatic," I mutter, letting him lead me toward the bedroom where I spend twenty minutes getting a hissing and spitting Leo into his kennel, and then another thirty minutes packing enough clothes to last a week. As soon as we're done and our bags are zipped, I take one last look around and make sure we didn't miss anything we may need.

"Get Leo, baby. I'll get our bags," Dillon says as I start to pull my suitcase across the wood floors. Knowing it's pointless to tell him I can get my own bag, I pick up Leo's kennel and carry it downstairs to the garage behind him.

"Should I follow you in my car?" I ask as he puts our stuff in the trunk of the Mercedes and slams it closed.

"No," he practically barks, and I feel my spine tingle and goose bumps break out across my skin from the intensity of that one word. "Sorry," he softens his voice and steps toward me, reaching out, touching my cheek gently with the tips of his fingers. "I don't want you out of my sight."

"It's okay," I assure him, breathing through the overwhelming fear in the pit of my stomach. I know the worry I'm carrying around like a weight won't go away until the person responsible for the murders is caught, but I hate feeling like I do. I hate feeling on edge and jumpy. I hate not knowing if I'm in danger, and I hate that Dillon is so stressed out about it, too.

"I'll watch your alien show if you get that look off your face." His words bring me out of my head, and I feel a smile touch my mouth as I hold out my hand toward him.

"You've got a deal."

"The things I do for you," he grumbles, making me laugh as he tucks a piece of hair behind my ear. "Come on." He opens my door, helping me into the car. Once he's sure I'm buckled in, he slams the door and heads around to the driver's side, getting in behind the wheel he presses the button for the garage door and starts up the engine. The drive to my old place takes less than fifteen minutes, and as soon as Dillon pulls into my driveway and shuts the car down, I suddenly feel like Goldilocks when she was trying to find a comfortable bed to sleep in. My house looks exactly as it did everyday I lived in it for the last two years, only now it doesn't look like home anymore.

"Are you okay?" he questions, and I turn my head to look at him, pulling in a breath as I do.

"Yep," I lie, and he searches my face, squeezing the steering wheel so tight his knuckles turn white.

"I don't think you'll feel safe anywhere until this is done." He's right, I wont feel safe anywhere until this is done or until I know the police have a suspect. Not knowing who I need to be cautious of is what is making me crazy.

"I'm sorry." I rest my hand over his on the steering wheel and pry his fingers loose, twining them with mine. "I'm fine."

"You don't have to apologize for anything, baby. If I have to drive back and forth between houses all night, that's what I'll do. Hell, we can go stay at your parents' if that's what you want, or even leave town."

"We can stay here. I'll be fine," I reassure him with a smile, reaching to open my door.

"If you change your mind, just say the word and we'll go wherever you want." He lifts my hand to his mouth, placing a kiss on my knuckles.

"Thank you."

"Anytime, babe, you know that." His free hand comes up and wraps around the back of my neck. Forcing me to lean across the console, he lowers his voice as his eyes lock on mine and fill with possessiveness. "You know I love you, right?"

Even though it sounds like a question, I know it isn't. I know it's a statement and a claim. I am his and he will take care of me. "I love you too," I say without the normal, 'I know,' and his fingers still linked with mine tighten. Closing the slight distance between us, I brush my lips softly against his then lean back and smile. "You're not getting out of watching *Ancient Aliens*," I inform him, needing to take the intensity out of the situation, and he laughs letting me go.

"I didn't think I would be able to." He grins, opening his door and sliding out from behind the wheel. Opening my own door, I grab Leo's kennel from the back seat while he gets our bags from the trunk and then wait for him on the sidewalk, since I'm too lazy to search through the contents of my oversized purse for my house keys. "Once we're settled, you need to tell your mom and dad that we're staying here. I know they have a tendency to show up at the house and I don't want them freaked when they find we're not there," he says, putting the key in the lock before opening the door, and I nod.

"I'll call after I release Leo," I murmur, heading down the hall to the living room while he takes our bags to the bedroom. Setting Leo's kennel on the couch, I open the door and wait. "Come on," I coax as he sticks his head out to look around. Realizing where he is after a moment, his eyes come to me and I swear he glares before taking off to hide.

Listening to my stomach remind me I haven't eaten much today, I walk across the living room to the kitchen and open the fridge door, shaking my head when I see we only have a can of Coke and a box of baking soda. "We have no food. Should we order pizza, or Chinese?" I shout toward the mouth of the kitchen. "Dillon?" I prompt after a long moment, feeling my hairs stand on end and my breath suddenly become choppy.

Concentrating closely and hearing nothing, I silently move across the tile floors and open the drawer with the knives, feeling my heart skip a beat as the metal clangs together. Listening for any sound at all, I carefully pull out one of the knives on top, wrap my fist firmly around the handle, and pray.

"Bab—" Spinning, my arm shoots out holding the knife as a horrified scream leaves the back of my throat. "Jesus fucking Christ." Dillon stumbles back wide-eyed, looking at the knife in my hand.

"Oh, God." The knife clatters to the floor as I stare at him in horror, feeling my knees give out.

"Fuck." He scoops me up into his arms before I can crumple to the ground and tucks me against him.

"Did I..."

"No." He carries me toward the bedroom without another word and lays me gently on the bed, hovering over me. "What the hell happened?"

"I... you... I..."

I close my eyes as he whispers, "Breathe," then open them back up on the third full breath I'm able to take.

"You didn't answer me," I finally get out, and his jaw tics.

"Baby, I did answer you."

"You didn't," I deny, and he drops his forehead to my chest.

"Swear to God, baby, I wouldn't play like that. I answered you." He *wouldn't* play like that; he would never do that to me. He would never purposely scare me, which means I'm really losing my mind.

"I thought... Oh, God, I could have killed you." I cover my face as realization and panic set in.

"I'm fine. You're fine. We are both fine." He tucks me against him, and I sob into his chest.

"I'm so sorry."

"It's okay." He shushes me, palming the back of my head and keeping my face pressed into his neck. Lying there, I cling to him until the tears dry up and my stomach reminds me that we need to eat.

"No!"

My eyes fly open as my heart thunders against my ribs and nausea turns in my stomach.

"No, please no," a woman screams off in the distance. Blinking, I try get my eyes to focus, but my vision is distorted and my head is pounding, making the task almost impossible. Closing my eyes, I shake my head realizing I'm drunk, even though I don't remember drinking.

"Dillon," I call, reaching out to wake him, and my blood runs cold when my hands don't move. "Dillon?" I jerk my hands again, feeling a rope bite into my wrist. "*This is just a dream,*" I whisper, swallowing down the bile burning the back of my throat. This has to be a dream. I fell asleep in bed with Dillon after eating Chinese food and watching the news. I know I did.

Hearing a door open, I still, then feel something thud against the floor at my feet. *Oh, God, wake up*, I beg, digging my nails into the palms of my hands, feeling the crescent moon shape of my nails imprint into my skin.

"Please."

I don't want to do it. I don't want to open my eyes and have reality crash down around me, but that plea was full of fear and desperation. Opening my eyes again, I blink, trying to clear the haze, then feel bile crawl up the back of my throat as I look into Kim's pain-filled eyes staring back at me. *Please*, she mouths, and I notice blood at the corner of her lips then move my gaze down her naked body. Fear like I have never felt in my life rips through me as I take in the bruises, welts and stab wounds covering her torso.

"Oh, God, please no," I choke, closing my eyes, wishing I'd wake up but knowing that will never happen because this isn't a dream. I'm awake in a living nightmare. "I'll get help," I promise as she reaches out toward me, and her eyes slide shut. Watching her chest heave unnaturally, my hands start to shake and my mouth dries up. "Stay awake," I beg, moving my hands back and forth, trying to get the rope around my wrist to loosen enough for me to slide free. "Please stay awake," I sob.

"Nuh-uh-uh."

Jumping, my head flies up and a new wave of fear washes over me as I watch the guy from the coffee shop step into the room and close the door behind himself.

"I can tell you recognize me." He grins, shoving his hands in the front pockets of his jeans. "Do you know how badly I wanted to take you the day we met face to face? Do you know how hard it was to let you go?" he asks as I lean back, trying to avoid his touch as his blood-covered fingers slide down my cheek.

"Please don't do this, please, just let me go."

"Now why would I do that?"

"You don't want to do this," I plea, trying to get my hands free.

"You're wrong. I very much want to do this." He smiles, grabbing a fistful of my hair and jerking my head back so hard I cry out. "I thought you wanted to be dominated? I thought you wanted someone to stalk and rape you."

"That wasn't me, I swear it wasn't me," I cry as his fist in my hair tightens and pulls harder, forcing my head over the back of the chair, and pain from my recently removed stitches to shoot through my scalp.

"Do you know what I did to my fiancée when I found out she was asking men to beat her? When I found out she was letting men take her like a whore?" he shouts, and I flinch, shaking my head again while tears fall silently down my cheeks. "I gave her what she wanted. She wanted to be beaten, so I beat her until she couldn't open her eyes. She wanted to be fucked like a slut, so I fucked her like the slut she was, until she was bleeding from every hole in her body." He pets my hair, almost gently, and softens his voice. "You were the first profile I saw after her, the first one I responded to. At first, I wasn't going to hurt you. At first, I was going to save you like I couldn't save her. But then I saw you with him, saw what you were doing to him without him knowing. I saw that you were just like her," he roars, and I squeeze my eyes as tight as they will go.

"Oh, God." *Dillon, where are you? Please be okay.*

"God isn't on your side." He grins an evil grin, and then bites my neck so hard I feel my flesh tear while his hand circles my throat.

"Please! Stop," I rasp, and he squeezes harder. Struggling for breath, my body shakes and stars dance before my eyes, then everything goes black.

Coming awake suddenly, my hands fly to my throat and I gasp for air. "Oh, God." I look around, feeling fear consume me once more as tears fill my eyes. I'm still in my nightmare. I cover my mouth then realize my hands are free, and I sob.

I don't give myself time to think. I quickly untie my ankles and move to Kim, seeing the rope that was around my wrists is in her hand. "Kim." I roll her to her back, press my hand to her chest, and shake her. "Kim," I repeat, but she doesn't move; she doesn't even take a breath. Swallowing through the realization that she's dead, I drop my head to her chest and fight the urge to gather her against me.

I know this may be my only chance to get out of here alive. Moving to the door, I press my ear to it. Hearing nothing on the other side, I put my hand on the knob, turn it, and say a silent prayer when the door clicks open. Peeking out the small crack, I find nothing but hallway and dim light. Ducking low, I scoot into the hall, close the door, and look both ways, debating what way to head. I don't know where I am, but if I had to guess it's an old warehouse.

Tugging my T-shirt down, I creep silently on my bare feet along the hall, then feel a surge of adrenalin and hope course through my veins when I spot another door. As soon as I can reach the knob, I place my hand on the metal, turn it, and push, breathing in a deep breath of cold night air as it skims across my face. Opening the door another inch, I want to scream as it clanks and I see a large chain on the outside. Looking back down the hall to where I came from, I feel my eyes widen as I see the guy head into the room I just left. Knowing I don't have a choice, I push the door as far as it will go, get my head out through the space, and scream as I hear him running toward me, roaring, "What the fuck?" Getting my shoulders and arms out, I use the doorjamb to push myself the rest of the way through, and scream in pain as my chest is crushed as he pulls on the door. "You fucking cunt!" he snarls, tugging me toward him as I kick as hard as I can, refusing to give up now.

"Fuck you!" I kick and twist wildly, and finally, by some miracle, get free from his hold, falling hard to the ground just outside the door. I don't pause. I don't take a chance to look behind me. I run as fast as I can toward the woods, letting the darkness engulf me and keep me safe.

Dillon

HEARING THE NAME Trent Denton, I turn and watch the small television on the wall across the room. A clip of Trent being escorted into a police station with his hands cuffed behind his back appears on the screen before the newscaster reappears, shuffling the papers in her hands, speaking. "*Trent Denton, an upstanding citizen, a doctor, and a man many people in the community looked up to, is also the man police arrested today for six murders in the Nashville area over the last three months, along with the attempted murder and kidnapping of a Murfreesboro woman. The FBI was called in to assist the police with the case after four of his victims were found to be linked together through the website Dominate Me, a fetish website the accused used to find his victims. Tonight at eleven we will have more on this story, along with the interview of Trent Denton's still missing fiancée's mother.*" Finding the remote I turn off the TV, not wanting to hear more. Resting my head on Ashlyn's stomach and my hand over her chest, I let the feel of her heartbeat remind me she's here with me and safe.

"Dillon." I lift my head and watch Lilly walk toward me. "Why don't you go on home and shower, I'll sit with her while you're gone."

"I'm good," I mutter, pulling my eyes from hers when Ashlyn's hand resting under mine tenses. Sliding my hand up her chest to her cheek, her body relaxes and I study her beautiful face, making sure she isn't having another bad dream. For the past four days, sleep for her has been a struggle and I finally convinced her a few hours ago, after getting word that Trent was arrested, to take a sleeping pill. Thankfully, it seems to be helping.

"Honey, you need to shower and you need to eat something," she says gently, almost pleadingly, and my jaw clenches.

"I'm not leaving her side." I try to keep the bite out of my tone, but it can't be helped. The woman I love is lying in the hospital, having suffered from a fractured larynx, two broken ribs, and hypothermia, after being kidnapped by a serial killer and hiding in the cold over night, wearing nothing but the T-shirt she went to bed in.

"Honey." Lilly's hand rests lightly on my back.

"He took her from our bed and I couldn't do one goddamn thing to stop him."

"He drugged you," she reminds me quietly. "He drugged both of you."

"I watched him take her, I watched him take her right from my arms and I couldn't even move." My throat burns as I think about the moment I saw him lifting her limp body from our bed. I thought it was a bad dream. I couldn't move, couldn't speak. I could only watch him carry her out of the room while I lay there completely helpless to do anything to save her.

"Stop," I hear whispered hoarsely, and my head flies up. "Pl—ase." Ashlyn's voice cracks and I reach over, grabbing her cup of water then holding the straw up to her mouth. Watching her take a few sips, I pull the cup away when she's done and set it down.

"You're not supposed to be talking," I remind her gently, running my hand over the top of her head, pressing my lips to hers softly.

"Some—one h-as to stop yo-u from be—ating yourself up," she croaks, patting my cheek. Turning my head, I kiss her palm then link our fingers together.

"She's right you know," Lilly says quietly, walking around to Ashlyn's other side, taking her opposite hand. "It's absolutely horrible what happened, but there is nothing you could have done." Even knowing she's right, my mind won't allow me to accept the fact that she is. I should have left town with Ashlyn the moment the FBI approached us. I should have taken her away where she would have been safe. "You heard Agent Torres yesterday, Trent Denton knew what he was doing. He knew the alarm codes for both your houses, he knew the lay outs and your schedules. I hate to say it because he took my baby and hurt her, but it was just a matter of time before he did what he did," Lilly says, and I watch her eyes fill with tears then watch as she struggles to breathe. "If Kim's sister…"

"Don't." Ashlyn shakes her head at her mom. "Pl—ease don't." Tears fill her eyes, and I carefully gather her against me. The moment she got away and was finally able to find help, she told the police about who she thought was Kim still being there. When the police finally found the abandoned building where Trent had taken her, the body was missing. She didn't know at the time, none of us knew at the time, that it was actually Kim's identical twin sister, Kelly, who was there with her. "S…she sav…ed me," her voice cracks as her tears wet my neck.

"I know baby," I say, gently stroking my hand down her back, then hear her inhale sharply as she moves to hold me tighter. "You need to lay down. This isn't good for your ribs," I whisper, placing a kiss to her ear and she nods. Adjusting her back onto the bed I take a seat in the chair and watch as Cash comes back into the room, followed this time by Sage and Jax. I swear, every time he leaves he comes back with someone who wants to check on her for themselves, since the hospital won't allow more than a few visitors at a time.

"H… how's Kim?" she asks, looking at Sage as Cash comes over to kiss her cheek, and Jax waits to do the same.

"She's okay, she wanted to come see you but…"

"It… It's okay." Ashlyn tears up once more and his face softens.

"Tell her I lo… love her."

"I will." He comes around the side of the bed and bends to kiss her forehead. "I can't stay, I need to get back to her," he says softly, and her eyes close as she whispers,

"Take care of her."

"Always." He states with determination as he stands, then reaches over to pat my shoulder before saying a quiet goodbye to everyone and leaving the room.

"Did they find Kelly's body yet?" Lilly asks Jax as he takes a seat next to me, and he shakes his head.

"They're still searching, hopefully the police can convince him to tell them where he dumped her," he says quietly while Ashlyn's hand around mine tightens almost painfully. "Sorry." He looks away, and I watch his eyes get wet. I know he's thinking exactly what I'm thinking. I know he realizes that we could be out searching for Ashlyn's body right now instead of sitting in a hospital room waiting for her to recover enough to go home.

"I love you all," Ashlyn whispers, and I run my fingers down her cheek then look at her mom and dad and Jax. We may have had a rough start, but like family does, we worked through our shit and we will be stronger because of it.

Ashlyn

LOOKING INTO THE fire in front of me, I watch the flames dance in the fireplace, feeling the warmth seep into the skin on my face. It feels like it takes forever for me to get warm. No matter what I do, it feels like a constant chill has burrowed its way through my skin, muscle, and bone, straight to the marrow inside. Making me wonder If I will ever be warm again.

Studying the flames, I think about my phone call with Agent Torres this morning. He said they finally got the confession they had been hoping for from Trent.

He told me Trent cried when he explained to them how it all started, how he found out his fiancée was on the website Dominate Me looking for kinky sex while in a relationship with him. He said he came across my profile after her death and was planning on scaring me off the site. But then saw me with Dillon and thought I was just like her, so he tried to kill me then by running me over. Agent Torres said it was that moment that sent him over the edge completely, the moment he started using the site as a way to hunt for victims. The really sad part is, Trent's fiancée's mother told the police when she went missing that she suspected him of killing her daughter, but they never had any evidence to prove he was responsible for her disappearance, let alone her murder. So they were forced to let him go, even after believing he was guilty themselves.

Rubbing my wrists, I close my eyes. I still have no idea why he didn't kill me when he had the chance. The what ifs are enough to make me crazy. I know how close I came to death, and I know that if Kelly hadn't found the strength to untie me before she died, I wouldn't be here today. She saved my life; whatever she had done before that did not matter. Her last moments were spent helping someone she didn't know, and I will forever be grateful to her for saving me.

"Baby."

Jumping, I turn my head on the pillow and watch Dillon walk toward me.

"I didn't mean to scare you."

"It's okay. What's up?" I ask, pulling my feet back to make room for him on the couch, but instead of taking a seat, he holds out his hand for me to take.

"I got something for you."

"You did?"

"Yeah, come on." He pulls me up, then leads me by the hand out of the library toward the front door then outside. As soon as we're down the steps, he leads me over to the fountain.

"You didn't." I smile, and his face softens.

"You said you wanted to put fish in it, so I had your dad and brother help me put in the filtration system, and Jax just dropped off the fish a few minutes ago."

"I was joking." I grin, leaning over the side, watching the goldfish swim around, and then see a wooden stick on the ledge. Picking it up, I notice a line tied to the end. Pulling it out of the water, I gasp when I see my rings.

"You..." My eyes fill with tears as he unties the rings from the line and takes my hand in his. Feeling my hands shake, I watch him slide both rings back onto my finger. The day the police came to the hospital to tell me they got Trent, Dillon asked them if he had my wedding rings on him. It wasn't until that moment I noticed they were missing and realized that at some point he had taken them from me. "How?" I swallow, studying the rings that represent more than just me being his wife.

"I had this one sent from the chapel we got married at in Vegas. It's not the same ring. And this one is from the jeweler I purchased your other one from," he says, moving his fingers from one ring to the other.

"Thank you." I lean into him, pressing my face into his chest. "I love you," I breathe, feeling his breath at the top of my head then his lips there.

"Thank you for coming back to me," he whispers, and I squeeze my eyes tight.

"I will always find my way back to you," I promise.

WALKING OUT OF the bathroom, rubbing lotion into my hands, I climb into bed, and then watch Dillon walk out of the closet a minute later, wearing nothing but a pair of dark blue boxers that are molded to his thighs like a second skin.

"I'm not going to my appointment tomorrow," I inform him and he frowns.

"Pardon?" He gets into bed next to me then pulls the covers up over us.

"My appointment for my birth control. I'm not going."

"Baby," he whispers, sounding conflicted. I climb onto him, straddling his waist, placing my hand against his solid chest.

"I want to start a family with you."

"I thought you wanted to wait," he murmurs, resting his hands on my hips, and I shake my head.

"I don't want to wait anymore." I run my hands up his chest to rest on the underside of his jaw and his eyes harden.

"He is not going to change the course of your life anymore than he already has," he growls. I know he's talking about Trent, and that he believes this is because of what happened, but it isn't.

"He's not. *You* did. You make me want more," I say, and the hardness seeps out of his eyes as his face softens. "I want to be a mom. I want to fill this monster of a house with screaming kids, and I want to see you tucking our babies into bed at night. I can still have a career, but that isn't what I know will make me happy anymore."

"Are you sure that's what you want?"

"Down to my bones, I know it is," I mutter, then squeak as he flips me to my back and looms over me.

"Maybe we should start practicing, just so we know we're good at it before it's time to start trying." He grins, and I laugh, tugging him down to me.

"That sounds good," I agree against his mouth, smiling.

Epilogue

One year later

"BABY, I'M HOME," I call, walking through the front door and dropping my suitcase to the ground next to the stairs, placing my coat on top of it. Gaining no reply, I fight back the ever-present fear that lives inside of me and head toward the kitchen to look there.

I know she's home; I've talked to her every couple hours since I left and spoke to her as soon as my plane landed. Honestly, I didn't want to leave her, but it couldn't be avoided due to her current condition. Breathing in a sigh of relief, I smile when I spot her lying on one of the lawn chairs with her feet up, and Michelle sitting next to her, rubbing her very large stomach. She's already eight months along. It doesn't seem possible, and I have no idea where the time went. Sliding the door open, both women's heads turn toward me, but I'm focused on my wife.

"You're home." She starts to sit up, but I shake my head and move to where she's lying, resting my hand on her stomach and my mouth against hers.

"I missed you," I grumble, and she smiles, resting her hand on my jaw and running her fingers across it.

"You were gone one night."

"I know, and I swear, without you, it was hell."

"It was kind of nice having you out of my hair and not bickering at me." She laughs, and so does Michelle, who I lift my head to look at.

"Hi, Michelle."

"Hey." She stands then leans over, kissing Ashlyn's cheek and mine. "I'm gonna head home, so you guys can naked fight it out." She winks, making me chuckle.

"Bye!" Ash shouts as Michelle heads into the house, leaving us alone, and then her eyes come to me and her hands rest over mine on her stomach. "We missed you."

"I thought you said it was nice having me out of your hair."

"I lied. I hate going to bed without you."

"Me too." I lean in, kissing her softly, and then rest my lips against her stomach. "How was my girl?"

"Good, active as ever. I swear she sleeps all day then keeps me up all night, dancing on my bladder."

"Sounds like her mama."

"I know." She grins, running her fingers through my hair, and then her face softens and I know what's coming. "How was everything?"

"I told you it was okay when I talked to you this morning."

"I know, but—"

"No buts. After what that bitch did, after the way they reacted? Trust me, it wasn't hard to watch her be sentenced."

"Okay." She presses her lips together as rage simmers through me. Finding out Isla was the one who put up the fake profile on Dominate Me for Ashlyn was a slap in the face and a kick to my gut. I have no pity for the cunt, and I hope she finds out firsthand what the fuck it means to be someone's bitch.

"Because of that selfish cunt, I almost lost you. So, sorry, but I have no fucking sympathy for them or her."

"I didn't say anything," she mutters, and I realize she didn't say anything; I'm just still that fucking mad. Waking up drugged, and having my wife taken from my arms while I was helpless to do anything, will forever torment me. I had never felt as much fear as I did then, and will thank my lucky stars if I never feel it again. "Please get that look off your face. I'm okay, remember?" She touches my jaw and I close my eyes.

"I know."

"Good, then help me up. I'm kind of stuck." She laughs, and I smile while helping her up off the chair and then leading her toward the house.

"Are you hungry?"

"When am I not hungry?"

"Good point," I mutter, watching her smile. Since almost the moment she found out she was pregnant, she has been sending me on food runs, even waking me in the middle of the night to go out and get whatever she's craving. "Where do you want to eat?"

"Mexican sounds good to me."

"At this point, my daughter is going to come out speaking Spanish with as much time as we spend eating at the Margarita House."

"That wouldn't be a bad thing." She laughs again, and her belly bounces then her eyes widen.

"What?" I rush to her, but she slaps me away.

"Nothing. I'm fine." She waves me off, but I know she's lying. I also know she's become more stubborn with pregnancy. Helping her out to the garage and into the car, I drive us across town to the restaurant she has become obsessed with and help her inside. Before we are even through the door, Maria, the owner, is there with two menus and a smile on her face.

"Not much longer, is it?" Maria smiles over her shoulder at Ashlyn, leading us to our table.

"Nope, a few more weeks and she'll be here," Ash agrees, holding her belly while scooting into the booth before I take my own seat.

"Would you like your regular?" she asks, and Ashlyn nods.

"Yes, please."

"And you?"

"I'll have what she's having, but if you could bring me a Miller with mine, I'd be thankful."

"I can do that," she assures, walking off and coming back a minute later with chips and salsa, a bottle of beer for me, and a glass of apple juice for Ashlyn.

"Thanks." I lift my chin then move my eyes to Ashlyn and see her flinch. "What's wrong?"

"Nothing, I think I'm having more Braxton Hicks contractions."

"Pardon?" I stand suddenly, and she grabs my arm.

"It's okay. Sit down. It's normal."

"How do you know they're not real contractions?" I question without taking a seat, and she glares at me.

"I don't kno—oh, God." Her eyes tighten, and I mutter a curse under my breath, scoop her up into my arms, and apologize to Maria, who is looking like she might pass out with worry.

"You are so damn stubborn," I grumble, glaring at my wife an hour later as the anesthesiologist leaves the room, having just given Ash her epidural.

"How was I supposed to know I was going into labor weeks early?" she asks on a huff, rolling her eyes, and my jaw tics.

"I don't know. Maybe the contractions you had been feeling all day but somehow forgot to mention to me or anyone else," I bark, standing to pace back and forth at the end of the bed, feeling restless.

"Stop being an angry bear," she yawns. Pulling in a breath, I move to the bed and scoot her over to lay down next to her.

"Sorry."

"I know you are. You always act like a madman when I'm in the hospital. Trust me, I'm used to it by now."

Ignoring her statement, I hold her against me as she falls asleep, keeping my eyes glued to the monitor next to the bed.

"I hate you so fucking much I hope your penis falls off!" Ashlyn screams

as another contractions hits, and I wince from the sound and the feel of her nails digging into my hand.

"Breathe, baby," I urge her softly as the doctor tells her to push again.

"You fucking breathe!" she cries.

I hate this. We are not having any more kids after this. No fucking way can I stand to see her in this much pain ever again.

"Ash, just one more push and she will be here," the doctor says, and Ash bears down hard. So hard, her face turns red.

"Holy shit." My head lightens and stars dance in front of my eyes as I watch my daughter's head, shoulders, and then body appear.

"Someone catch him!" I hear someone shout, and I shake off the shock.

"I'm okay." I pull in a breath, and then watch the doctor drop Destiny to Ash's chest and wipe her off as she cries.

"You did so good, baby." I kiss my wife's brow, resting my hand on our little girl. "So fucking good. Look at her. She's perfect."

"She is perfect." Her watery eyes meet mine, and I know in that moment I truly have everything.

Ashlyn

WAKING, I ROLL over in bed and sigh at the sight that greets me. I don't think I will ever tire of seeing my big, strong husband with his daughter. Sitting up carefully, as not to wake them, I smile as his big palm on her tiny diaper-covered bum holds her more protectively against his bare chest as she stirs. As I look at the two of them, I wonder what my life would have been like if I didn't wake up married to Dillon in Vegas. I was always happy, but until him, I never knew what true happiness felt like.

"Come here." My eyes fly to his, finding him watching me. Reaching out, he tugs me against him and settles me against his side under his arm.

"Perfect," he whispers, and he's right. This is perfect.

Dillon

Five years later

"CAN I SLEEP with you and Mama?"

"No, baby, remember you're a big girl now, big girls sleep in their own beds," I tell my baby girl as I tuck the covers in around her, silently praying this is the time.

"I don't want to be a big girl."

"You want to wear nail polish and only big girls get to wear nail polish," I remind her, watching her bottom lip pop out making her look just like her mom.

"Can I have some water?"

"You already had water," I remind her, since we just got back from getting water three minutes ago.

"Can I go potty?" Jesus, this kid doesn't stop.

"Do you really have to potty?" I ask and she shrugs.

"I think so."

"Okay, come on." I help her up and lead her across the hall to the bathroom. "All done." She grins at me mischievously after washing her hands four times.

Jesus, I love my girl. I love her with everything I have in me. But there are times, like right now when I know her mom is in bed awake and waiting for me, that I wish I could send her away for a night or three.

"Are you ready?"

"Can I have water?"

"Sorry, no more water tonight. Tomorrow you can have more."

"Okay, Daddy." She holds her arms out toward me and I pick her up, feeling her heavy weight against my chest as I carry her back to bed. Tucking her back in for the tenth time since putting her to bed over an hour ago, I kiss her forehead then stand.

"Night, baby." I head for the door then stop when her soft, sweet voice asks quietly,

"Can you read me another story?" Turning to look at her, I watch her give me the puppy dog eyes that are my kryptonite.

Sighing, I pick up a book off her desk and head back toward her, watching her smile.

It's going to be a long damn night.

Waking with my body aching, I carefully climb out of Destiny's tiny toddler bed, making sure not to wake her then head down the hall to mine and Ashlyn's room. As soon as I walk through the door, I smile. The TV's still on and Ashlyn is asleep on her side with a box of cookies against her round stomach, her hand still in the box where it obviously was when she fell asleep. Shaking my head, I carefully dislodge her hand and set the box on the bedside table before settling into bed next to her. "Wake up baby." I kiss her ear and run my hand over her breast and stomach, then freeze as her nails run over my abs and our daughter asks,

"Daddy, can I sleep with you and Mama?" from the doorway.

"Christ," I groan in frustration as Ashlyn carefully turns and sits up, giving me an apologetic smile before looking at our daughter.

"Come on up, baby." She pats the bed, and Destiny grins then runs across the room and climbs up next to her. Watching her tuck our daughter into her side, I pull both my girls close and rest my hand over my son, who will be here in a few months. Holding everything that is important, I close my eyes and fall asleep.

Until Sage

Coming 2017

I'M SORRY BUT *your sister's dead.*

Those words replay over and over in my head while I watch the celling fan spin in circles. I keep telling myself to get up, to shower, to call my parents back so they don't worry about me, but I cant force myself to move. All I can do is think about Kelly, she was my identical twin. We shared the same hair, the same face, the same everything, down to the freckles across the bridge of our nose, and yet with all of that in common, I hated the person she was.

Hearing pounding on the door to my apartment I try to sit up, but I can't force myself to move. "Kim, open the door." *Sage.* I'd know his voice anywhere. "Open the goddamn door." He bangs harder and new wave of tears fills my eyes. "Kimberly, if you don't open the fucking door I'm gonna break the motherfucker down." He roars making me jump.

"I'm fine, go away," I attempt to yell back, but the words come out in a whisper through my dry throat as my heavy eyes slide closed and I finally give into the darkness surrounding me.

"Jesus, baby?" I hear growled through my subconscious as warm fingers rest against my neck under my ear. My eyes open slowly, and I blink. "Baby," Sage whispers, taking a seat on my bed next to my hip, pushing my hair away from my face gently.

"Kelly's dead." I breathe staring into his sea foam green eyes resting softly on my blue ones.

"I know," He pulls me against his chest and I sob clinging to him.

Other books by this Author

The Until Series

Until November – NOW AVAILABLE

Until Trevor – NOW AVAILABLE

Until Lilly – NOW AVAILABLE

Until Nico – NOW AVAILABLE

SECOND CHANCE HOLIDAY – NOW AVAILABLE

Underground Kings Series

Assumption – NOW AVAILABLE

Obligation – NOW AVAILABLE

Distraction – NOW AVAILABLE

UNTIL HER SERIES

UNTIL JULY – NOW AVAILABLE

UNTIL JUNE – NOW AVAILABLE

UNTIL ASHLYN – NOW AVAILABLE

UNTIL HIM SERIES

UNTIL JAX – NOW AVAILABLE

UNTIL SAGE – COMING SOON

Shooting Stars series

Fighting to breathe – Now available

Wide open spaces – Now available

Alpha Law CA ROSE

Justified – NOW AVAILABLE

Liability – NOW AVAILABLE

Verdict – Coming Soon

Acknowledgment

First I want to give thanks to God without him none of this would be possible.

Second I want to thank my husband and son. I love you now, always and forever. Thank you both for the joy and happiness you bring to my life.

Thank you Nat for your friendship and encouragement.

Thank you Ro for always being honest with me.

Thank you my twin beauties. I LOVE YOU GIRLS.

Thank you mom for all your help we would be lost without you.

Thank you Sain, you are an amazingly beautiful friend.

Thank you Alycia for your constant support.

Thank you my ROSES. I love each of you for the support and encouragement you give me daily.

Kayla, you know I adore you woman. Thank you for all your hard work and for being an editing rock star and the other part of my brain when I need you to be.

PREMA Editing thank you for everything from your amazing advice to your hard work I love working with you. I really love that I learn something new with each edit.

Thank you to my cover designer and friend Sara Eirew your design and photography skills are unbelievable. I love that you accept my craziness and that you know what I'm looking for even when I just have a vague idea. This cover is as gorgeous as all the others.

Thank you to TRSOR you girls are always so hard working, I will forever be thankful for everything you do. Lisa I love you woman.

To every Blog and reader thank you for taking the time to read and share my books. There would never be enough ink in the world to acknowledge you all but I will forever be grateful to each of you.

XOXO Aurora

About The Author

NEW YORK TIMES & USA TODAY BESTSELLING AUTHOR Aurora Rose Reynolds started writing so that the over the top alpha men that lived in her head would leave her alone. When she's not writing or reading she's spending her days with her husband and beautiful son.

For more information on books that are in the works or just to say hello, follow me on Facebook:

facebook.com/pages/Aurora-Rose-Reynolds/474845965932269

Goodreads

goodreads.com/author/show/7215619.Aurora_Rose_Reynolds

Twitter

@Auroraroser

E-mail

Aurora she would love to hear from you Auroraroser@gmail.com

Sign up now for Aurora's Alpha-Mailing list where you can keep up to date with what's going on.

http://eepurl.com/by57rz

And don't forget to stop by her website to find out about new releases, or to order signed books.

AuroraRoseReynolds.com

CPSIA information can be obtained
at www.ICGtesting.com
Printed in the USA
LVOW12s1802310817
547116LV00005B/904/P